Alok Ray

Reminiscences and Anecdotes of Great Men of India

Alok Ray

Reminiscences and Anecdotes of Great Men of India

ISBN/EAN: 9783744618021

Printed in Europe, USA, Canada, Australia, Japan

Cover: Foto ©Raphael Reischuk / pixelio.de

More available books at **www.hansebooks.com**

RAM GOPAL SANYAL

REMINISCENCES AND ANECDOTES
OF
GREAT MEN OF INDIA

INTRODUCTION WITH NOTES

By

ALOK RAY

R I D D H I - I N D I A
28 BENIATOLA LANE
CALCUTTA-9

INTRODUCTION

Scholars have often differed in their opinion about the nature of the 19th century Indian renascence. May be they would agree as far as to say' that there had been some kind of awakening. But there has been no end of controversy about describing the social phenomenon as 'Renaissance.' Not that scholars have always agreed about the nature of the European Renaissance either. At least Jacob Burchardt's analysis of the European Renaissance is no longer accepted by the majority of scholars. The new attitude that has emerged from the broader perspectives which historical analyses receive today from sociology. politics and economics calls for a new angle of vision, a new method of dissection. However, no historical study can do without facts, even when these are insufficient or contradictory. History not merely presents facts. The historian has certainly the right to lead such facts towards a well defined opinion, a definite view. Facts that have been known for ages may be illuminated differently by a historian. Facts that have just come to light may also be put to new analytic prisms to yield areas of understanding not seen before. But the collection and preservation of historical facts have always been neglected in India. The result is a certain dwarfing of historical research. Any research even about the 18th and 19th century India has to depend today on histories written by English scholars. The English have written our histories as much in pursuit of knowledge as of political ends. Therefore, a total dependence on the crutches of these studies which include or eschew facts according to political exigencies and betray a flimsy knowledge of our thoughts and societies can never be conducive to proper historical research. But Indians have seldom, cared to write about themselves and their own country. Autobiographies and memoirs, for instance, were seldom written in the 19th century India. Not many people kept diaries or preserved personal letters. Even the 19th century Indian newspapers and magazines are not easily available. In the light of this enormous lack of historical facts it is not very difficult to understand why historical research in India can never make do without books written by foreign scholars. Sometimes historical research in this country has shown definite originality of treatment and a broadening of vision, but the inadequacy of facts has always proved to be the grit in the mill.

In his collection of the 'Reminiscences and Anecdotes of Greatmen of India' what Ramgopal Sanyal aimed at in the last decade of the 19th century was 'a well-written and authentic Indian History from a purely native point of view.' Ramgopal Sanyal did not certainly attempt a complete history, but he certainly collected some valuable data to be put to use by future historians. He performed the unique task of collecting social, cultural, governmental and biographical facts mostly from contemporary newspapers and periodicals which no longer exist. News, obituaries and controversies published in newspapers and periodicals are basic to all historical research. Ramgopal also culled material from printed biographies, official documents and books of history which may not be as rare as the data collected from contemporary newspapers and periodicals, but in compiling them all into one volume Ramgopal certainly did some considerable service to the future historians. Ramgopal also collected some personal letters, and printed them in his book. Today these precious letters exist only in print. Besides Ramgopal's book has a collection of interesting anecdotes which the author heard at different times of his life. We have no way to know how much sea-change these ancedotes must have suffered in transition from Ramgopal's memory into his writings, but these certainly give some inkling of how the common people were reacting to contemporary realities and happenings.

Ramgopal was no historian. He is best described as a chronicler. He took the first step towards a National History, although the very concept seemed unreal in a country where even a dictionary of national biography is yet to be written. Ramgopal therefore had to remain content merely with the collection of data. But the unique leaning of his mind has revealed itself through his collection, arrangement and explanation of facts. He was personally involved in the Hindu Revivalism and National Movement of the late 19th century. Naturally he has not been totally objective in his presentation of facts. At times his nationalistic sympathy has surfaced in his writings. For instance, he has described the characters of his book as 'great men of India.' We have certainly our doubts about the appropriateness of Ramgopal's description. Ramgopal's heroes do not at least have greatness of the same measure. The ambiguity in Ramgopal's mental makeup was also typical of the century he lived in. He was somewhat torn between nationalistic enthusiasm and loyalty to the British Raj. Although we often take up an attitude of derision towards the 19th century hero-worship, but a knowledge of this basic ambivalence is essential for a fuller understanding of the 19th century.

Ramgopal Sanyal is well known for his biographical sketches, but ironically enough, very little is known about the biographer himself. He was the son of Iswar Chandra Sanyal, and was born in Meherpur subdivision in the district of Nuddea. His year of birth is not known to us, but it was probably a few years before 1850. The Sanyals used to live at Goari, near Krishnanagar, and had marriage relations with the Lahiri family of that area. ·Ramgopal married the daughter of Sripada Lahiri, brother of Ramtanu Lahiri. After passing the Entrance and F. A. examinations, he became the Headmaster of A. V. H. E. School at Krishnanagar. Dwijendralal Roy was one of his students at that time. Afterwards, Ramgopal taught in many schools at various places, e.g. Chuadanga H. E. School, Kusthia H. E. School and Mamjoani English School, retiring finally from the teaching profession as Headmaster of Sambalpur H E. School in Orissa. While staying at Krishnanagar in his early life, he was connected with some newspapers, published from Calcutta as their 'Mofussil correspondent' sending letters and news regularly to them. On 4th May 1883, he organised a 'Protest Meeting', the first public meeting to be held at Krishnanagar, to express sympathy with Surendra Nath

Banerjea. He came to Calcutta in or about 1890, and bought a house at Doctor's Lane, Taltala. Ramgopal started his new career from that time as a fulltime journalist. For a few years he worked as Manager of the *Bengalee* and thereafter as the sub-editor of the *Indian Mirror*. His connections with the last mentioned periodical continued for a decade or more. During this period, he contributed many articles to various English periodicals and also published the following books : *The Life of the Hon'ble Rai Kristo Das Pal, Bahadur C.I.E.* (1886), *The Life of Babu Hurrish Chunder Mookerjea* (in Bengali, 1887), *History of celebrated criminal cases and resolutions recorded thereon by both provincial supreme governments* (1888) *A General biography of Bengal celebrities* (1889), and *The Life of Babu Kristo Das Pal* (in Bengali, 1890). Ramgopal also compiled a book called *Record of criminal cases, as between Europeans and natives, for the last sixty years* (1893). He died in 1921.

Ramgopal Sanyal's books have never been reprinted, and as such his works are not easily accessible to present day scholars, and this is specially true of his *Reminiscences and anecdotes of great men of India* (1894, 1895). Riddhi–India has already reissued *Bengal celebrities* (1977), and now offers a facsimile print of the *Reminiscences and anecdotes* in two volumes. Additional notes and information are supplied by the present editor at the end of the second volume, and an index, lacking in the original work, is added in this edition for ready reference.

Scottish Church College,   **ALOK RAY**
Calcutta.

REMINISCENCES AND ANECDOTES

OF

GREAT MEN OF INDIA,

BOTH OFFICIAL AND NON-OFFICIAL FOR THE LAST ONE HUNDRED YEARS.

———————

EDITED & PUBLISHED
BY
RAM GOPAL SANYAL.

AUTHOR OF THE LIFE OF THE LATE BABU KRISTO DAS
PAL AND OTHER WORKS.

———————

PART I.

———————

Calcutta.

PRINTED BY WOOMA CHURN CHUKERBUTTY,
AT THE HERALD PRINTING WORKS.

189, Bow Bazar Street.

———————

1894.

Price Cloth-bound Rs. 2-8.   *Paper-bound Rs. 2.*

DEDICATED

TO THE

Sacred Memory,

OF

SREEMUTTY MON MOHINY DABEE,

AND

SREEMUTTY RAJUBALA DABEE,

My first and Second Wives whose untimely death in Rapid Succession had made the life of this poor contented Author miserable for ever.

PREFACE

It has been said that the 'Reminiscences and Anecdotes" of the great men of a nation are the "marrows and bone" of its true history. If the aphorism be true, why should not the educated natives India store up in their minds the reminiscences and anecdotes of the immortal Hurish Chunder Mukherjea, Ram Gopal Ghose, the Rev. K. M. Banerjea, Dr. Bhau Daji, Sir Monguldas Nathubhai, the Hon'ble Biswanath Mundlik, Mr. Patcheapah Moodelly, Sir Mathuswami Iyer and others equally distinguished. Most of the educated natives can recite, with perfect ease, what Boswell had said and Macaulay written about Johnson for instance, but they know not, whether Patcheapan Moodelly or the Hon'ble Bishwanath Mundlik was a Hindoo or a Christian.

For the last thirty years, since my connection with the Metropolitan press, I have been collecting these materials from various newspapers from the year 1837 down to the present time. In the absence of a well-written and authentic Indian History from a purely native point of view, I have ventured to publish this my humble work, with a view to rescue these precious Anecdotes and Reminiscences of the Great men of India, from the dark shade of oblivion, with what success, it is for the readers to say. The main portion of my materials having been picked up from nearly a hundred isolated old files of newspapers that are to be found in the Metcalfe Library, I have failed to arrange them in a strictly chronological form.

In arranging these materials, I have, in certain places, reproduced the extracts verbatim, and in other places abridged and annotated them for the sake of brevity. For these and other defects, of which no one is more conscious than myself, I crave due indulgence from my readers.

No one who has had experience in hunting up old records will under-rate the trouble that has been incurred. This is a country in which records themselves are few and meagre, so indifferent are our countrymen to the necessity of preserving a history. And such records as existed at one time it is difficult to lay hands on, so little care has been bestowed on their custody. This little work, therefore, has no pretension to exhaustiveness, and it does not claim to be monumental. But for its shortcomings I may be permitted to plead in all humility that the fault is not wholly my own. To make a full use of existing materials it is necessary that the compiler should have some facilities given to him and should have the necessary material resources. I have not received help enough in either of these directions. My efforts to obtain information concerning the distinguished men of other presidencies than my own, have been very little success- ful, owing to the indifference of the gentlemen appealed to, and the difficulty of obtaining access to the newspapers of those presidencies. About Bengal Celebrities I believe I have made a fair collection, but I regret that I have not been able to present the full results of my researches in this volume. Should the present effort receive due encouragement I would be in a position to give to the world all that I am now com- pelled to withhold, with such additional information as I may be fortunate enough to collect in the meantime. It is un- fortunate that we have no Dictionary of National Biography nor a National History, and I trust it will be no presump- tion if I say that my humble volume and its successor. if one should appear, may in some small measure lighten the work of the future historian. A nation never makes progress or grows in self-respect without an appreciation of its great men. We have, as a rule, shown little appreciation so far, for we have generally allowed our great men to be forgotten, and I trust that my poor effort, whatever its literary worth, may at any rate be found to have a moral value. One word only it it necessary to add, to close a preface already too long for a work so little. History is no respecter of persons, and I hope I shall be pardoned if I have unearthed some records the memory of which will be a sad one to all who care for the good name of great men, official or non-official.

It would be ingratitude on my part, if I did not take this opportunity to acknowledge that the publication of this book is greatly indebted to the munificence of Her Highness the Maharanee Surnomoye C. I., Sir Maharajah Jotindra Mohun Tagore, the Hon'ble Justice Gurudas Banerjea, and the Hon,ble Doctor Rash Behary Ghose.

CALCUTTA,
23, Doctor's Lane, TALTOLLAH,
15th August, 1894.   RAM GOPAL SANYAL.

CONTENTS

Reminiscences and Anecdotes of Great Men of India, both European and Native.

CHAPTER I.

RAM GOPAL GHOSE

(Born in October 1815, Died in 1868.)

THE STATUE OF DAVID HARE AND RAM GOPAL GHOSH'S EXERTIONS.

Before we narrate this unpublished, though not the less authentic anecdote of the noble endeavours made by Babu Ram Gopal Ghose for erecting the statue of David Hare, "the Father of English Education" in Bengal, we must premise by saying that, in attempting to write a life of the immortal Orator, Ram Gopal Ghose in my work called the *Bengal Celebrities*, published in 1889, we could not publish all the anecdotes then unknown to us. After a full and persistent enquiry, we have come to learn these facts from our dear venerable uncle-in-law Babu Ram Tonoo Lahiry, the most intimate friend of the illustrious patriot of Bengal.

It was on the 17th June, 1841, a public meeting was called by Rajah Krishna Nath, the illustrious husband of the Moharanee Surnomoye, to perpetrate the sacred memory of David Hare. It took place in the theatre of the Medical College, under the presidency of Babu Prusunna Kumar Tagore. The idea of erecting a statue was not at all liked by

the aristrocracy of Calcutta, and overt and covert oppositions
were shewn to the cherished idea of Baboo Ram Gopal Ghosh
and his friends.   This show of opposition from so influential
a quarter doubl⸗ d the zeal of Babu Ram Gopal who, with a
view to carry out his idea, issued a kind of manifesto to all
the pupils and friends of David Hare to pay without any
loss of time one month's pay for raising the statue in
question.   In response to this urgent and most enthusiastic
call for subscriptions from every student who was then in
some sort of employment, almost every one of David Hare's
pupils and friends sent his quota of a month's pay for the
purpose.   The sum thus collected was no doubt a decent one,
but Ram Gopal with his characteristic liberality contributed
a very large sum to the fund which amounted to about half a
lack of rupees with which the statue was raised in 1847.   The
zeal and enthusiasm of Babu Ram Gopal Ghosh who could always make a tremendous sacrifice of his own hard-earned
money is well worthy of imitation by the present generation.

THE STATUE OF LORD HENRY HARDINGE AND
BABU RAM GOPAL GHOSE.

It was on the 24th December, 1847, a public meeting was
held in the Town Hall under the presidency of MR. Charles
Hogg, the then Sheriff of Calcutta to consider the propriety
of voting an address to Lord Hardinge, and to raise a memorial in his honour.   Sir Thomas Turton proposed that an
address should be presented to his Lordship.   Babu Rashamoy
Datta seconded this motion.   The Rev. K. M. Banerjee then
addressed the meeting "to remove the impression from the
minds of certain parties, if it existed, that the native community were not disposed to appreciate the government of Lord
Hardinge."   In a very eloquent address, this native Christian
patriot, " the hoary-headed political Padri " of Kristo Das Pal
pointed out to the meeting, that the natives of India appre-

ciated as much as Europeans the military achievements of Lord Hardinge. He then moved an amendment to the address to the following effect.

"We can not on the occasion of your Lordship's departure refrain from expressing our grateful admiration of the lustre, which your beneficent policy in the encouragement of education, your resolute adherence to the peace until war became inevitable, and your paternal solicitude for the welfare of the people entrusted to your charge have shed on your administration. Brief as your sojourn has been, you have represented the high-minded benignity of the British sceptre, no less than its majestic splendour, the peaceful virtues of Christian Statesman, no less than the indomitable courage of the British warrior, the humanizing influences of British ascendancy, no less than the invincible force of the British arms."

Mr. James Hume and Sir Thomas Turton objected to this amendment. Babu Ram Gopal Ghosh then rose, and in a telling speech supported the amendment moved by his friend the Rev. K. M. Banérjee. After a discussion it was agreed that, a line should be inserted in the address expressing the gratitude of the native community for the great encouragement his Lordship had shewn to the cause of public education. Sir Thomas Turton then objected to the erection of a statue to the memory of the Governor, as recommended by the Lord Bishop of Calcutta. He said that as "the Sutledge Column would be placed in a prominent part of Calcutta, the erection of a Statue, would be, as it were, gilding refined gold." He proposed that a piece of plate and a picture in the Town Hall should be sufficient for the purpose. To this proposal Babu Ram Gopal Ghosh objected, and moved an amendment for the erection of a statue. Captain Ramsey seconded his motion. After a good deal of discussion, the proposal of Babu Ram Gopal Ghosh was carried. The following gentlemen were then elected to form a committee for the carrying out of the object of the meeting.*

The Hon'ble Mr. Hay Cameron, Mr. G. A. Bushby, Mr.

---

* For the full report of the speech, see our work *Bengal Celebrities*, p. 190.

James Colville, Major Bygrave, Babu Ram Gopal Ghosh, Rushamoy Datta, and the Rev. K. M. Banerjee. Babu Ram Gopal Ghosh, and Frederick J. Mouat were appointed Joint Secretaries to the Hardinge Memorial Committee. Babu Ram Gopal Ghosh, with the liberality of a prince, contributed Rs. 500 to the Memorial Fund.

THE BLACK ACTS PAMPHLET AND BABU RAM GOPAL GHOSH.

The four Draft Acts, with titles specified in the margin, commonly called the "Black Acts" were published in the Government Gazette, of the 31st October and 21st November, 1849. A General meeting of the Europeans was held on the 29th December 1849, to memorialize the Government against these Acts. Babu Ram Gopal Ghose wrote a pamphlet in support of these Acts, and thereby incurred the displeasure of some of the Anglo-Indians.

(1) An Act for abolishing exemption from the jurisdiction of the East India Company's Criminal Courts.
(2) An Act declaring the Law as to the privilege of Her Majesty's European subjects.
(3) An Act for trial by Jury.
(4) An Act for the protection of Judicial Officers.

THE AGRI-HORTICULTURAL SOCIETY OF CALCUTTA, AND RAM GOPAL GHOSE.

We learn from the *Friend of India* of 1850, that at a meeting of the Society held in January of that year, Babu Ram Gopal Ghose was removed from the Vice-Presidentship of that Society for having supported the "Black Acts." Another native gentleman was nominated in his place. The *Friend of India* of the 17th January, 1850, in a leading article under the heading "The Black Act, Babu Ram Gopal Ghose, and Mahomedan Law," condemned the Society for this ungrateful act. Mr. (afterwards Sir) Cecil Beadon and Babu Ishan Chander Ghosh resigned their Memberships of this Society for the removal of Babu Ram Gopal Ghosh. *En-passant* we may remark that this Society was established in 1821 by Dr. Carey, the well-known Missionary.

THE CHARTER ACT MEETING OF 1853 AND BABU RAM GOPAL GHOSE.

A public meeting of the native inhabitants of Calcutta was held on the 29th July, 1853, under the presidency of Rajah Radha Kant Deb Bahadur to consider the question of the renewal of the Charter in that year. Babu Ram Gopal made an eloquent and masterly speech which earned for him the *sobriquet* of Indian Demosthenes from no less an authority than the *London Times*. In this speech he severely criticized Mr. (afterwards Sir) Frederic Halli-day's evidence before the Indian Committee of enquiry appointed in 1852 by the British House of Commons, consisting of Sir. H. Inglis, Sir. J. Graham, Mr. Ellice, Mr. Cobden, Sir. J. Hogg, and Mr. Macaulay. He called in question the veracity of the evidence of Mr. Halliday. The Rev. K. M. Banerjee also criticized the evidence of Mr. John Marshman, Editor of the *Friend* of *India.* Babu Ram Gopal read the following letter of Babú Horro Chunder Ghosh in refutation of what Mr. Halliday had said in his evidence.

MY DEAR RAM GOPAL,

I am very sorry to notice Mr. Halliday's statement, and I regret to say that he must have evidently misunderstood me. I never complained of my countrymen generally, for I really had no cause whatever for doing so. When I did speak to him, to you and my other friends of annoyances, I alluded, not to my countrymen generally or as a body, but to a certain quarter whence I believed for special reasons all those annoyances proceeded.

July 23, 1853. } I remain, my dear Ram Gopal, yours &c.,

(Sd.) HURRO CHUNDER GHOSH,

Mr. HALLIDAY'S EVIDENCE.

"I am sorry to say that there is a very strong tendency amongst the natives to regard with unappeasable jealousy, amounting to animosity, any member of their own class raised above themselves, especially among the natives of Bengal, with whom I am most familiar. I will give a recent instance of it, which was very well known in Calcutta at the time I left. Lord Dalhousie took what was considered one of the boldest steps towards the advancement of the natives which had been taken for many years, namely, the careful selection and appointment of one of the very best of them ; a man against whom his fellows could not possibly utter one word of accusation or reproach. He was a Hindoo of high caste and high family, who had borne an irreproachable and unreproached name in the public service for many years. This man, Lord Dalhousie, very much to the annoyance of a great number of English claimants, and particularly to the annoyance of the English bar, who were candidates at the same time for the office of which I am about to speak, appointed as a stipendiary magistrate of Calcutta. He had on that occasion to sustain, not only the very loudly expressed anger of the English claimants, but the still more loudly expressed annoyance of the natives ; and the natives exhibited in so many ways their jealousy and dissatisfaction with this appointment, arising simply out of the fact of this man being placed over their heads, that he repeatedly came to me, and to other friends, to complain of the bitterness of his position, and the pain and misery which had been brought upon him by the constant attacks, public and private, and the annoying petty jealousy which he had experienced from his countrymen in consequence of his elevation".

For this fearless independence shown by Babu Ram Gopal Ghose in criticizing the evidence of Mr. Frederic Halliday, his name will remain ever memorable in the Annals of Indian History. The low servile speakers and writers of our own days ought to take encouragement from this noble example of Babu Ram Gopal Ghose.

THE PUBLIC MEETING OF 1858 AND BABU RAM GOPAL GHOSE.

A public meeting was held in the Town Hall of Calcutta on the 3rd of Novr. 1858, to vote a Loyal Address to Her Majesty. Babu Ram Gopal Ghosh said :—

If I had power and influence, I would proclaim through the length and breadth of this land from the Himalayas to Cape Comorin—from Brahmapootra to the Bay of Cambay, that never were the natives more grievously mistaken than they have been in adopting the notion foisted upon them by designing and ambitious men that their religion was at stake ;—for that notion, I believe, to be at the root of the late rebellion. (Cheers) They do not understand the English character ; (hear hear,) they donot understand the generosity, the benevolence of the governing power, the evenhanded Justice with which that power is willing and anxious always to do that which is right between man and man, without any reference whatever to the fact whether the men belonged to the governing or to the governed class."

BENGAL BRITISH INDIA SOCIETY, AND BABU RAM GOPAL GHOSE.

At a Special Meeting of the Members of the Bengal British India Society, held at the Fouzdari Balakhana on the 19th of December, 1845, it was proposed by the Rev. K. M. Banerjea, seconded by Babu Dwarka Nath Gupta that Babu Ram Gopal Ghose be requested to fill the office of President, vacant by the resignation of W. Theobold Esq. The Rev. K. M. Banerjea presided at this meeting.

RAM GOPAL GHOSE & THE SHRIEVALTY OF CALCUTTA.

Sir James Colville had all but promised the honours of the Shrievalty to the late Babu Ram Gopal Ghose, but somehow or other it miscarried.

THE Rev. K. M. BANERJEA.
SON OF BABU JIBUN KRISTO BANERJEA.
(BORN IN CALCUTTA IN 1813 AND DIED IN MAY 1885.)
THE Rev. K. M. BANERJEE AND THE HON'BLE K. D. PAL.

On the introduction of the elective system of Municipality in Calcutta, the Rev. K. M. Banerjea once stood as a

candidate for one of the elected seats on that corporation.
The late Rev. K. M. Banerjea was a fearless and most out-
spoken member of that civic body. The Hon'ble Kristodas Pal,
therefore, asked Babu Irosau Das Dutta, his most intimate
friend, to exercise his influence with the voters of the ward
for which the Rev. K. M. Banerjea stood as a candidate to
elect him by a large majority of votes. It was, thus, through
the influence of Kristo Das Pal that the Rev. K. M. Banerjea
was elected to a seat in that corporation. Kristo Das used to
say that the "hoary-headed political padre" was a fearless
man and never shirked the duty of criticizing the actions of
government and its representatives in a sledge-hammer and
uncompromising style when occasions required it. It was
for this reason Kristo Das always helped the return of the
Rev. K. M. Banerjea.

THE REV. K. M. BANERJEE AND LORD HARDINGE.

We learn from the *Englishman and Military Chronicle* of
22nd August, 1846, that Lord Hardinge presented a beautiful-
ly bound copy of "Elphinstone's India" through the Honourable Mr. Hay Cameron to the Rev. K. M. Banerjea, as a mark
of his approbation of the first and second numbers of the *En-
cyclopœdia Bengalensis.*

The third number of the *Bengalensis* appeared in July 1846.

HIS BAPTISM.

The following letter addressed by the Rev. K. M. Banerjea to his intimate class-friend Babu Gobind Chunder Bysak
who was a Deputy Magistrate of Midnapore will be now read
with interest.

WEDNESDAY, 16th October, 1832.

MY DEAR FRIEND,

Through the mercy of a Gracious Providence, I intend being baptized
this evening at the house of the Rev. A. Duff, and as you were one of
those with whom last year about this time, I began first to examine the
claims of Christianity, it will give me great pleasure to see you witness

my declaration before God and man, of what is now my faith, and my admission into the visible Church of Christ.

Your's most affectionate friend,

KRISHNA MOHANA BANERJIA.

THE EFFECT OF BAPTISM.

The defunct Bengali Monthly Journal *Nabajiban* thus described it in 1889, in an article containing a sketch of his life.

"After his conversion to Christianity, he never wore his Native dress (*Dhuti* and *Chadur*), but never adopted the European hat and coat. In the latter days of his life he became a great lover of his country, but in his earlier days he was reckoned as one of the greatest enemies of the Hindus. In days gone-bye, he was generally called by the Calcutta people "house-spoiler Kristo" (*Ghur majana* Kristo.) The guardians of boys used to take fright when they saw their children in company with him. He had a great hand in the conversion of many Hindu boys. Take for instance, the case of Michael Madhu Sudan Datta and Gyanendra Mohun Tagore.

In his younger days the Rev. K. M. Banerji was a great hater of the Hindus. Such was his hatred towards them that, when the Calcutta Hindu community, amidst drenching rain and foul weather, mustered strong to show their respect at the time of David Hare's interment, the Rev. K. M. Banerji was conspicuous by his absence. To David Hare, to whose kindness he was greatly indebted for his education in the Hindu College, the Rev. K. M. Banerji cherished no feeling of respect, as David Hare was a great friend of the Hindus. At his funeral ceremony, the Rev. Doctor James Charles took as his text for his sermon "Ye fight not with the dead," and from this many inferred that the Reverend gentleman was, as if it were, alluding to the absence of Mr. Banerji. Then, again, when a large Memorial meeting of the Hindus was held on the 17th June, 1841, in the Medical College Hall in honor of David Hare, Mr. Banerji kept aloof from it.* The secrecy of his absence was that David Hare was no admirer of Christianity, and never liked the idea of conversion of the Hindus to Christianity. He (the Rev. K. M. Banerji) cherished an ill-feeling towards the Hindu College. With a view to convert the students of the College, the Rev. K. M. Banerji once thought of establishing a

---

* This version does not tally with the report given in the biography of David Hare by Babu Kishori Chand Mitter.

Church in the vicinity of it at the present site of the Presidency College.
He arranged secretly for the construction of the Church, when at the ele-
venth hour when the foundation stone of it was about to be laid, the secrecy was known to David Hare, Sir Rajah Radha Kant Deb Bahadur,
Babus Ram Komul Sen, Dwarka Nath Tagore, and Mutty Lall Seal, who
represented the matter to Lord Auckland, and the Rev. K. M. Banerji's
design fell to the ground. At last, the Church was built on the western
side of the Hedua tank. The Christian Missionaries cherished a deep
hatred towards the College. On one occasion Babu Ishur Chunder Mitter
(now a Government pensioner), student of the said College and a pupil of
the celebrated mathematician, Mr. Rees, calculated the date of an eclipse
of sun and published the result of the calculation in the *Bengal Hurkara*
newspaper. The Missionaries, who watched the progress of Hindu students, contradicted the statement, and this was done by the Rev. Mr.
Smith of the General Assembly's Institution. A counter-reply appeared
under Mr. Rees' own signature, vouching for the correctness of Ishur
Babu's calculation, and in order to ascertain the truth, a bet was laid at
Rs. 1,000 between Mr. Rees and the Missionaries, and on the day of the
eclipse it was seen that the calculation of Ishur Babu was right. The
Rev. K. M. Banerji used to throw bones of cows into the houses of his
neighbours, and to write declamatory things against the Hindus in newspapers. Once[*] he wrote a novel[†] against the respected head of the Hindu
community, Sir Raja Radha Kant Deb Bahadur, and called him Gadha
Kant or Rashava Kant (Ass). To this a rejoinder was given by an unknown writer who in his book, called "Spunjy Redivivus," called Kristo
Mohun "*Dhini-Kristo-tini ta*," and gave him the title of *Beef-fed ass.*
His brother, Kally Mohun, was called "*Harkally*", and a Christian
woman was named "Mrs. Eliza *Bhuter-Ma.*" [‡] The Missionaries also
indulged in similar invectives against the Hindus. The late Dr. Duff,
once in 1849 § either in September or August, wrote to the *Bengal
Hurkara* that the Bengalis would kill him for his having converted
several Hindu children. To this a contradiction appeared, written by a
student of the College, who signed the letter "Mac Bamboo."

---

[*] In 1850.

[†] A Squib in a phamphlet form under the name "Report of a grand Brahminical meeting, against the Lex Loci Act, to which are appended petitions from
the Khoonds and the Thugs in behalf of their rights". (Fr. I. May 1, 1850.)

[‡] Vide F. I. Aug. 29, 1850.

§ In 1847.

THE Rev. K. M. BANERJI AND
BABU PROSUNNO KUMAR TAGORE.

"Gyanendra Mohun married the Reverend gentleman's daughter at a mature age, and we do not blame Mr. Banerji for it. By this conversion and marriage, a deep mortal wound was given to the heart of the late Prosunno Kumar Tagore. The Reverend K. M. Banerji added sometimes fuel to the fire that burnt in the heart of the Tagore.

We know from personal experience that, on one occasion, Babu Prosunno Kumar arrived at the Howrah Railway Station with his wife in order to go to his summer retreat at Pirpabar in Mongbyr and accidentally, at the very same time Rev. K. M. Banerji and his wife came there in order to go to a place by the same train. When he saw Prosunno Kumar, he said in a loud tone to Mrs. Banerji, "Look, look, our *Bayi* (bridegroom's father) is going there." On hearing this, Prosunno Kumar became somewhat ashamed, and with a quicker motion he tried to evade his presence. But the Reverend K. M. Banerji was irrepressible. He, with a still louder voice, called out, "*Bayi;*" *Bayi*, !! (Oh bridegroom's father ! ! come, come, let us travel in the same compartment with our *Bayin* (bridegroom's mother.)" Thus insulted, Prosunno Kumar abandoned the idea of travelling with him in the same train, lest he should insult him more, and returned home on that day."

THE REV. K. M. BANERJEE AND Mr. MICHAEL
MUDHU SHUDHUN DUTT

The Same writer in the *Nabajibun* who was Babu Ganga Churn Sirkar, the father of Babu Akshaya Chandra Sirkar, the Editor of that paper thus wrote on the subject :—

"Although we were senior to him by some few years, yet Michael, by obtaining double promotion, reached our class, and we (the writer of this article) and Modhu read together in the 3rd class of the Senior Department of that College. While we read together, we knew him to be a jolly fellow, fond of humour, and very fastidious in dress. From his early days he showed a tendency to dress himself like a European, and he used to come to the College always without his *chadur*. This *chadur*-less boy was known to us by the nickname of *Akohuta* (এক‍হুট)boy. While we thus studied together, one day we came to learn, all on a sudden, that Michael had gone to the Missionaries for conversion. Rumours were afloat that *shurkiwallas* and *lattials* had been engaged ·by Michael's father, in order to snatch him away form the custody of the Missionaries. In the meantime, the late Rev. K. M. Bannerji came to our lodging, and told my maternal uncle with whom there was a great friendship with the father of Michael, that Michael had been, according to his own suggestion, kept in the Fort of Calcutta under Brigadier Powners, and that he, of his own accord, would accept Christianity. The suggestion of keeping him concealed in the Fort was not really Michael's, but it originated probably, from the Rev. K. M. Banerji himself. My maternal uncle and myself accompanied by Babu Ram Chunder Mitter, a teacher of the Hindu College, went to the Fort, and got an interview with Modhu, and my maternal uncle requested him to go back to his parents, who were bitterly crying for him, but Machael summarily dismissed them with "a good morning," and we had to come back greatly disappointed. We then heard that Modhu was baptized in the church, situated in Mission Row, by Archdeacon Daltry, with great pomp. Modhu was so much delighted that he composed a piece of poetry, called "On My Seeing the light." and got it published in a local newspaper. The old venerable Babu Rajnarain Bose of the 1st class of the Hindu College, wrote another piece of poetry "On my circumcision," by way of ridiculing."

The above extracts appeared also in the *Indian Mirror.*

THE REV. K. M. BANERJEE, AS EDITOR OF
A VERNACULAR NEWSPAPER

We learn from the *Friend of India* of September 12, 1850, that a Bengali hebdomadal called (সংবাদ সুধাংশু) *Sangbad Shudhangshu* was edited and published by the above gentleman, the first number of which appeared in September, 1850.

THE REV. K. M. BANERJEA AND
BABU RAJ NARAIN BOSE.

The latter kindly wrote us a letter from which, we extract the following :—

"I had a fierce discussion with the Rev. K. M. Banerjea in 1851 about the relative merits of Christianity and Vedantism (we, Brahmas, were Vedantists at that time.) A man of Hindoo predilections as he was, he inadvertently called

Noah and Moses his ancestors in one of his lectures. I availed myself of this careless merry expression, and taunted by saying, "forsaking his national ancestors Manu and Jagya-walkya &c. &c. &c". He used to call our Vedan-tism *Belatee* Vedantism, as we availed ourselves of English Theology and English Science to interpret Vedanta."

BABU RAJ NARAIN BOSE'S LETTER CONTINUED.

We extract the following from the same letter of Babu Raj Narain Bose.

"He was very fond of nationality. He used to join in Native Christian *sangkirtan* and *kathakatha.* He used to like them very much. With *khol* round his neck, he used to join in the former. He made it a point not to marry his daughters except to Brahmin converts, or to English Reverend gentlemen who are the Brahmins of their community. His sons-in-law were my college fellows, Mr. Gyanendra Mohun Tagore, and the Reverends Sale and Wheeler. As a proof of his Hindoo predilections it may be instanced that, at a বিদ্বজ্জন সমাগম or Literary Reunion held at the house of the venerable Debendra Nath Tagore, (this বিদ্বজ্জন সমাগম was a suggestion of mine), he ate (ফলার) feast with *luchis* and sweat-meats with great gusto like a regular Bhattyacharya. Love of ফলার (feast) is ineradicable from men of Brahmin lineage, however hetrodox or religiously perverted they may be. At one of these Reunions, on Rev. Lall Behary Dey's asking him for his *hookah,* he repeatedly refused to give it to him, but was at last obliged to yield, exclaiming that a *sonarbania* should not smoke the hookah of a Brahmin. His near christian rela-tives after his examples were very Hindoo in their predilec-tions. Mr. Gyanendra Mohan Tagore in one of his lectures called himself a "Brahmin Christian." The Rev. K. M. Banerjie's brother Kali Bundo kept matted hair like a Hindu ascetic, and used to call the Bible not by its own name, but as

Veda. Whenever he wished to read the Bible, he used to
tell his friends, "let us now read Veda."

BABU RAM TANOO LAHIRI AND THE HON'BLE SIR. E. DRUMMOND, LIEUTENANT-GOVERNOR OF THE NORTH-WESTERN PROVINCES.

Babu Ram Tanoo Lahiri went to Allahabad sometime in
1865. Sir E. Drummond was then the Lieutenant-Governor
of the North-Western Provinces. Babu Ram Tanoo Lahiri
knew him while he was the District Magistrate of Burdwan.
To renew his old acquaintance, and perhaps to pay
respect to a high official then on the musnud of the Allahabad
Government, Babu Ram Tanoo Lahiri expressed a desire
to see the Lientenant-Governor. Most simple minded
as he is, he communicated his desire to Babu Nil
Kamal Mitter with whom he was then putting up at Allahabad. The idea of a Native, however educated and enlightened he might be, desirous of paying a visit to the exalted
officer in the position of the Lieutenant-Governor of the
North-Western Provinces and Oudh was simply laughed out,
and Babu Ram Tanoo Lahiri was dissuaded by Babu
Nil Kamal Mitter not to stultify himself as he had proposed.
They thought that, it would be impossible for a poor school-
master like himself to get an interview with the Lieutenant-
Governor. In spite of their protest, Babu Ram Tanoo wrote
a letter to the Private Secretary to his honour the Lieutenant-
Governor, asking his permission to appoint a time for the
interview. The letter from this poor school-master of Bengal,
the jewel among the Barendra Brahmins of Krishnagar, no
sooner reached the Government House, than a reply was immediately ordered to be sent to him, appointing a time for it.
On receiving this letter from the Private Secretary, he drove
to Government House in a barouche belonging to Babu Nil

Kamal Mitter. No sooner the carriage arrived in the gari-varenda of the Gubernatorial Palace at Allahabad, one of Sir E. Drummond's sons, then scarcely out of his teens, accosted him thus "Well Babu ? "What business have you here?", "Do you intend seeing Sir E. Drummond." In, reply to this abrupt and uncouth question, Babu Ram Tanoo with his characteristic modesty said, "Yes, Sir, I have come to see the Lieutenant-Governor". The boy then asked the old man " Do you come by appointment ? " The answer being in the affirmative, the boy muttered something expressing his view that it would be simply impossible for him to see the Lieute-nant-Governor. In the mean time liveried Chaprasies surrounded him from all sides, and took him to Sir, E. Drummond. But before he was led into the room, the Chap-rasies requested him to leave his shoes behind. To this he mildly protested in his soft sonorous voice, as befitting his high position as the most moral man of Bengal, but the Chaprasies grew relentless in their demand. The more they pressed the question, the more the grand old man became courteous to them. In the meanwhile the Lieutenant-Governor finding the delay too much ordered this Private Secretary to see why the man was detained. The Private Secretary reported the matter to Sir, E. Drummond who immediately ordered Babu Ram Tanoo Lahiri to see him with his shoes on. In this way the long sought-for interview was granted to his old acquaintance, the old school-master of Burdwan, with all the courtsey and honour due to him Sir, E. Drummond greatly respected Babu Ram Tanoo Lahiri for his unexampled moral courage and purity of character, while he was a school-master at Burdwan, and threw off his Brahminical holy thread without any fuss or noise.of any kind in 1851.

RAJA ROMANATH TAGORE.

The first obituary notice of this gentleman appeared in the *Hindoo Patriot* of the 11th June, 1877. Babu K. D. Pal,

its Editor having been away from the town, the notice was
written by Dr. Rajendralal Mitra. Kristo Das wrote a second
notice of the late lamented deceased from which we glean the
following reminiscences of that great man.

"He remembered the days, when a native could not see
a civilian, without paying nuzzer, generally a gold mohur,
and how happily he used to contrast those days with the
present time, when the Viceroy and Governor-General does
not consider it *infra dig* to admit a native to his august presence without exacting that tribute. With his able and
patriotic cousin, the late Prasuna Kumar Tagore, C. S. I., he
conducted a newspaper called the *Indian Reformer* under the
suprintendence of one Mr. Crow.* It was his privilege,
in the absence of his brother (Babu Dwarka Nath Tagore)
who was then ill, to acknowledge the toast in honour of the
people of India at the Free Press Dinner at the Town Hall
in 1835. It is not perhaps generally known that he was the
soul of the movement on the great Burning Ghat question
of Calcutta. When the question came before the Justices at
a Meeting, it was he who chiefly urged Babu Ram Gopal
Ghose to make that now celebrated speech on the subject."

"He was one of the chief movers of the agitation, which
was set on foot by the Hindu community against what was
commonly called the Native converts' Inheritance Act passed
by Lord Dalhousie in 1850. He was ably seconded by the late
Babu Promotho Nath Deb, who chiefly supplied funds."

BABU ROMA NATH TAGORE AND BABU
ROMESH CHUNDER MITTER.

"Now that Lord Northbrook has retired from the Viceroy-
alty and the Moharajah has been snatched away from the
scene of his earthly labours, we think we may mention
without breach of confidence that, he was the only native

---

* Mr. Crow, a Roman Catholic gentleman was its editor.

gentleman, whom his Lordship consulted on the appoint
ment of Babu (afterwards Sir) Romesh Chunder Mitter, as
a Judge of the High Court. The Raja strongly supported
his nomination.

BABU DWARKA NATH TAGORE AND
Mr. MONTGOMERY MARTIN OF THE *BENGAL HERALD.*

The Surgeon had a shop close to the *Hurkura* office. It
happened that Dwarkanath Tagore's horses ran away with
him, overturned his carriage, and broke his leg; and Mr.
Martin standing at his door, was the first to offer professional
assistance. Dwarkanath always liberal, easily listened to the
persuasions of Mr. Montgomery Martin to establish a newspaper for him. He thus became Editor of the *Bengal Herald,*
soon tiring out his proprietor by involving him in several
libel cases. The *Bengal Herald* was sold to the proprietor of
the *Hurkura.* (Vide Englishman, Aug. 11, 1845.)

RAJAH GOPEE MOHUN DEY, FATHER OF
SIR RAJAH RADHA KANT DEB BAHADUR.

The Strand Road was constructed in 1820-21, over a
"chur" that passed through two zemindaries, that of Calcutta, and that of Sootanaty, which was then the property of
Raja Gopee Mohun Dey. In 1824, he filed a bill in Equity
against the Company for building a road over the land which
had accrued to his zemindary. On the death of the Raja,
his son Radha Kant continued his suit, and after sixteen
years, the Supreme Court came to a decision that the Raja
had a right to the price of his land, but as the suit had been
brought on the Equity instead of the Common Law Side of
the Court, he was not to have it. At last, government paid
two lakhs of rupees to the Rajah, as value of the land in
dispute. (Vide F. I. Sept. 8, 1853.)

RAJA RAM, THE FOSTER SON OF RAJA RAM MOHUN ROY, AND BABU NOGENDRA NATH TAGORE.

"In the East India Company's Charter of 1833, the broad principle of the employment of natives in the public service of India was first declared, but it was soon after put to the test by an application made by the foster son of Raja Ram Mohun Roy, and as usual, he was humbugged. Even the influence of the late Babu Dwarka Nath Tagore, the Indian Crœsus, could not obtain for his son Babu Nogendra Nath Tagore, who accompanied him to England, a niche in the temple of the favoured service. In later life, Raja Ram became a convert and got a writership in the Foreign Secretariat. Lord Dalhousie appointed Babu Nogendra Nath Tagore as an Assistant Collector of the Calcutta Customs.

In 1836 Sir John Cam Hobhouse (afterwards Lord Broughton) the President of the Board of Control, presented a writership to Raja Ram ; but the Court of Directors refused to confirm the nomination."

Was Raja Ram, a foster son of the Rajah ? We have doubts on that point. The late Dr Sumbhu Chunder Mukherjea, Editor of *Reis* and *Rayyet* held a contrary opinion.

RAM GOPAL GHOSE, MUTTY LAL SEAL AND OTHERS, AND THE MEMORIAL OF Mr. W. W. BIRD, DEPUTY-GOVERNOR OF BENGAL.

In 1844, the native inhabitants of Calcutta subscribed for a portrait of this eminent man, which was to be kept in the Hindu College. The following is the list of subscribers to the above memorial fund :—

Babu Dwarkanath Tagore	...	Rs. 1,000
Mutty Lal Seal	... ...	„ · 100
Ranee Katayani	... ...	100

Bobu Ram Gopal Ghose ... „ 100
„ G. D. Dutt ... ... „ 50
„ H. C. Ghose ... ... „ 16

Babu Dwarka Nath Tagore as one of the proprietors of Messrs. Carr Tagore & Co., advanced Rs. 3,000 to an English painter for the portrait. But some of the subcribers having failed to pay, Messrs. Carr Tagore & Co., notified that the portrait would be sold by public auction, if the subscribers did not pay the balance Rs. 1500, due to them. Babu Ram Gopal Ghose, thereupon tried his best to induce the non-paying native subscribers to pay off their subscriptions, but all his efforts were in vain. The European friends of Mr. W. W. Bird then paid the balance, and hung up the portrait in the Town Hall of Calcutta.

THE LATE BABU KUNJA LAL BANERJEE.

Babu Kunjalal Banerjee, the late second Judge of the Calcutta S. C. Court, objected to the practice of hearing cases of European suitors first, and then those of the natives. It was on his representation, Sir Ashley Eden put a stop to it in 1878.

BABU DUKHINARANJUN MUKHERJEA.

Died in 1878. He was a grandson of Babu Surjee Kumar Tagore of Calcutta. He was one of the first fruits of the late Hindu College, and gave early promise of future excellence. He was a prominent member of the first batch of the Hindu College *alumni*, whom Mr. James Hume gave the *sobriquet* of Chuckerbutty Faction, and who in after life distinguished themselves by their patriotic and public spirited labours. Babu Dukhinaranjan started the *Bengal Spectator*, an Anglo-Indian periodical with the co-operation of Babu Rushik Krishna Mullic and Peary Chand Miter. As a member of the British Indian Association, he made a speech in 1859 on Lord Canning's Oudh policy, for which, Lord Canning, as recommended by the Rev. Dr. Duff, his patron, granted him a sunud conferring on him the Taluk of Sun-kurpur in Rai Bariely in Oudh, which was forfeited to the British Crown by the rebellion of its chief Bani Madho, who refused to avail himself of the mercy offered to him. He was the personal friend of Sir Charles Wingfield, and the successive Chief Commissioners of Oudh, and was honored with their confidence. He was the trusted friend of Maharaja Maunsing and the other Talukdars of Oudh, and for their common benefit established an Association known as the "Talukdars' Association," of which he was the first Secretary. His zeal for the interests of the Association was so great that he often risked the friendship of his English friends and went the length of offending his best friend Sir Charles Wingfield and the Hon'ble Mr. Davis, rather than yield an iota of his convictions as to what was right for the good of the Talukdars and the people of Oudh. To the credit of those honorable gentlemen, be it said, that they were soon convinced of the singleness of purpose of Babu Dukhina-runjun Mookerjee and the clouds that hung over the horison of his fame soon passed way, and they were again as warm friends as ever. Sir Charles Wingfield obtained for him the sunud, and the award of the Taluq from Lord Canning, and the Honorable Mr. Davis recommended him highly for the Rajaship. He established the *Samachar Hindoosthani* and purchased the *Lucknow Times*, as the organ of the Talook-dars of Oudh. He made a free-gift of some portion of the land on which the Bethune Female school was erected in 1850. Sir John Littler, the Deputy-Governor of Bengal laid the foundation of this building on the 6th of November, 1850.

BABU PEARY MOHUN BANERJEE,
THE "FIGHTING MUNSIFF."

Babu Peary Mohun Banerjee, Senior Government Pleader of the North Western Provinces, died in 1874. He was a native of Ooterparah, and was first brought up in the local school, and subsequently in the Hindu College. He was serving as a Munsiff in the district of Allahabad, when the hurricane of the Sepoy revolt came, and he was found foremost in braving the danger, though many a stout British heart had sunk under it. For the bravery he displayed in that crisis, he was dubbed the "Fighting Munsiff." A writer in the *Calcutta Review*, No. XLI, in an article, headed "A district during a rebellion," thus testified to his services :

"In one remarkable instance the native Civil Judge—a Bengali Babu by capacity and valor—brought himself so conspicuously forward, as to be known as "the fighting Munsiff." He not only held his own defiantly, but he planned attacks, he burnt villages, he wrote English despatches thanking his subordinates, and displayed a capacity for rule and a fertility of resource very remarkable for one of his nation,

Apropos of the "Fighting Munsiff's" case, Mr. Townsend, the then editor of the *Friend of India* thus wrote :

"We are not slow to scold Bengalees when required, but if in India there is a race to whom God has given capacity, real clearness of brain, it is the Bengalee."

The Government of India rewarded the loyal services of Babu Peary Mohun Banerjee with a Jaighir in the district of Goruckpore worth Rs. 10,000. Babu Peary Mohun would not however allow his mind to rust in the pigeon hole of the Munsiff's office, and so he resigned it, and was soon after installed as the Dewan of the Maharaja of Benares. After a few years' service at Benares he joined the bar of the North West High Court, where he soon distinguished himself, and was ultimately appointed Senior Government Advocate. He published a Fouzdari Guide in English and Urdu.

THE PSEUDO RAJA PROTAP CHAND.

He was released from Jail on the 3rd Feb., 1837. Babu Raj Krishna Raichowdry and Gopee Kishen Raichowdry tendered their shares of the extensive Talook of Gouripur in

16068

the 24-Purgnahs as security for the release of Protap Chand.
(vide *Englishman*, Jan. 26, 1837.)

BABU CHUTOORDHURY SHAHAI OF PATNA,

The evil practice of conferring titles on Zemindars and
monied men for their handsome subscriptions for public
purposes is not confined to our own times. For, we learn
from the *Gyananasun* of May, 1837, that the above gentleman
received the title of "Maharajah Bahadur" for subscribing
Rs. 50,000 to the "Education Fund."

BABU ASUTOSH DEB, AND OTHER NATIVE
GENTLEMEN ; AND THE HINDU ANTI-
CHRISTIAN MEETING.

On the 19th of September, 1847, a public meeting was
held in the house of Babu Gora Chand Basak and Hindoo
society was formed, binding every member not to send
his children to Missionary Institutions at Calcutta. The
meeting was called by Babu Promotho Nath Deb, and
attended by Rajas Radha Kanta Deb, Satya Charan Ghoshal,
Babu Asutosh Deb, * and his brother Babu Promotho Nath
Deb, Babus Hara Kumar Tagore, Debendra Nath Tagore,
Romanath Tagore, Kashi Prasad Ghosh, and others.

The object of this meeting was vilified and misrepresent-
ed in a series of letters published in the *Hurkura* of September, 1847, written by an anonymous correspondent "Indophilus". We suspect "Indophilus" was the Rev. K. M.
Banerjea who charged the Hindoos with maltreating him and
other Christians. In the *Hurkura* of September 3rd, 1847,
appeared a letter from the Rev. Alexander Duff to Babu
Promotho Nath Deb, asking his party to discuss the relative

---

* Died in 1849. He was known in Calcutta as Chatu Babu, while his brother Babu Promotho Nath Deb as Latu Babu.

merits of Christianity and Hindooism with him. Babu
Promotho Nath Deb declined to hold any controversy on that
subject. The moral of this highly interesting episode in the
history of Hindoo Society of days gone-bye is too apparent
to us all. The illustrious successors of these old Hindoos
should always keep this noble example before their eyes.

BABU KASHI PROSAD GHOSE, PROPRIETOR
AND EDITOR OF THE HINDU
INTELLIGENCER.

He was one of the first fruits of the Hindoo College. He
distinguished himself greatly in the College by his intelligence,
industry, and thorough mastery of the subjects which he
studied. He soon became a favorite of Dr. Horace Hayman
Wilson, the then Secretary to the Hindu College. He wrote
both in prose and verse, and contributed literary papers to
almost all the leading journals and periodicals of the day. The
most valuable papers were those entitled "Historical Sketches
of the Maharatta Dynasty" Bristling with facts, some of which
he had collected after considerable pain, industry, and research, and containing fair and accurate delineations of
scenes and characters, these papers were highly appreciated
by Indian critics. Babu Kasiprosad was however better
known as the Indian Bard. He contributed poetry to the
Bengal Hurkara, *John Bull*, the *Literary Gazette*, the *Bengal
Annual*, and other periodicals. Babu Kasiprosad Ghosh
was the first native gentleman, who conducted newspaper
exclusively in English. He founded * the *Hindu Intelligencer*,
a weekly chronicle of news, politics, and literature. Before
the *Intelligencer*, there were native papers like the *Gyanane-
shana* and the *Bengal Spectator* † conducted by Babus Russick

---

* It was established in Nov. 1846.

† He edited the paper up to January 1837, when he was nominated a
Deputy-Collector of Burdwan. He was formerly in the Bengal Revenue
Board office.

Krishna Mullick, Dukhinarunjun Mookerjea, and Peary Chand Mitter, and the *Reformer* by Babus Prossunno Coomar Tagore and Romanath Tagore, but the former were diglots, while the latter was under European superintendence. *   He was opposed to female education, and the late Mr. Bethune found in him a stout opponent to his philanthropic efforts to ameliorate the condition of the Hindu woman. He was a zealous member of the Dhurma Sabha established by the late Raja Sir Radhakant Deb, and lent his ready pen against such social movements as the remarriage of widows and the suppression of polygamy.   He was, however, an earnest advocate of his country's cause, and never shrunk from exposing abuses and oppressions.   He took a delight in nursing the literary ambition of many a struggling educated native. Both Babus Hurrish Chunder Mookerjea and Grish Chunder Ghose learnt the art of journalistic warfare from him. Lord Canning's Gagging Act of 1857 gave a quietus to the *Hindu Intelligencer*.   Babus K. D. Pal, and Sumbhu Chunder Mukherji first fleshed their pen in the columns of this paper.

SIR RAJA RADHAKANT DEB BAHADUR,
BABU HURI MOHUN SEN, AND
THE HINDU MEMORIAL
AGAINST THE LEX
LOCI ACT.

A memorial against the Lex Loci Act (XXI of 1850) was held in the house of Babu Udoy Chand Bosak of Jorasanko, on the 14th of May, 1850, under the presidency of Raja Radha Kant Deb.   It was resolved at that meeting to present a memorial to the Court of Directors against the Act through Mr. John Farley Leith, a barrister of the Supreme Court.   Babu Huri Mohun Sen was appointed secretary to the committee. (*Hindoo Intelligencer*, June 4, 1850.)

---

* Mr. Crow a Roman Catholic edited the *Reformer* which was afterwards incorporated with the *Hurkura*.

THE HON'BLE JUSTICE DWARKANATH MITTER AND SIR GEORGE CAMPBELL.

"Sir George Campbell, if we are informed aright, actually entered a protest against the independence of the late Justice Dwarkanath Mitter, particularly in reference to the notorious Maldah case, and advised against the policy of appointing natives to the bench of the High Court, but not only Lord Northbrook took no notice of this policy, but marked his confidence in natives by appointing a native successor to the lamented Justice Mitter, though there was a widely circulated rumour at the time that no native would be appointed to the Bengal High Court." (H. P. May, 1, 1876.)

BABU RADHANATH SIKDAR.

We publish the following extract from a letter from Lieutenant Colonel Sherwill to the *Friend of India* of 1876.

"A friend has just sent me a copy of the *Friend of India* of the 24th June, all the way from Germany, in order that I might be made acquainted with the *sad fact* that, when bringing out a third edition of "Smyth and Thuillier's Manual of Surveying for India," the much respected name of the late Babu Radhanath Sikdar, the able and distinguished head of the computing department of the Great Trigonometrical Survey of India, who did so much to enrich the early editions of the "Manual," had been advertently, or inadvertently, removed from the preface of the last edition ; while at the same time all the valuable matter written by the Babu had been retained, and that without any acknowledgment as to the authorship.

As an old Revenue Surveyor who used the "Manual for a quarter of a century, and as an acquaintance of the late Radhanath Sikdar, I feel quite ashamed for those who have seen fit to exclude his name from the present edition, especially as the former Editors so fully acknowledged the deep obligations under which they found themselves for Radhanath's assistance, not only for the particular portion of the work *"which they desire thus publicly to acknowledge.*—so runs the preface of the 1851 edition,—*but for the advice so generally afforded on all subjects connected with his own department.*

Yesterday only I mentioned the circumstance of the omission of Radhanath's name to one of the Tagores, an old and intimate friend of

Radhanath's and who is now travelling in Scotland ; he was pained beyond measure, but made the significant remark "you see, he is a dead man."

Yes, who cares for the dead, particularly when the dead man is a native of India !

RAJA PRASUNA NATH ROY OF DHIGHAPUTYA.

Was dubbed a Raja by a pretended Prince named Ferozeshah who received a nuzur from him. Sir T. Metcalfe of Delhi reported that he was a pretended Prince.

Hurk. Aug. 1, 23, 1847.

PUNDIT ISHUR CHUNDER VIDYASAGUR
(BORN IN 1820, DIED IN 1891.)
HIS MOVEMENT AGAINST HINDU POLYGAMY.

The Dharma Sabha, with a boldness, reopened the question of prohibiting kulin polygamy, and some warm discussions on the subject took place in that assembly. Adverting to the revival of the discussion, the venerable Pundit Iswara Chunder Vidyasagur published a most powerful pamphlet on the subject. That pamphlet was not only a model of political controversy in Bengali, but a most able resume of the arguments against the practice of polygamy. The materials of that pamphlet had been collected long ago. So long back as 1856 he commenced to collect statistics and information on the subject, but the Sepoy Mutiny broke his plan, and he kept quiet till 1862, when he resuscitated it on the offer made by Raja Sir Deonarain Sing to introduce a Bill in the Council. Some progress had been made in it, a bill had been drafted, but Lord Elgin was opposed to the measure, and Sir Deonarain also soon after went out of the Council by rotation, and so the project dropped. In 1865 the subject was again revived by the monster petition, which the worthy Pundit was instrumental in presenting to Sir Cecil Beadon, it led to the appointment of a Committee, who counselled a policy of non-interference, in which the Government of India acquiesced. An accident also interfered with Pundit Iswar Chunder's plan.

PUNDIT ISHUR CHUNDER VIDYASAGUR
ON THE SAME MOVEMENT.

We heard the following account of this movement from the Pundit himself.

He told us that at his repeated and urgent request, Sir Cecil Beadon, the then Lieutenant-Governor of Bengal, consented to take the initiative for the suppression of polygamy, and advised him to send a memorial, signed by the heads of aristocratic families in Bengal, in support of the movement. Agreeably with this request, the venerable Pundit Iswar Chunder went to Krishnaghur, and saw Maharajah Srish Chunder Roy, Bahadur, (grandfather of the present Maharajah), and took his consent in the matter. He then saw the Maharajah of Burdwan, who heartily thanked him for his project. The signatures of the Rajahs and Maharajahs in the Mofussil Districts were not enough for his purpose, and so he went personally to all the leaders of Hindu society in Calcutta, and obtained their assent to it. The petition was drawn up, and the Maharajah of Burdwan headed the list of its signatories. Sir Cecil Beadon, with the sanction of the Supreme Government, appointed a Committee to report whether, in the interest of the Hindu marriage system, it was desirable to put a stop to polygamy, as prevalent in Bengal, by any legislative enactment. The Committee was composed of members, both official and non-official. Among these latter, were some of the leaders of the Calcutta Hindu society, who had previously pledged themselves to Vidyasagur to support the movement. But at Committee meetings, they opposed the project almost unanimously, and the idea of putting an end to the polygamous marriage system of Bengal was thus abandoned. From that day, Vidyasagur 'never crossed the thresholds of these men, who had deceived him with false hopes in this matter.

of the reasons why these Calcutta Zemindars betrayed him was, said Vidyasagur to our anxious enquiry, that they took umbrage at finding the Memorial signed at first by the Maharajah of Burdwan, to whom they were reluctant to give precedence in such a matter.

BABU RAM GOPAL GHOSE AND PUNDIT ISHUR CHUNDER VIDYASAGUR, AS MEMBERS OF THE CALOUTTA UNIVERSITY.

When the Calcutta University was established in 1857, Pundit Ishur Chunder Vidyasagur, Babu Ram Gopal Ghose, Babus Prasuna Kumar Tagore, and Roma Prosad Roy, were the only four Hindu gentlemen, who were first appointed. Fellows of the University. Among the Mahomedans, Moulvi Abdul Wazid, Principal of the Calcutta Madrassa, was the only man who was appointed a Fellow.

Babu Ram Gopal Ghose was appointed a Member of the Council of Education in Oct, 1848.

HIS GRATITUDE TO THE BENEFACTORS OF HIS FATHER BABU THAKUR DAS BANERJEA.

His gratitude towards Babu Bogobut Churn Singh and his son Juggut Durlub Singh was as undiminished as ever. It was in the lodgings of these gentlemen at Doyahatta in Burra-Bazar (which is now occupied by Babu Kartic Johuri) Vidyasagur's father used to remain as their Sirkar on a salary of Rs 10 per mensem. It was here, his uncles, brothers and he himself used to remain, while they were poor. On the death of Babu Juggut Durlub, he used to pay a monthly allowance of Rs. 10 to Srimati Mokhyadayini, widow of the son of the said Juggut Durlub. A similar pension was paid to his daughter. These pensions were paid continually for more than 19 years. His charity was of a cosmopolitan character. Sometimes, he used to succour the distress of the public women of Calcutta.

PUNDIT ISHUR CHANDER VIDYASAGAR AND THE AFFILIATION OF THE METROPOLITAN INSTITUTION, AND THE OPPOSITION OF DR. DUFF.

We read the following in the *Hindoo Patriot* of March 24, 1873, anent this question.

The Friend of India in quoting our statement regarding the difficulty experienced by the managers of the Metropolitan Institution in getting it affiliated to the University seems to think that the opposition came from the Education Department alone. The Missionaries were not, however, altogether blameless. We believe Dr. Duff was at the time a member of the Syndicate, and he could not bear the rivalry of Pundit Iswarchunder Vidyasagar as the supporter of an independent Native College, and hence we believe the first application was rejected, though Bishop Cotton had in a manner promised to pass it.

In 1866 the affiliation of the Metropolitan Institution which had the warmest support of Sir Cecil Beadon, Bishop Cotton and other influential Fellows of the Calcutta University, was opposed by Mr. Sutcliffe who "pulled the wires from behind." The privilege of affiliation was granted to the Institution in 1873, mainly through the generous support of Mr. Atkinson. Vidyasagar got the management of the "Training School" from Babu Thakur Das Chuckerbutty, formerly one of the clerks in the Secretriat in 1859.

VIDYASAGUR AND THE FIRST WIDOW MARRIAGE.

It is said that he asked Rajah Roma Proshad Roy to be present on the occasion of the marriage of Pundit Srish Chunder Vidyarutna. The Rajah having expressed hesitancy in the matter, he (Vidyasagar) left the Rajah's place in disgust, and pointing out to the photo of his father, said, "You had better throw that photo in the street."

Babu Ram Gopal Ghose and the learned Pundit walked by the side of the palanquin of the bridegroom.

THE LEARNED PUNDIT AT THE ROYAL
PROCLAMATION MEETING.

In 1858, soon after the Mutiny, it was arranged that the Bengali translation of the Royal Proclamation should be read by Vidyasagur at the Durbar room from which he was driven away by the Durwans for having slippery shoes on. The Durbar commenced at the usual hour, but the venerable Vidyasagur was not to be seen. Sir Cecil Beadon made enquires, and made a search after him, when he was found at the door in his usual Oriental dress, with Taltollah slippers on. He was allowed to come, and read the translation from his seat at the Durbar."

PUNDIT ISHUR CHANDER VIDYASAGUR, AND
THE SHOE QUESTION.

One day in 1874, Pundit Iswar Chander Vidyasagar accompanied by a native friend from the North West went to the Indian Museum located in the Asiatic Society's building, and was asked by the porters to leave his shoes at the portico, or rather to take off his shoes and keep them in his own hand if he wanted to go in. To this he did not of course consent, and on return home, wrote a letter to the Trustees of the Museum enquiring as to whether they had passed any rule of the kind, and observing, that if such a rule has been passed, it would deter respectable native gentleman, who wore shoes of the native pattern, from visiting the institution. He also wrote to the Council of the Asiatic Society that, if the Museum authorities enforced such a rule, it would discourage respectable Pundits, who like him wore native shoes, from visiting the Society's Library, in as much as both the institutions were located in the same building. The Museum Trustees replied that they had not passed any such rule on the subject, but did not say whether they would pass any order for the discontinuance of the practice. They also seemed to doubt whether the complaint applied to their servants. The Council of the Asiatic Society went further, and wrote to the Pundit in reply that native gentlemen ought · to know the Indian etiquette in the matter. The Pundit, we learn, has sent rejoinders to both. To the Trustees of the Museum he has written to say that it was the servants of the Museum, as he had distinctly stated in his first letter, who had required him to take off the shoes. To the Council of the Asiatic Society he has explained that the Indian custom is not to take off the shoes as a mark of respect, that the Indians do not leave their shoes behind in visiting each other if they are seated in rooms furnished with chairs, but that they do so when they sit on the farash or carpet for their own comfort and convenience. The question is accordingly pending before the Trustees of the Museum and the Council of the Asiatic Society.

BABU RUSHOMOY DUTT, AND THE HONOURABLE MR. CHARLES RAY CAMERON

The natives of Calcutta presented an address in 1848, to this gentleman, adopted at a public meeting held in the Medical College Hall under the presidency of Babu Russomoy Dutta.

SIR MAHARAJA JOTENDRA MOHUN TAGORE, K. C. S. I., AND THE CIVIL PROCEDURE CODE AMENDMENT BILL.

We read the following in the *Hindoo Patriot* of 1877.

" The country is indebted to the Hon'ble Maharaja Jotendra Mohun Tagore for a grand moral victory. The new Civil Procedure Bill withdrew the jurisdiction of the Munsiff and Subordinate Judge over suits against Government and public officers, thereby casting a great slur upon the native judiciary. The British Indian Association and the public meeting convened by the Association had strongly protested against this retrograde move. His Honor the Lieutonant-Governor also wrote in his usual incisive style against this provision. In Select Commitee the Maharaja had fought stoutly against it, but he was defeated. In the Council

he brought forward a motion for the omission of the section
and put the case ably and clearly. He was hotly opposed by
Sir Arthur Hobhouse, Sir John Strachey, Mr. Cocherell, Mr.
Hope. He was however, powerfully backed by his Honor
the Lieutenant Governor. When the motion was put to the
vote, there was a tie, seven members voting for and seven
against the motion; at this dilemma His Excellency the
Viceroy came to the rescue of the Maharaja, and gave his
his vote in favor of the motion. Thus the Maharaja carried
the day, and the conspiracy to put back the clock of progress
was frustrated. This chapter in the history of Indian legis-
lation will be long remembered by the people."

SIR MAHARAJAH, JOTENDRAMOHUN TAGORE, K.C.S.I.,
VERSUS
GYANENDRA MOHUN TAGORE.

We take the following from the *Home News* of 1872.

"Jotendromohun Tagore and Another vrs: Gyanendramohun Tagore.
Judgment.—These were cross appeals from the High Court in Bengal
and involved important questions under the Hindoo law relating to pro.
perty of between £40,000 and 50,000 a year. The testator, the Hon-
Prosonocoomar Tagore, was a Hindoo inhabitant of Calcutta, and the
corpus of his estates exceeded half a million sterling. He made a gift
to his son, Gyanendramohun Tagore on his marriage, when he was of the
same religion as his father, and when he died left him nothing, the son
having in 1857 become a Christian and been baptized. The large property was left under various trusts in perpetuity, and it was submitted
that under the Hindoo law of inheritance, such trusts were invalid.
There were besides legacies and annuities, which it was not sought to
set aside, but the principal question in the contention was as to between
£40,000 and £50,000 a year. Gyanendromohun Tagore, who is a barrister-
at-law, claimed to be considered as heir-at-law of the vast estates for the
reasons alleged in his appeal. Mr. Justice Willos attended to deliver the
judgment of the committee, and was nearly an hour and a half in reading
an elaborate review of the facts, and the Hindu law applicable thereto.
The effect of the judgment was that the first estate for life was held to be
good, and the subsequent estates created by the will to be contrary to the
power of a Hindoo to create,- and therefore, on the termination of the life

estate of Jotendromohuu Tagore the Plaintiff, Gyanendromohun Tagore, (who had embraced Christianity in the lifetime of his father) would succeed as heir-at-law to the whole of the real estates of the testator, and to the surplus of the personalty, after payment thereout of the legacies and annuities bequeathed by the will. Their lordships directed accounts to be taken, and on the ground of the important and novel questions involved, decreed the costs of the parties up to the present time to be paid out of the surplus of the personalty."

Babu Gyanendra Mohun Tagore since died, leaving a daughter to inherit this splendid property.

THE HON'BLE K. D. PAL, C. I. E.,
(BORN IN 1838, AND DIED IN 1884.)
MR. ANSTEY, BARRISTER-AT-LAW, AND K. D. PAL.

The Hon'ble Kristo Das Pal related the following anec-dote in the *Hindoo Patriot* of August 25, 1873.

"As so many anecdotes of the late Mr. Anstey are afloat, we may mention one within our knowledge. The present writer took to him a draft-petition to the Secretary of State, and requested him to settle it. Mr. Anstey read the draft, but refused to have any thing to do with it, because it began with the words—"the humble petition of—". He said he could not understand why the petition should be styled "humble." The Indian subjects of the Queen were on an equal footing with her English subjects, and, it was not the custom of the latter to style a petition to any authority as "humble petition." He could not be made to understand that the Indians, notwithstanding "humble" petitioning in all manner of ways, were seldom heard."

THE HON'BLE KRISTODAS PAL, AND THE
HOUSE OF COMMONS.

Kristo Das was once offered a seat in the House of Com-mons. We read the following in the *Hindoo Patriot* of 1879.

"The Brahma Public Opinion hears that the Home Rulers of Ireland may return Mr. Lalmohun Ghose to Parliament. About three years ago a similar offer was made to the editor of this journal."

THE MEMORIAL FUND OF BABU HURISH CHUNDER MUKHERJEA, EDITOR OF THE *HINDOO PATRIOT*, AND BABU K. D. PAL.

The immortal Hurish Chunder Mukherjea edited the *Hindoo Patriot* from June, 1853, down to the middle of the year 1861, when he died of consumption, leaving a widow, a brother, and an old mother in a state of quite helpless poverty, and a little property consisting of a house and a press with its broken types and appurtenances, which the Indigo-planters of the district of Nuddea attached, by virtue of a civil decree obtained by them against the deceased Editor for libel. He made a tremendous sacrifice of his time and money for maintaining and editing that paper, and died a pauper for the cause of his country. No other native of India, since his time, has been able to show that amount of self-sacrifice for the good of his native land. To perpetuate the memory of this great journalist, no adequate steps were taken at the time by his Calcutta or mufusil friends, and we must candidly say that, the people of his time were not advanced enough to appreciate the worth of the great departed. A feeble attempt at perpetuation of his memory was made, however, both in Calcutta and mufusil towns. In the town of Midnapore, Babu Rajnarain Bose, held a public meeting, and raised public subscriptions for the purpose. The late Babu Dinobundhu Mitter, then a Superintendent of Post-offices in the district of Nuddea held a similar meeting at Krishnaghur, and collected public subscriptions for Hurish memorial. In this way more than Rs. 10,000 was raised, and Babu Kristo Das was appointed Secretary to the Memorial Fund. After a lapse of full sixteen years, a dark room in the lower floor of the building of the British Indian Association was solemnly inaugurated and declared as "Hurish Chunder Library." The truth of the matter is that some of the influential members of the Association who had contributed handsomely to the fund, contrived, in collusion with Babu Kristo Das Pal, to appropriate the entire fund to the erection of the building of the Association, and a nominal memorial was raised, to the great shame of the entire Bengalee nation. The moral effect of this misapplication of public fund has been felt in our times. The public have come to the conclusion from this and other instances in which public money has been misused, that it is not safe to contribute to public funds which are not scrupulously utilized by those who are entrusted with them.

THE HON'BLE KRISTO DAS PAL, AND THE JUVENILE. YOUNG ZEMINDARS IN THE CALCUTTA WARDS' INSTITUTION.

We have heard the following anecdote from Raja Soshe Shekhurashur Roy Bahadur of Tahirpur in Rajshaye

About thirty years ago, the question of fixing the maximum limit of age at which the minor zemindars under the Court of Wards should attain their majority was under the consideration of Government, The wards in the Calcutta Institution then under the superintendence and management of Dr. Rajendra Lall Miter, requested Babu (afterwards Hon'ble) Kristo Das Pal to agitate in the columns of the *Hindoo Patriot* to fix the maximum age at 18 instead of 21, but the Editor, in an article, strongly recommended that the maximum should be fixed at 21. The young zemindars of the Institution thereupon got offended with Kristo Das Pal, and thought of insulting him on the occasion of his visit to it. The young Zemindars of Goberdanga, Muktagacha, Tahirpur, and the Raja of Cooch Behar and others one day assembled together, prepared a mixture of cowdung with water, and with a show of broomstick, insulted Kristo Das Pal who had come to the Institution, alone, by throwing the cowdung water upon his body. Kristo Das Pal with his usual calmness, and gravity left the place immediately, trying to appease the wrath of the youngsters with soft soothing words. The mischievous foolish lot thought that Kristo Das Pal would take revenge with a double interest, and make it a grievance not only in his own newspaper, but that he would lay the whole matter before the government and Dr. Rajendra Lal Miter. But contrary to their apprehensions, the Hon'ble Kristo Das Pal next day came to the Institution with his friend Dr. Rajendralal, and spoke in most kind terms with those who had insulted him day before without letting any body know, not even the Doctor himself, what had happened. The moral of this authentic anecdote, we leave our readers to draw and reflect upon.

THE HON'BLE KRISTO DAS PAL'S VISIT TO KRISHNAGHUR.

It was in 1881, the Hon'ble Kristo Das Pal came to our native town of Krishnaghur, having been summoned by the Sessions Judge of Nuddea to give evidence in a criminal case. We were then absent from home. Babu Kristo Das Pal put up with the late Babu Ram Chunder Mukherjea, government pleader. The elite of the native community shewed him every mark of respect to him, and numerous were the visitors who came to see him during his short stay for a few hours only. Amist these busy hours, Kristo Das Pal expressed a desire to come to our lodging-house and see own poor little children and family. Those who knew not the relationship of mutual affection that subsisted between us and the renowned Editor of the *Hindoo Patriot* looked askance at this proposal, and dissuaded him from going to a poor man's house. Kristo Das Pal, however, with his usual smile, took leave of the vast influential assembled guests for a few minutes, came to our lodging at Goari, took his seat on a *taotaposh* (a broad wooden bench) with a dirty mat spread over it, took a *pan* and a glass of water offered by our poor little children, made a *pronam* to aunt and wife and departed.

It was this high moral quality of largeness of heart, his humility and courtesy to the poorest of his friends, and not his superior intellectual gifts that made him so great in his life.

***

HIS HIGHNESS THE MAHARAJAH OF VIZIANAGRAM,
AND THE BIOGRAPHY OF THE HON'BLE KRISTO DAS PAL.

THE late lamented Hon'ble Kristo Das Pal, Editor of the *Hindoo Patriot* died in 1884. We expected at the time that his biography would be written by some of his old friends, and published at the cost of the British Indian Association of which he was the "mainstay and guide." Babu Kristo Das Pal was worshipped in his life time, but was forgotten immediately after his death. Not a word was whispered for two subsequent years about the preparation of his biography. In this state of most culpable oblivion shewn towards his sacred memory, we, as an humble tribute of our respect and gratitude to the great departed man, thought of writing a sketch of his valuable life, and secured the co-operation, to that end, of Babu Surendra Nath Banerjea, and the late Dr. Sumbhu Chunder Mukerjea, Editor of *Ries and Rayyet*. We appealed to his Calcutta friends to help us in this undertaking with materials and money, but we regret to say, that we received not the least encouragement from them. The materials for the book we collected after a diligent search from various quarters, and again appealed to the numerous wealthy friends of the deceased for a little pecuniary help for the publication of the book, but our earnest and humble appeal was made in vain.

Hoping against hope, we then appealed to Sir Rivers Thompson, the then Lieutenant-Governor of Bengal for a little monetary help, and we must record here, with deep obligation to Sir Rivers Thompson, that on receiving our letter, his Honor sent us Rs. 25 from Monghyr, where he was then halting on his gubernatorial tour. We required the paltry sum of Rs. 500. for the purpose, and even this small amount, there was no one among the native millionaire friends of Kristo Das Pal willing enough to pay us at the time.

In this state of hopeless despondency, we appealed to HIS HIGHNESS ANUNDA GAJAPATI ROW, MAHARAJAH OF VIZIANA-GRAM, through his agent, Babu Radha Nath Sirkar, and received forthwith a telegram from His Highness granting us Rs. 500 for the publication of the book. It was in this way, through the generous liberablity of HIS HIGHNESS THE MAHARAJA OF VIZIANAGRAM, the biography of Kristo Das Pal was published by us in 1886.

RAJA RAJENDRA LAL MITER, L. L. D. C. I. E.
(BORN IN 1824 &. DIED IN 1891)
DR. RAJENDRA LAL MITER, AND THE PHOTOGRAPHIC SOCIETY.

At a monthly meeting of the Photographic Society held on the 19th of August, 1857, it was proposed by Mr. Durrsch-midt, and seconded by Mr. Church, that Babu Rajendra Lal Miter and Babu (Raja, we believe,) Ishur Chunder Sing should be expelled from the society, and the following resolution was adopted :—

"In consequence of the language used by Rajendra Lal miter in a speech made by him at the Town-Hall, and which he subsequently admitted to have been correctly reported, this society feeling highly indignant at the tissue of falsehood contained in the said speech, consider the speaker unworthy of the honor of continuing to be a member of the society, and as the rules make no provision for the expulsion of members, it is resolved that the said Rajendra Lal Miter be requested to retire from the society."

A PORTION OF THE FAMOUS SPEECH OF THE LEARNED DOCTOR.

" Is it for the interlopers to make such accusations? Devoid of the merits which characterise a true Englishman, and possessing all the defects of the Anglo-Saxon race, these adventurers from England have carried ruin and devastation to wherever they have gone. Ask the red Indian in the prairies of South America, and he will say that the antagonism of the Anglo-Saxon adventurers has within a hundred years reduced their number from half a million to forty thousand. What is it, but the antagonism of the sweepings of England and Holland that has driven the Bosjeman and the Caffre to the inhospitable sands of Central Africa? In Australia and New Zealand, the battle is still being fought, and ere long the natives of those places will be numbered with the things that were; and yet it is these adventurers who pretend to dread the antagonism of the Hindoo, these are the men who having made England too hot for their residence, come *admissericordium* to complain of our rivalry. They talk of their energy, education, and high civilization. They boast of the capital that they bring to India, and the vast number of men who find employment from their wealth. Surely never was a more consummate case of making a mountain of a molehill. Taking the cost of the whole of the Indigo produced in this part of the country at a million and a half, we shall have scarcely a crore of European agricultural capital in all India, and for its sake the country could not have a greater curse than the Anglo-saxon planters, who have been by their own missionaries denounced as the greatest tyrants, who have ever been permitted to fatten on the ruination of the offensive and helpless peasants, men whose like can be had only in the above owners of Virginia."

The only apologists for the learned doctor were Major Thullier, who stated that Europeans had made use of language to natives of a grosser description than that used by Rajendra Lall Miter, and affirmed that. the vituperations of the Babu were only directed against Indigo Planters, and not against Englishman in general, and Mr. Hume with some few others who, however, did not take any prominent part in the proceedings. Babu Rajendra Lal was expelled from the society by a majority of six, but Raja Ishur Chunder Singh having previously sent in his resignation, and declared that he did not coincide in the view of Rajendra Lal was saved the indignity of expulsion.

Major Thullier resigned for this gross insult to Raja Rajendra Lal Miter.

RAJA PETAMBUR MITER,
GRAND-FATHER OF Dr. RAJENDRALALA MITER.

A correspondent of the *Delhi Gazette* wrote the following in 1876.

"Looking over a file of old Calcutta newspapers, I learned that it was customary in the City of Palaces in 1792 for native princes, when they were about to leave the city, to announce their approaching departure. Perhaps such a measure was made compulsory by the Government of the day. In the announcement all creditors were called upon to make known their claims, so that such as did not come forward would be debarred from all claims after the prince had gone to his own country. Here is an advertisement of the sort alluded to:—"Rajah Petambur Mitter, intending to retire from Calcutta, requests that all persons who have demands on him will make the same known," &c. &c.

This was a very good practice and it would be well, were it renewed in the present day.

THE LATE DR. RAJENDRALALA MITER, AND THE BIOGRAPHY OF KRISTO DAS PAL.

It was in 1885, we began writing the Life of Babu Kristo das Pal. We wrote a letter, on the 21st. september, 1886, to Dr. Rajendralala for a copy of the Trust Deed of the *Hindoo Patriot*, to which, he replied as follows:—

The *Bengalee* Office, Taltolah,
Calcutta, 21st. Sept., 1886.

To

Dr. Rajendralala Miter, L. L. D. C. I. E.,

MY DEAR SIR,

I have been requested by the numerous subcribers to my book (K. D. Pal's Life) to insert therein, the full text of the Trust Deed that was drawn up when Babu Kristo Dass Pal took the editorial management of the *Hindoo Patriot.*

May I request the favour of your kindly giving me a copy of it, if there is no objection to your doing so, on the part of the Trustees. An early reply is solicited.

If the Trust Deed cannot be made public, will you kindly let me know at least the purport of it.

I have   &c.   &c.   &c,

RAM GOPAL SANYAL.

THE REPLY.

8, *Manicktola, Calcutta.*

Sept. 23, 1886.

DEAR SIR,

In reply to your letter of the 21st instant, I have to state that no "trust deed was drawn when Babu Kristo Das Pal took the editorial management of the *Hindoo Patriot.* He was appointed editor by a resolution of the Trustees, and a letter of appointment was given him. The trust is older than the editorial career of my late friend, and has no concern with him.

Yours faithfully,

(Sd.) RAJENDRALALA MITER.

Babu Ram Gopal Sanyal.

In this politely evasive way, the learned Doctor refused to furnish us with a copy of the Deed which, we at last got from Babu Prosad Das Dutt. The doctor's account of how Kristo Das became the editor does not tally with what we had heard from the late venerable Pundit Ishur Chunder Vidyasagur. He told us that he appointed Kristo Das, as Editor, having taken the management of the paper from Babu Kally Prosunna Shinghee. Kristo Das afterwards became "impatient" to remain under his control, and clandestinely carried on negociations with Babu Kali Prosunna to

6

make over the paper to a body of Trustees composed of Raja Romanath Tagore, Babu Rajendralala Mitei, Raja Ishur Chunder Shing, and Babu (afterwards Sir Maharajah) Jotendra Mohun Tagore.*

DR. RAJENDRA LAL MITER AND DAVID HARE.

At the thirty-ninth Hare Anniversary meeting, Dr. Rajendra Lal related the following anecdote :--

"He was a student of the Calcutta Medical Collge, and was making practical experiments in chemisrry. He was fusing some metals, and took out a platinum crucible from the laboratory worth about Rs. 500, and placed it on the fusing vessel. After a few minutes, he wanted to test his operation, when 'lo! the crucible was gone—it had melted away! He was non-plussed and reported the accident to his professor, Dr. † O'Shaughnessy, who of course got very angry and gave him a scolding. He did not, however, fine him, degrade him, or suspend him, far less expel him—under the rules of the College he was, however, obliged to report him to David Hare, who happened to be the Secretary to the College. David Hare knew Rajendralala, sent for him, gave a few shrugs to his own shoulder, no "jerks to the throat' of the offending student, told him to be careful in future and not to do the like again. He did not even call upon him to replace the crucible, which was worth Rs. 500."

HER HIGHNESS THE MAHARANEE SURNOMOYE C. I., AND HER TROUBLES IN 1847,

BEFORE we narrate the circumstances of the law-suit instituted against her in 1847 by the East India Company to disposess her of the property left by her husband, Raja

---

* (Vide our biography of K. D. Pal, p. 171.)
† Afterwards Sir William Brook O'Shaughnessy.

Kishennath, we annex below a genealogical table of this aristocratic family.

KRISTO KANT NUNDY.—Founder of the family.

RAJA LOKENATH BAHADOOR.

RAJA HURY NATH   ,,

KRISTO NATH   ,,

RAJA KRISHEN NATH'S DEATH.

Having been implicated in a murder case of his servant, he committed suicide on the 31st October, 1844, in his mother's house in the Chitpur road in the Cubberdanga Division of the town. He executed a Will in the presence of Mr. Strettel, the attorney. By this Will, as stated in the *Calcutta Star* of Nov. 2, 1844, he left the bulk of his property to the Court of Wards for the purpose of founding "Kishenath Roy's University," Moorshedabad. He provided a small sum for the marriage of his daughter and allowed Rs. 1500 a month to his widow, prohibiting adoption. The coroner held an enquiry and examined Dr. Robert Young, the Raja's medical attendant, Mr. Herklotts, Mr. Hedger, Mr. Strettel, Keshub, the Rajah's head *furash*, and Sree Nath Chatterjea, Dewan of the Rajah's mother. The jury gave in a verdict of *felo-de-se*. The coroner's charge to the jury appeared in the *Englishman* of Nov. 1st, 1844, and repoduced in the *Calcutta* Star of 12th Nov, of that year.

MAHARANEE SURNOMOYEE DASEE.
VERSUS
THE EAST INDIA COMPANY AND OTHERS.

SUPREME COURT,—MONDAY, NOVEMBER, 15, 1847.

(BEFORE A FULL BENCH.)

WE read the following in the *Hurkura* of Nov. 16, 1847, · nent this *cause celebre.*

This cause came on for hearing on the 8th upon the issues which had been directed on the common law side of the Court, and found in favour of the Ranee in February last. In the absence of Keshub's leading counsel, however, the Court heard only the argument of Mr. Strettel's Counsel as to the revival of a former will under which he was appointed executor ; (but without renumeration.)

Mr. Clarke, Mr. Morton, and Mr. Taylor, for the Ranee.

Mr Cochrane and Mr. Macpherson for Mr. Strettel. The Advocate General, Mr. Prinsep and Mr. Ritchie for the East India Company.

Mr. Sandes for Keshub Chunder Sirkar, Mr. Dickens being absent.

The will now in question bearing date January 7, 1841, (and the particulars of which are mentioned in Mr. Strettel's evidence reported by us on the hearing of the issues) was executed in the most solemn manner, in the presence of the subscribing witnesses Mr. Turton, Mr. Morton, and Mr. Blacquire, authorising the Ranee to make six consecutive adoptions, and in failure of them for a College to be super-intended by Government. Mr. Strettel and Mr. Lambrick his former tutor (since deceased) being appointed executors. This will was afterwards altered by the Rajah by erasing a salary of Rs. 500 a month to the executors, and omitting several legacies. The original will was left by the Rajah in Mr Strettel (his attorney's) office, where it remained until after the Rajah's death, when Mr. Strettel gave it into the Registrar's office.

The Rajah came down to Calcutta in 1842, and requested Mr. Strettel to send him a copy of the above mentioned will with the interlineations with a view of framing another will on the basis of it. Mr. Strettel did so accordingly, taking the opportunity, however, (without instructions) of inserting several formal clauses, and amongst others the usual clause of revocation of all formal wills. He also left the places for the names of executors blank. The second will also was duly executed, and attested in the presence of Mr. Duff, (since deceased) and a Native Dr. Nobin Chunder, and the Rajah filled up the blanks by reappointing Mr. Strettel and one Degumber as executors. This second will has not been heard of since then, and was not forthcoming at the Rajah's death.

Mr. Cochrane and Mr. Macpherson now contended that the will of January, 1841, was now a good and subsisting will, standing unrevoked. The Chief Justice delivered a long judgment, which, for want of space, we cannot reproduce here. The Chief Justice said that "the evidence failed entirely of the existence, in fact, of any intention, to revive the first will." Then as regards the the second will, he said that "the time of the destruction of the second will was unknown, it might have been coeval with or shortly prior, to the preparation of the last instrument propounded, but not established as the last will of the testator The time of the preparation of that instrument was also unknown to us, for Ram Chunder's evidence we disbelieved. No instructions for its preparation was proved, and no aid of any kind in its preparation was proved. The evidence led us to think that the Rajah alone unaided incompetent to compose such an instrument. We viewed as to *testamentary capacity* (which we did not confound with insanity) that is of the existence of such testamentary capacity at the time of the execution of the instrument, the critical time, to be also insufficient. There were circumstances also suggestive of grave doubt as to the free exercise of such capacity as he might have had." On these and other grounds he (the Chief Justice) set aside the will, and decreed in favour of the Ranee.

HER INTERMEDIATE TROUBLES. RAJA KRISHNA NATH'S WILL BEFORE THE FULL BENCH OF THE SUPREME COURT, CALCUTTA.

Mr. Dickens, Mr. Sandes, and Mr. Fulton moved from new trial on behalf of Keshub on the ground of new and material evidence, upon affidavits and correspondence consisting of letters from the Raja to one Nobin Chunder. The motion was refused. (Vide *Hurkura* July 22, 1847).

MOHARANEE SURNOMOYE AND THE WILL CASE.

We read in the *Hurkura* of Aug. 20., 1847 that Rance Hurosoondary, the mother of the late Raja Krishna Nath Roy, filed in the court of Babu Huro Chunder Ghose Bahadoor, Principal Sudder Ameen of the 24-Purgunahs, a bill against Rance Surnomye, for obtaining possession of all the real and personal property left by her husband. The claim is based upon the *incapacity* of the widow and daughter of Krishna Nath to inherit the property, in consequence of *his* having forfeited all right to inheritance by reason of his eating and drinking with Europeans. The will of the widow against the Government and Keshub Sirkar in the Supreme Court was not yet disposed.

ANOTHER CASE IN THE CALCUTTA SUPREME COURT AGAINST HER HIGHNESS, THE MAHARANEE SURNOMOYE.

We cull the following from the *Friend of India* of May 2, 1861 :—

"In a recent case in the Calcutta Supreme Court, the Crown claimed a portion of the large sum of Rs. 6,86,700, held in the custody of the Court for the maintenance of the grandmother, mother and sister of Krishnanath Roy, who committed suicide in 1844. The grandmother having died, the Indian Government, to whom the Crown resigned the claim, applied for as much of the principal as was not required for the maintenance of the relations of the suicide. The Chief Justice said t that the law of forfeiture in the case of *felo-de-se* has never been introduced into Calcutta, and consequently did not operate to forfeit the estate of Raja Kristonath Roy to the Crown.

It was through the exertions of the late Babu Huro Chunder Lahiry, the famous Attorney of Sreerampore, the property was secured to Her Highness the Maharanee Surnomoye, C. I., who has been making a noble use of it for the benefit of mankind. Maharanee Surnomoye, it is said, paid a bonus of Rs. 10,000, with valuable shawls to this Barendra Brahmin Attorney, as a reward for his labours.

BABU RAMDULAL DEB OR DEY *ALIAS* DULAL SIRKAR.

In 1882 appeared in *St. James' Gazette*, an article on the Bengali millionaire, Ramdulal Dey. We give the following extract regarding his charities.

"But the charities of Ramdulal were on a magnificient scale. A famine broke out in Madras, and a public meeting was held at Calcutta, and largely attended by members of Government and the leading merchants, for the purpose of raising subscriptions to mitigate the calamity. On this occasion Ramdulal paid down a lack of rupees, or £10,000, in current coin. He subscribed £3,000 towards the foundation of the Hindu College for the education of the sons of Natives. He set aside seventy rupees a day about seven pounds sterling, for the relief of distressed person who applied at his office. He gave monthly supplies of rice and other necessaries to 400 of his poor neighbours, together with monthly stipends in cash to defray other expenses. He was always surrounded by candidates for employment, and frequently gave a bank-note enclosed in an envelope to one or other of them, according to what he knew of their necessities. He retained one Native in his employment whose sole duty was to visit his poor neighbours every day, and bring him news concerning their difficulties and wants.

He engaged three native physicians to visit the sick, and to administer medicines and medical comforts at his expense. On Sundays he went out in person, with a train of no fewer than fifty native gentlemen, paid visits to his friends and often after seeing a wealthy master in his drawing room, he would enter the hovel of a sick servant and enquire how he did and whether he wanted anything   Five hundred poor persons were fed every day at Ramdulal's house in the city; and if a beggar asked for rice at his door, the servants were under orders to pour upon his rags as much rice as he could carry.   Any person having a daughter to marry, or a *shraddha* to perform for a deceased parent had only to apply to Ramdulal, and would then receive a present, generally of five hundred rupees, or 50 pounds sterling.   At his villa in the country, he opened an asylum for the needy, where thousands obtained their daily food at his expense, and continue to receive it down to the present time.   This asylum is open to comers of all castes, for the provisions are made over before they are cooked together with the necessary pots and firewood, so that men of every caste can prepare food for themselves."

Oh ! for a Ramdulal at the present time !

BABU ANNODA PROSAD MUKHERJEA,
ZEMINDAR AT ULLA, AND
THE LATE Mr. ROBERT KNIGHT.

On the institution of the Hydrabad libel case in 1881, Mr. Robert Knight, the late Editor of the Calcutta *Statesman*, appealed to the Indian public for pecuniary support. In response to this appeal, we called a public meeting in our native town of Krishnaghur, to raise public subscriptions from the people of the District of Nuddea.   The late lamented Rai Jadu Nath Roy Bahadur presided on the occasion, and Mr. Lal Mohun Ghose, Barrister-at-law, who was then at Krishnaghur, at our request, addressed the meeting.   A committee was formed at Krishnaghur, the local gentry of which contributed about a hundred rupees to the Defence Fund of Mr. Knight. We then went into the interior of the district where many Zemindars were found willing to contribute their mite to this fund. Amongst these enlightened and liberal village Zemindars, was the late Babu Annoda Prosad Mukherjee, brother of the well-known Zemindar Babu Bamun Das Mukherjee of Ulla (otherwise called Birnugger) in the District of Nuddea. We went to him with an introductory note from the late Babu Ram Chunder Mukherjee, Government Pleader of Krishnaghur. It was at dusk that we came to his place where we saw the old Brahmin Zemindar then bordering on three-score years and ten in his *Boithukhana*, pulling a silver *gurguri.* We made a *pronam*, and handed over to him the letter of introduction. He read it in a minute, and requested us most politely to take our seat in a chair placed by his side. The time for evening prayer was then come, and we were requested by Babu Annada to make *Sundhya* (or evening prayer) with him. We both went to make *Sundhya* in a large hall attached to the drawing room. When we finished our prayer, two servants came with silver plates filled with all sorts of delicious fruits, sweetmeats, *Khyr* &c. for our refreshment. No distinction was made between our poorselves and the great Zemindar whose annual income was over fifty thousand. We pertook of this splendid repast along with him. The old Zemindar kept us three days in his house, shewing every courtesy due to our position, and paid Rs. 200 as the quota of his subscription to the Fund, and requested us to remit the amount in his name to Mr. Paul Knight, the eldest son of Mr. Robert Knight, at Calcutta. Babu Annoda Prosad knew not a syllable of English, yet he entertained a high regard for Mr. Knight, having read what that veteran journalist had done to this country, from the *Shomeprokash* newspaper. Such example of unselfish liberality has become almost a rare thing in our own days.

7

We collected more than Rs. 500 on this occasion from all classes of people of our native district of Nuddea, as a mark of our respect and gratitude to the great journalist.

BABU NORENDRA SEN, EDITOR OF THE *INDIAN MIRROR*, AND LORD DUFFERIN.

Babu Norendra Nath Sen, Editor and Proprietor of the *Indian Mirror* is a fearless man of great independence of spirit. One day in 1887, he along with Babu Surendra Nath Banerjea, Editor of the *Bengalee*, Mr. Anunda Mohun Bose, Barrister-at-Law, the late Dr. Sumbhu Chunder Mukherjee, the Editor of *Reis* and *Rayyet*, Babu Dwarka Nath Gangooly, and several others waited upon Lord Dufferin in the White House of Calcutta, on behalf of the Indian Association. Lord Dufferin, before formally receiving the members of the deputation first enquired, whether Babu Norendra Nath Sen, Editor of the *Indian Mirror* was present among the party. On coming to know that he was there, he abruptly and without any show of ceremony asked him, "how did he come to know that the Viceroy had sent a "secret despatch" to the Secretary of State for India, recommending the gagging of the Indian Press ?" Babu Norendra Nath with his characteristic boldness refused to answer the question, and respectfully pointed out to the Viceroy, that to put such a question to an Editor on such a public occasion was simply against all etiquette.

The conversation between the Viceroy and the native Editor took a somewhat unpleasant turn, but fortunately for the party, the great English Statesman, and a diplomat to boot, soon acknowledged his error, apologized to the offended Editor, and the party separated, after having transacted the business of the day.

THE CRIMINAL CASE AGAINST RAJA RADHA KANT DEB BAHADOOR, HIS SON, AND BABU RAM RATUN ROY OF NARAIL.

The case was instituted against them for "having insti-
gated a conflict between two bands of lattials," as stated in
the *Friend of India* of Nov. 30th, 1848. It was tried at first
by the Joint Magistrate. of Sreerampore who refused
to take bail. A motion was thereupon made to the Su-
preme Court of Calcutta, by Messrs. Clarke and Morton,
Barristers-at-Law, and Messrs. Oehme, Wight, and Hedger,
Solicitors for the Raja. A Division Bench consisting of
Sir Robert Barlow, and Mr. Hawkins ordered the Joint-
Magistrate of Sreeram pore to accept bail from the accused.
The case was afterwards committed to the Sessions held at
Hoogley, presided over by Mr. Torrens, Judge of the 24-
Purgunahs. The trial took place on the 24th October, 1848,
before the Sessions Judge and four Assessors, viz., Messrs.
Dampier, Russel, Patton, and Major Birch. The accused
were acquitted.

Dr. Maxton, as stated in the *Friend* of *India*, was dismissed by Lord Dalhousie, for having given a "false certificate"
to the Raja when he was incriminated in this case. In the
same Journal of Dec, 14, 1848, appeared a letter from Mr.
F. J, Holliday, then Secretary to the Government of Bengal,
to the Superintendent of Police, dated Fort William, 26th,
July, 1848, in which the Government requested to enquire
into this case and take action "without respect of persons."

The prosecution of the Raja produced an uncommon
commotion among the native community, and it is said, that
a vast concourse of Rajas and Zemindars both of Calcutta
and the Mufusil came to Hoogley, and lived there for days
together, to shew sympathy with the Raja. The town of
Hoogley was overcrowded, as if a Mela had taken place there,
This laudable example of sympathy between Zemindars

and Zemindars, in hours of trial, has now become a thing
of the past ! ! !

Babu Ram Rutun Roy, the Patriarch of the famous Narail
Zemindars, exclaimed, on his release, to the Rajah, "Bayai !
of what avail your empty titles of "Sir, Rajah" &c., have
proved to be in this hour of danger." Well said, the great
Ram Rutun !

SIR RAJAH RADHA KANT DEB BAHADUR, AND LORD ELGIN.

"It was Lord Lawrence who excluded native gentlemen
from State balls, but the severe condemnation which his
action met with in England, made him rectify the omission
on the next occasion. Lord Elgin invited Raja Sir Radha
Kant Deb Bahadur to his Fancy Balls as the representative
of the native community."

"In 1842, a Durbar was held by Lord Auckland in celebration of the
birth of Prince of Wales. Rajah Radhakant Bahadur was the spokesman
of the native community of Calcutta. The speech of Raja was reproduced in the *National Magazine* in 1876, when the Prince came to
Calcutta." (Vide H. P. January, 10, 1876.

SIR RAJAH RADHA KANT'S LIBERALITY TO A POOR GERMAN SCHOLAR.

We take the following from the *Indian Mirror* of the
25th December, 1891.

About three decades and a half ago, there lived in Bielefeld a Prussian
town in Westphalia, a scholar, Dr. L. Schutz, who was a teacher of the
High School there with an income of £90 annually, which was barely
sufficient to supply the most urgent wants of his large family. He had
dedicated all his leisure hours to the study of Sanskrit, and spent much
money for the purchase of Sanskrit works—"more than" as he used to
say—"I ought to have done." His urgent needs at one time suggested to
him the painful necessity of selling his library unless he could obtain any
assistance from some friendly quarter. The fruits of his labours at that
period were translations of various Sanskrit works, and partial prosecutions of others which he could not finish on account of his pecuniary

difficulties. In this plight, he communicated his difficulties to a counrry-man of his—a brother-scholar, the late Dr. E. Roer, who in a letter dropped a hint about this matter with great delicacy to the late Rajah Sir Radha Kant Dev. The Rajah promptly responded, in a communication, dated the 21st August, 1857, of which the following is an extract :—

"With respect to the note of your friend, Dr. Schutz, which you sent me in original * * I thank you to have given me an opportunity of serving a worthy man. Most cheerfully I enclose a Bank Note of Rs. 400 which you can send to your friend in time to relieve him from the neces-sity of parting with the precious jewels in his thesaurus, earned with his heart-blood. Surely, it is a source of the highest gratification to me to become the instrument of preventing the scholar from echoing the strain of Roscoe.

"Thus loved associates, chiefs of elder art, Teachers of wisdom, who could once beguile."

"My tedious hours, and lighten every toil,—I now resign you."

May the great God free the indefatigable scholar from his present hardships, and enable him to prosecute his labours in the intellectual field, which would, no doubt, reward him with a rich harvest.

Dr. Roer wrote in reply ;—"Permit me to express my admiration and thanks for your noble and generous act towards me, who in every other respect, but in the common pursuit of learning, is a stranger to you. The beautiful sentiments, which you express in your letter tenfold enhance the gift."

Dr. Schutz acknowledged the Rajah's gift thus, in his letter of 21st October, 1857 :—

"Words cannot express the feelings by which I was overwhelmed, when I had read the letter of Dr. Roer, and the noble lines you had addressed to him on my account. If I could transport myself 'to India, my eye would tell you more of heart-felt gratitude than words are able. Your kind relief came in a time when it had become nearly imperatively ne-cessary to part from my dear Sanskrit books, acquired in a period of thirty years.

BABU RAM LOCHUN GHOSE, FATHER OF Mr. M. M. GHOSE, AND MAHARAJAH SRISH CHUNDER ROY BAHADUR.

THE FOUNDATION OF THE KRISHNAGHUR COLLEGE.

A public meeting was held at Krishnaghur on Tuesday, the 18th of Novr., 1845, to raise public subscriptions for the support of the college as well as to thank Lord Hardinge for having sanctoned its establishment. Amongst the influential Zemindars of the district, there were present MAHARAJA SRISH CHUNDR ROY BAHADUR, Babus Bamundas Mukherjee, and his brother Shumbhu Nath Mukherjee, Zemindars of Ulla, Sree Nath Pal Chowdry, Chundra Kumar Pal Chowdry, Sreegopal Pal Chowdry, (father of Babu Surendra Nath Pal Chowdry of Ranaghat), Messrs Bruce, Trevor, Fowle, and Hobhouse, and Babu Ram Lochun Ghose, subordinate Judge (father of the illustrious Messrs. M. M. Ghose, Lal Mohan Ghose, and Muruli Mohun Ghose).. Babu Ram Lochun Ghose explained to the meeting the purport of the letter of Government to the Local Committe of Public instruction at Krisnaghur on the establishment of the college. On the motion of Babu Ramlochun Ghose, seconded by the Brahmin Zemindar, Babu Bamundas Mukherjee of Ulla, a suscription list was opened for the purpose of providing a building for the college. It was proposed to thank the Government for the boon thus offered. At that meeting more than Rs. 13000 was subscribed. It was formally opened in January, 1846, with captain D. L. Richardson, as its first Principal. MAHARAJAH SRISH CHUNDER ROY BAHADUR gave a donation of Rs. 3,000 for this College, and held an illumination on the day of its opening, at a considerable cost. Babu Ram Tonoo Lahiri was also transferred, at this time from the Hindu College as a teacher to that of Krishnaghur.

The commitee of Public Institution at Krishnaghur consisting of Mr. J. C. Brown, the District and Sessions Judge of Nuddea, as president, Mr.

H. F. James, Mr. E. F. Trevor, Dr. Charles Archer, MAHARAJAH SRISH CHUNDER ROY BAHADUR, Babu Ramlochun Ghose, Sub-Judge Nuddea, as members, presented an address to Captain D. L. Richardson, on his transfer at the close of the year, to the Hoogley College which was then called the "college of Hadgi Mohomed Mohim." The masters and scholars of the Krishnagur College also presented an address to the Captain, but it was not published in the *Calcutta Star* for "not being written in proper English"! Such was the condition of our *Alma Mater* which has produced such brilliant scholars as Professor Omesh Chunder Dutt, Babu Radhika Prosuna Mukherjee, Rajkrishna Mukherjee, Messrs. M. M. Ghose, Lal Mohun Ghose and others.

RAJA SRISH CHUNDER ROY BAHADUR.

Mr. Money, Collector of Nuddea handed over a firman or a letter of Government to the Rajah conferring on him the "title of Maharajah" on the 9th Sept. 1848. Babu Ram Lohun Ghose, father of Mr M. M. Ghose read the firman which was in Persian language. (F. I. Sept. 14, 1848.)

DR. MOHENDRA LAL SIRKAR'S CONVERSION TO HOMŒOPATHY.

Dr. Sircar furnished the following account of his own conversion in 1867.

"The case of Raja Radhakant, the conversion of Vidyasagar, and the persistent appeals of Babu Rajender for a fair hearing and above all for a fair trial, forced Homœopathy upon my attention. I remember how a second reading of Morgan's *Philosophy of Homœopathy*, which I was asked by a friend to sharply review for a local paper, made such an impression upon my mind that I ceased to think homoeopathy was the great humbug that it was represented to be. Sharp's *Investigation of Homœopathy* and *Letter to Sir B. Brodie* placed the subject in the clearest light, and removed many doubts and difficulties. Singularly enough, the *Organon* of Hahnemann made the strongest impression in favour of homoeopathy. There, notwithstanding many inaccuracies, obscurities, and even inconsistencies, I found a master-mind dealing with his subject in the most thorough and scientific manner. Thus prepared I thought looking through the telescope, and look what was the result. The revelation of a most beneficent truth dawned upon the mind. I declared my convictions (Feb. 1867) at the Fourth Annual Meeting of the Bengal Branch of the British Medical Association, of which I was then vice-president. I advocated as worthy of trial by the profession a system of medicine which four years ago, at the inauguration of the Association, I had in utter ignorance denounced as a baseless quackery! What the result of this open confession of faith was is not unknown to my colleagues in England. It was of course no other than professional excommunication, but this has been nothing to me compared to the benefits my patients have enjoyed, and the consequent consolation I have myself enjoyed of an approving conscience. To the honour of the lay press of India, it must be said, that they, both European and Native, one and all denounced the conduct of the medical men of Calcutta towards me as the most intolerant and bigotted that could be imagined, unworthy of men who belong to a noble and sacred profession, and pretended to be men of science."

Dr. SUMBHU CHUNDER MUKHERJEE.

EDITOR OF *REIS AND RAYYET*.

(BORN IN 1839, DIED IN 1894.)

His protest against the Memorial Meeting of Lord Northbrook.

On the 8th April, 1876, a public meeting was held in the Town Hall to vote an address to Lord Northbrook under the presidency of Sir Richard Temple, then Lieutenant-Governor of Bengal. Babu Sumbhu Chunder Mukherjee and the following gentlemen viz., Babu Jodu Nath Ghose, Head Master, Seal's Free College, Mr. Monmotho Nath Mullick, Barrister-at-law, Babus Probodh Chunder Mullick, Hem Chunder Mullick, Jogesh Chunder Dutt, Debendra Nath Dutt, Upendra Chunder Dutt, Noresh Chunder Dutt, Bhanu Chunder Dutt set a noble example of fearless and unselfish patriotism by shewing an active opposition to this movement. Never in the history of this country, such a bold front was presented to the voting of an address and a statue to the deposer of Mulharo Rao Gwekwar. In his famous Baroda pamphlet written by Dr. Mukherjee against the deposition of the Great Maharatta Chief, there was a proof positive of the patriotic spirit with which he thought it right to protest in the name of the nation against this memorial. Not being a practised speaker himself, he requested Babu Kally Churn Banerjea, then a young orator of great promise to stand up at the meeting and protest. But the orator Kally Churn funked, and so Mr. Monmotho Nath Mullick had to speak on behalf of these "immortal ten." They sustained a defeat no doubt, but their moral example will ever live in the pages of Indian History.

Dr. SHUMBHU CHUNDER MUKHERJEA.
EDITOR OF *REIS AND RAYYET*.

A PROPOSAL TO INVEST HIM WITH A TITULAR DISTINCTION.

We heard the following anecdote from the learned Doctor himself :—

It was during Sir Steuart Bayley's regime, his Chief Secretary, Sir John Edgar, wrote a letter to Dr. Mukherjea one day, to see him in his private house, without letting him know of the object of the interview. Sir John Edgar simply expressed "anxiety" to see him without fail. On receiving this letter, Dr. Mukherjea went to Sir John's place, and was most cordially received. The Chief Secretary to the Government of Bengal then intimated to Dr. Mukherjea that Sir Steuart Bayley wanted to recommend to the Supreme Government for the bestowal of a title upon him for his distinguished career as a journalist and scholar. Sir John also told him that the bestowal of the title was contemplated by Government on the ground that, as is usually done by title-seekers, Dr. Mukherjea never aspired to it. "It is the desire of the Government," said Sir John, to bestow the honorific title upon him unsolicited and unasked for. In answer to this request, Dr. Mukherjea gravely declined the offer so seriously made by the Chief Secretary. Sir John first took no denial from him and tried to induce him to accept the honor. But Dr. Mukherjea frankly told the Chief Secretary, that a poor man and scholar as he was, he did not like the distinction and honor which the Government wanted to bestow upon him. The Bengal Government finding it a hopeless task to honor him in this way, recommended his nomination to a Fellow-ship of the Calcutta University.

8

Dr. SHUMBHU CHUNDER MUKHERJEA, AND
Dr. HUNTER.

We heard the following story from the learned Doctor himself :—

The best reviews of books that appeared in the *Hindoo Patriot* from 1871 to 1876 were from Dr. Mukherjea's pen. Babu Shumbhu Chunder Mukherjea told us once that when he reviewed the "Annals of Rural Bengal," the author of the book, Dr. Hunter, who was then in England, wrote to Kristo Das Pal, thanking him for the ablest review of his work. Dr. Hunter came back to Calcutta very soon, and put up with Sir Richard Temple, who was then Financial Member of the Supreme Council. Shortly after, Dr. Hunter held an evening party to which Babus Kristo Das, and Shumbhu Chunder Mukherjea were invited. Dr. Hunter questioned Babu Kristo Das Pal as to his sources of information on the variety of subjects, omitted from the "Annals of Rural Bengal." Kristo Das, with a smile, pointed to his friend, Dr. Mukherjea, as the reviewer of his work. Dr. Hunter then congratulated Dr. Mukherjea, for the ability he has displayed in reviewing his work, and got much valuable information from him afterwards.

HOW WAS BABU SHUMBHU CHUNDER MUKHERJEA
MADE A DOCTOR.

The Amrita Bazar Patrica made the following announcement :—

"At the present time when Homœopathy is making so much progress in India, our readers will be interested to learn that our learned and versatile countryman Babu Shumbhu Chunder Mukherjea, minister to the Maharaja of Tipperah, has been elected an honorary member of the American Institute of Homœopathy. This is no small honor. The Institute is the Chief of the 4 national, 26 state, and 103 local societies in the United States, and the most important in the whole world. The rules for membership are very strict, and there are only 14 foreign members— 7 in England, 2 in France, 2 in Italy, 1 in Austria, 1 in Germany and 1 in India. That one is Dr. S. C. Mukherjea.

Babu Shumbhu Chunder Mukherjea knew more of Homœopathy than many a professed Homœopath."

THE *NILDARPAN* DRAMA BY BABU DENO BONDHU MITER, THE REV. MR. JAMES LONG, AND BABU KALLY PROSUNNA SINGHEE.

The *Nil Darpan* was written by Babu Deno Bondhu Miter, and was published from a Dacca Printing Press, and the date of its publication was the 2nd of Asin, corresponding to the middle of September 1860. We know not under what circumstances this drama was first published at Dacca. Mr. W. S. Seton-Karr, C. S., in his famous statement published in the *Friend of India* of August, 1861, said that the "drama was translated by a Native with his sanction and knowledge, as some persons were desirous of seeing it in an English form, and 500 copies were printed and sent to the Bengal Office. Out of these 202 copies were sent to England under official frank, and only 14 copies were circulated in India. The Rev. Mr. Long wrote an able preface to this translation, and published it in his own name. The Land-owners' and Commercial Association, as representing the Indigo planters, and Mr. Walter Brett, the Editor of the *Englishman* who was, along with the Editor of the *Hurkura*, described in the drama, as "having sold themselves, like Judas Iscariot, for Rs. 1000," first brought a libel suit against the Printer, Mr. C. H. Manuel who was fined Rs. 10 by the Supreme Court of Calcutta. They then brought a libel suit against the Reverend gentleman, which was heard at the Criminal Sessions, presided over by Sir Mordaunt Wells on the 19th July, 1861. The counts of the indictment were these :—

1st. Libelling the Editor of the *Englishman*. 2nd. Libelling the Indigo Planters of Lower Bengal. The Calcutta Grand Jury found a true bill for libel against him. Mr. Long was admitted to bail on his own recognizances and those of the Rev. Mr. Hutton, Presidency Chaplain, and the Rev. Mr. Stuart, Secretary to the Church Missionary Society.

Messrs. Peterson and Cowie appeared for the prosecution, and Messrs. Eglinton and Newmarch for the defence.

HIS CONVICTION.

He was found guilty and sentenced to suffer an imprisonment for one month, and to pay a fine of Rs. 1000. The late Babu Kally Prusana Shinghee paid the fine from his own pocket. The Hindu community headed by Sir Raja Radha Kant Deb presented an address signed by forty-three gentlemen to Mr. Long, expressing their gratitude to him for having advanced the cause of vernacular literature, and disseminated the views and feelings of the natives on topics of administration and social improvement, as reflected through the medium of the vernacular press! They also approved of what he had done in translating the *Nil Darpan,* expressing their views on the Indigo question. Another address signed by more than 30,000 natives was presented to him. The leaders of the native community expressed a desire to petition the Government on his behalf for a remission of his imprisonment, but the Rev. Mr. Long dissuaded them from doing so, on the ground that it would embarrass the Government.

Sir Mordaunt in the course of this trial made remarks casting reflections on the character of the natives which exasperated them very much, at the time.

A NATIVE PUBLIC MEETING FOR THE RECALL OF SIR MORDAUNT WELLS.

A public meeting was held on the 26th August, 1861, for the recall of Sir Mordaunt Wells. The following resolution was adopted.

"This meeting desires to record not without a feeling of regret, that its confidence in the Hon'ble Sir M. Wells, Knight, as a Judge of the Highest Court of Judicature in Bengal, has been impaired in consequence of his frequent and indiscriminate attacks on [the character of the natives of this country, with an intemperance inconsistent with the calm dignity of the bench, as well as from his repeated and indiscreet exhibition of strong political bias and race prejudices which are not compatible with the impartial administration of justice."

Dr. DUFF AT THAT MEETING.

Dr. George Smith, a quandom Editor of the *Friend of India* in the second volume of his biography of Dr. Duff made no mention of the fact that Dr. Duff took a part in this movement.

A memorial signed by 20,786 persons both of the town, and the mufusil was sent to the Secretary of State for his recall. Sir Charles Wood, the then Secretary of State for India censured the Judge for his indiscreet loquacity.

The sensation produced by the trial of the Rev. Mr. James Long was not confined to Bengal alone. The *Bombay Times* published in full the whole of the *Nil Durpan* drama in its columns. The *Samachar Durpan* translated it into Guzrati. The trial produced he famous song.

অসময়ে হরিষ মলো, লক্ষ্নে হলো কারাগার ।
ঝীল বানরে সোনার বাঙলা করলো ছার খার ॥

THE FOUNDATION OF THE CALCUTTA MEDICAL COLLEGE HOSPITAL, BABU MUTY LAL SEAL AND THE PAIKPARA RAJA.

On saturday, the 3rd, September 1848, the foundation stone of this building was laid by Lord Dalhousie. In 1843, Dr. Mouat, then secretary to the Council of Education, and a resident Professor of the Medical College, suggested to Sir John Peter Grant, the Chairman of the Municipal Committee which collected, by public subscriptions, a fund, for the foundation of a Fever Hospital for the Calcutta poor. Babu Muty Lal Seal granted a piece of land adjoining the College premises, valued at Rs 12,000, to form a portion of the site of the present building. The Municipal Committee transferred the Fever Hospital funds amounting to Rs. 55,462 to the Council of Education. Dr. Mouat published a pamphlet and a further sum of Rs. 36,000 was realized by public subscriptions. Rajah Protap Chunder Sing paid Rs. 50,000 to this fund. (F. I. Oct. 5 1848.).

NATIVE THEATRE AT THE GOVERNMENT HOUSE.

We read in the *Englishman* of the 30th March, 1837, that a dramatic performance was played by the Hindoo College students in the White House of Calcutta. Lord Auckland the Lord Bishop, the Hon'ble Miss Francis Eden, the Hon'ble Mr. Shakespeare were present on the occasion.

THE FOLLOWING WAS THE PROGRAMME.

THE KING AND THE MILLER.

KING	... ...	Gobind Chunder Dutt.
MILLER	... ...	Norrotum Das.
SOLDIER'S DREAM	...	Shoshee Chunder Dutt.
TOBY TOSSPOT ...	...	Gopal Nath Mukherjee.
SHAKESPEAR'S SEVEN AGES		Abotar Chunder Gangooly.
LODGINGS FOR SINGLE AGENT		Protap Chunder Ghose.

MERCHANT OF VENICE, ACT IV. SCENE I.

DUKE	... ...	Rajendra Nath Sen.
SHYLOCK	... ...	Uma Churn Mitter.
ANTONIO	... ...	Gopal Krishen Dutt.
PORTIA	... ...	Abhoy Churn Bose.
GRATIANO	... ...	Rajendra Narain Dutt.
BASSANIO	... ...	Rajendra Narain Bose.
SALARINO	... ...	Gopal Nath Mukherjea.
NERISSA	... ...	Rajendra Narain Mitter.
NELLYGRAY	... ...	Gobind Chunder Dutt.

THE DRAMATIC ASPIRANT.

PATENT	...	Kally Kishen Ghosh.
DOWLAS	...	Grish Chunder Ghosh.

BABU RUSIK LAL SEN, AND LORD AUCKLAND'S
SCHOOL AT BARACKPUR.

A private English School was established in 1837 by Lord Auckland for the eleemosynary education of native youths. The school-building in the Barrackpore Park was raised at a cost of Rs 3,500 paid by Lord Auckland from his private purse. Babu Russicklal Sen who was formerly an English teacher at Midnapore, was entrusted with the management of this seminary, the entire expense of which was paid by Lord Auckland. The boys were furnished *gratis* with books &c. It was opened on the 6th March 1837. (Gyananashun, March 29, 1837.)

BABU HURO CHUNDER GHOSE, AS A NATIVE PRIVATE
SECRETARY TO LORDS DALHOUSIE AND BENTINCK.

We read the following in the *Hindoo Patriot.*

"We believe an appointment of this kind was contemplated by Lord William Bentinck, and was actually offered to the late Babu Huro Chunder Ghose, but family circumstances prevented that gentleman from proceeding to the North-West, and the idea was then abandoned."

NATIVE ADDRESS TO LORD CANNING
DURING THE MUTINY.

Maharajah Satish Chunder Roy Bahadur of Krishnaghur, Rajah Protap Chunder Singh Bahadur, Rajah Promothonath Roy Bahadur, Babu Joykishen Mukherjea and the other zemindars, traders, merchants, agriculturists &c., presented an address to Lord Canning, expressive of their deep sense of gratitude for the several measures of security adopted by his Lordship. The address was published in the *Friend of India* of December 24, 1857. Sir Cecil Beadon, as Secretary, to the Government of India acknowledged it in a letter, dated the 17th December, 1857 in a suitable terms. (Vide *Friend of India,* December 24, 1857.)

BABU SHYAMA CHARAN DEY.

In 1845 a heavy defalcation having taken place in the Bengal Bank, he was along with two others to put the accounts of the Bank into order. Mr. Plumb was then its Secretary, and Mr. Cooke Accountant.

RAJA DEGUMBER MITER AND DAVID HARE'S STATUE.

Babu Peary Chand Miter in his biography of David Hare published in 1877, omitted to mention that Babu Degumber Miter moved a resolution at the memorial meeting held on the 17th. June, 1841, to the following effect.

"That a building be erected to be called Hare's Lyceum for the reception of the youths of Mr. Hare's school, in substitution of the present premises, and a book of subscription be opened for such purpose, and that after such building shall have been completed, the surplus fund be appropriated towards a marble statue, bust, or picture, as the funds may admit."

After a good deal of discussion. the proposal for a statue was unanimously accepted.

DWARK NATH TAGORE IN ENGLAND IN 1842.

We read the following in the *London Times* of 1842 :— "At a recent banquet given at the Mansion-house, the Lord Mayor said—"I now beg to propose the health of two distinguished strangers, whom I am happy to see to-day. The high character and great attainments of my friend on my right render him an ornament to society. The great kindness he has always shewn to our countrymen in India, entitles him to the gratitude of every British subject. I am sure you will all unite with me in drinking the health of Dwark Nath Tagore and Chunder Mohun Chatterjea.

The toast was drunk with great applause. Dwark Nath then rose to return thanks. The company could not, he said expect to hear him speak well in a language foreign to him.

* * * But he felt, as he ought, the distinction and friendship with which he had been treated, what must his country,
which had been saved from utter destruction by the national
friendship and humanity of England, feel upon looking to
the glorious result ; (cheers,) It was England who sent out
Clive and Cornwallis to benefit India by their counsels and
arms. * * * It was impossible for his countrymen to
treat the English with ingratitude. He was confident that
they could ever be such fatal enemies to themselves as to exchange for the benignant protection of the British, the awful
villany and tyranny of the Mahomedans or the Russians."

"Prince Dwarkanath Tagore Zemindar" was placed in a
dilemma on Friday last while present amongst the party invited by the Lord Mayor to an entertainment on the Thames
at Twickenham. When the barge was moored off Pope's
villa, about 6o'clock, a gentleman arrived with a despatch for
Lord Fitzgerald and Vesci with her Majesty's commands for
the Prince to be present at the Royal dinner-party on the
same evening. Unfortunately for His Highness no vehicle to
transferring him to London could be procured : at length
however, Mr. T. P. Austin, of Lambeth road, who had driven
a friend down in his stanhope to partake of the civic festivity
kindly offered His Highness a seat, and drove him towards
London. When on the road they met the Prince's carriage,
in which he was enabled to reach Buckingham Palace just
in time to escape a breach of etiquette."

DWARK NATH TAGORE'S VISIT TO ENGLAND IN 1846.

Mr. Stocqueler in his "memoirs of a journalist" thus
notices Babu Dwark Nath Tagore's visit to England :

"It was, with no small delight that I welcomed him on his visit to
England in 1846—if I remember rightly the date. His *bonhommie*, good
manner, and rare intelligence made him many friends in the highest
circle. The men who had governed India in his time, and who did not
forget how much he had contributed by his purse and his example to the

enlightenment of his countrymen and the establishment of useful municipal and educational institutions, were glad of the opportunity of bringing him into notice. He was for a time quite the pet of the aristocracy.
At length he became wearied of the constant succession of balls, *soirées*,
&c., and wished for a new excitement. He had seen the aristocracy of
wealth and the aristocracy of birth, he now was desirous of seeing something of the aristocracy of talent ; not of that higher order of ability
which adorned the Legislature and the walks of Science, or imparted lustre
to the Pulpit, the Bar, and the Bench, but the description of talent which
makes the press, the stage, and the arts galleries brilliant, pleasant, and
instructive. Did I know the men who belonged to that charming class,
and if I did, would I bring them together ? Of course I knew a considerable number, and equally, of course, I was delighted to be able to gratify
a man, who had been a first friend during the vicissitudes of my Calcutta
career. It was arranged that a dinner should be given at my house at
Notting Hill, and the party was to consist of twelve. It was really a
festive gathering. Of those who came, Oxenford and Kenny of the *Times*,
Tom Taylor and Shirley Brooks of Punch and Harrison Ainsworth, of the
Jack Sheppard school, still survive ; Albert Smith, always gay, Robert
Keely the actor, and his wife, Horace Mayhew, Forrester (Alfred Crow-
quill), and a lady aunt of mine are gone. Dwark Nath was supremely
happy and laughed heartily of the jokes and jokelets let off by the party.'

BABU DWARKANATH TAGORE AND THE
UNION BANK.

The Bank commenced its operations on the 17th August,
1829, and its original proprietors were Mr. William Carr, Mr.
William Prinsep, and Babu Dwarkanath Tagore. With them
Major H. B. Henderson, Mr. W. C. M. Plowden, Dr. Macpherson, Civil Assistant Surgeon of Rampore Boalia, Captain Taylor of the Madras Military Service, Babu Debendra
Nath Tagore, and Girindra Nath Tagore were subsequently
associated as partners. The Bank failed in 1846.

RAJA SHOOKMOY ROY AND THE BANK OF BENGAL.

It was established in 1806 at the instance of Government under the name and style of the Bank of Calcutta with a capital of sicca rupees 50,00,000 in five hundred shares of ten thousand sicca rupees each. The first Charter is dated the 2nd January 1809, and the designation was then altered to what it now bears viz., the Bank of Bengal. The Charter declared that the affairs of the Bank shall be managed by nine Directors, three of whom shall be nominated by Government to represent their interest, (100 shares), and six by proprietors. The first Board of Directors was constituted as follows :

Henry St. George Tucker, Esquire, *President.*

William Egerton, Esq.

Richard Waite Cox, Esq.

Alexander Colvin, Esq. James Alexander, Esq.

John Palmer, Esq. John W. Fulton, Esq.

George Tyler, Esq. Maha Raja Sookmoy Roy.

The first three were the ex-officio Government Directors ; the last six were elected at a public meeting, held at the Town Hall on the 15th December 1808. The Government has always had a direct interest in the Bank. It held, we believe, 275 shares of Rs. 4,000 each. The Government had further secured its voice in the management of the Bank by giving the Secretaryship to a Bengal Civilian. Since the establishment of the Bank all the Secretaries except four were Bengal Civilians, to wit :

YEAR.	NAME.	YEAR.	NAME.
1806	J. W. Sherer, Esq. C. S.	1830	Richard Uduy, Esq. C. S.
1808	W. Morton, Esq. C. S.	„	George Uduy, Esq. C. S.
1815	Henry Wood, Esq. C. S.	1840	Thomas Bracken, Esq. C.S.
1816	Charles Morley, Esq. C. S.	1847	Charles Hogg, Esq.
1820	W. H. Oakes, Esq. C. S.	1851	W. Grey, Esq. C. S.
1822	C. T. Glass, Esq.	1854	T. B. Plumb, Esq.
1829	J. A. Dorin, Esq. C. S.	1860	George Dickson, Esq.

THE LATE BABU BHUDEB MUKHERJIA, C. I. E.

A GREAT EDUCATIONIST IN BENGAL.

We take the following from the *Indian Mirror* of May 26, 1894.

"The following interesting anecdote connected with the life of the late lamented Babu Bhudeb Mukerjea, C. I. E., is related by the *Chinsura Bartabaha* :—"In 1849. he was appointed Second Master of the Calcutta Madrassa. In this capacity, he had to discharge the duties of the Head-Master of that institution. Mr. Clinger was the Head-Master of the Madrassa. The boys of the first class were more attached to Bhudeb than to the Head-Master. They used to take their lessons after school hours from Babu Bhudeb. It was for this reason, the Head-Master made private arrangements with Bhudeb Babu, and left the task of instructing the boys of the first class to him, except on Thursdays, when Colonel Railey visited the school, and taught the boys of the first class. The Head-Master also intimated to Babu Bhudeb that he would teach the boys music, and get extra remuneration from them. In this private arrangement, Babu Bhudeb acquiesced, as a matter of course, and taught the boys of the first class, except on Thursdays when the Head-Master himself took charge of the class. Colonel Railey got information of this private arrangement, and asked Bhudeb one day, whether it was true that he regularly taught the boys of the first class. To this query, he politely refused to make any answer, and requested the Colonel to question the Head-Master himself on the point. The more persistently the Colonel pressed the question, the more politely Babu Bhudeb referred the Colonel to the Head-Master. Babu Bhudeb told the Colonel that, subordinate as he was, it was not proper for him to say anything for or against the Head-Master, his official superior. Colonel Railey was a somewhat rough sort of man. But he was highly pleased with Babu Bhudeb's conduct, and told him, "Young man, always behave thus, and you will succeed in life." The Colonel then recommended him to Dr. Mouat, then Secretary to the Council of Education. After serving for only ten months in the Madrassa College, Babu Bhudeb was appointed, in 1849, Head Master of the Government School at Howrah, where he served for more than seven years till 1856, when he was appointed Head-Master of the Hughly Normal School, on a salary of Rs. 300 per mensem."

RAJAH KRISHNA CHUNDER BAHADUR

THE ILLUSTRIOUS HUSBAND OF HER HIGHNESS
THE MAHARANEE SURNOMOYE C. I.

The following letter signed by the Rajah himself appeared in the *Englishman* of Sept. 25. 1840, which speaks for itself.

A HARD CASE, ILLUSTRATIVE OF THE SUNSET LAW.

To the Editor of the *Englishman,*

SIR,

I beg to bring to the notice of the public through your valuable paper, the following grievance that has occured to me. Mr. Taylor, the Collector of Moorshedabad, advertised my eight annas and eight gundahs share of a talook, situated in the Zilah of Moorshedabad, Purgunah Coowar Protaup &c, containing 7 Purgunahs, for sale on the 6th of Srabun last, for the non-payment of Rs. 73, 291, balance of Government revenue for the last year, on which day my Muktear attended at the Collector's Cutchery and paid Rs. 20,000 in part, but the Collector did not attend on the day to sell mine or any other property, On the following day the 7th. my Mooktear again attended at the Cutchery, and paid the further sum of Rs, 24,000 and requested the Collector to give me further time to pay the balance, which had then been reduced to Rs, 25,291, which the Collector refused to do, and fined every word of my Muktear uttered; he was fined 10 times, which fines amounted to 420 Rs. After 5 o'clock in the evening when there was no purchaser present, my property was put up and sold for the sum of one rupee to Government; after the sale the Collector informed my Muktear that if I would pay the balance of the revenue, he would cancel the sale and at the same time he remitted Rs, 400 of the fine two days after the sale. My Muktear attended and paid into the Collector's Cutchery the whole of the balance of the revenue, which was reported by the Collector to the Commissioner, Mr. Jackson, with a recommendation that the sale should be cancelled. The Commissioner however instead of attending to the recommendation, confirmed the sale. Thus for the sum of one rupee have I been deprived of property of the value of five lacks of rupees and upwards, and Government have been the purchaser.

I am, Sir, your Obdt. Servant,

RAJAH KISHNO CHUNDER BAHADUR.

Calcutta Sept. 24, 1840.

It was in this year, Rajah attained his majority.

BABU RAM TONOO MULLIK.

We read the following in the *Englishman* of Sept. 29, 1840 :—

"We are informed that the Commissioners of the Court of Requests. (since called the Calcutta Small Cause Court) have received a letter from Babu Ram Tonoo Mullik to know the number of prisoners now imprisoned in the Great Jail for petty debts, and the aggregate amount of their debts which he has liberally offered to pay. We understand that the number of prisoners now in Jail is 155, and the amount is about 7,600 rupees. After getting them out, he paid to the Christians Rs. 4 each, and to the native Re. 1 and a suit of clothes."

Such a kind of charity is now almost unknown in our days. Our Zemindars are now fond of vying with each other in contributing to a fund inaugurated under official patronage ! ! !

RAJA RAM MOHAN ROY'S MEMORIAL MEETING.

We learn from the *Bengali Spectator* of July, 1842, that in April 1834, a public meeting was held in the Town Hall for the purpose of perpetuating his memory under the presidency of the Hon'ble Sir J. P. Grant. Messrs J. Pattle, Babu Rusik Krishna Mullik, H. M. Parker, T. E. Mr. Turton, and J. Sutherland addressed the meeting. A committee was formed consisting of Sir J. P. Grant, Messrs. T. E. M. Turton, L. Clarke, J. Sutherland, G. J. Gordon, W. H. Smoult, Rustomjee Cowasjee, Bishwanath Mutty Lal to carry out the objects of the meeting. Rs. 5000 were raised at the time.

THE HON'BLE SURENDRANATH BANERJEE.

HIS CASE BEFORE THE COURT OF QUEEN'S BENCH
JUNE 11, 1869.
(*Times* June, 12.)

(Sittings in Banco before the Lord Chief Justice, Mr. Justice Blackburn, Mr. Justice Mellore, and Mr. Justice Hannen.

Mr. Mellish (with him Mr. Bell) moved on behalf of the applicant, for a *mandamus* to the Civil Service Commissioners.

to hear him, and receive his evidence as to his age, with a view to his admission to the Civil Service. The application was made under the Indian Civil Service Act, 21 and 22 Victoria, Cap. one hundred and six. These regulations requir-ed the applicants to send in certificates of their birth, show-ing that on the 21st of March, 1869, they were above 17 and under 21. Babu Surendra Nath succeeded in passing among the first fifty, and so was admitted. The candidate who was 51 in the list and who had failed, sent in a complaint that the applicant was over the proper age, because at the time he entered at Calcutta he had, in the language of the Univer-sity certificate, "attained the age of 16." Babu Surendra Nath made an affidavit, that among the Bengalees, a person was understood to be 16 when he had entered his sixteenth year, and cited *Macnaughten's Principles of Hindoo Law* p. 117. He swore that he was born in November, 1848, and in support of his statement sent a deposition of his father's, and a certificate from the Hon'ble Mr. Dwarka Nath Mitter, Judge of the High Court at Calcutta. The Civil Service Commissioners declined to have evidence upon that point.

The Court then granted the rule *nisi*. The case was to be heard in Novr. 1869. (Vide *Englishman*, July 7, 1869.)

Mr. Gilbert Leslie Smith who was placed 51st on the list raised objections to the admission of Babu Surendra Nath Banerjee, Messrs. B. L. Gupta, and Sripad Babaji Thakur on the ground of their having exceeded the limits of age prescribed by the Civil Service Regulations. Mr. Behary Lal Gupta stood fourteenth and Babu Surendra Nath thirty-eighth on the list of successful candidates. They were final-ly admitted on their producing satisfactory evidence on that point. The entire correspondence that passed between Mr. Walrond, Secretary to Her Majesty's Civil Service Com-missioners, and these native Civilians was published in the *Englishman* of July 10, 1869.[*]

---

[*] As for the other anecdotes, see our *Bengal Celebrities*.

THE CASE OF MYSADAL RAJ FAMILY
SUTTEE.

The *Hurkura* stated that the Rajah of Mysadal died at
Kidderpur on the 1st of November 1840, without issue, leaving a widow named Bemola of about 12 years of age. She
immolated herself on the funeral pile, a few hours after his
death. (F. I. Feb. 11. 1847.)

BABU KISHORY CHAND MITTER.

A committee consisting Mr. Hinde, Babu Hurro Chunder Ghose, and Mr. Ferguson, was appointed to enquire into
his conduct as Junior Police Magistrate. He was charged
with having made interpolations in the deposition of witnesses examined by him. (F. I. Sept. 22. 1858.)

THE LATE DR. BHOLA NATH BOSE.

Dr. Bholanath Bose was born in A. D. 1825, in his paternal residence at Chanuk Bowbazar in South Barrackpore.
His father Ram Soonder Bose died when Bholanath Bose
was only about six years of age. He received his early
education in the Barrackpur School set up by Lord Auckland.

Lord Auckland and his friends used every now and then
to visit the Barrackpore School, and Bholanath soon attracted His Lordship's notice by his intelligence and progress in
studies. In the year 1840 His Lordship transferred him
to the Calcutta Medical College with a stipend of Rs. 10 a
month, which he paid from his own private purse. His career
in the Medical College was a brilliant one, and at the expiration of about five years since his admission into it, he
accompanied Dr. R. A. Goodeve to England as one of the
Tagore scholars. The circumstances which led to this then
novel and daring adventure may not perhaps be so well-
known. In the beginning of 1845 the late Babu Dwark Nath
Tagore proposed, through the then Council of Education, to

take with him to England two medical students at his own expense for the purpose of enabling them to acquire superior skill in their profession by a European education. The liberal offer having been cordially approved by the Council was announced to the students by Dr. F. J. Mouat, then their Secretary. No one responded to the patriotic call of Babu Dwaka Nath. At last when the project seemed doomed to failure, Bhola Nath stepped forward and volunteered to accompany the Babu on his intended journey. He did so, however, on certain conditions, which were approved and granted by Government, and Dr. Gooodeve was appointed to take charge and superintend the expedition. Bhola Nath Bose and Gopal Lal Seal were named Tagore students ; Surja Kumar Chakravarti was selected on the part of Government and Darka Nath Bose on that of the public, funds having been raised by public subscriptions for the purpose. At the time of their embarkation from India Bholanath, as already stated, had been nearly five years in College, Dwarka Nath and Seal three years, and Chakravarti a little more than one year.

One the eve of his return to India he received an autograph letter of which the following is a copy—from his distinguished patron and friend, the late Earl of Auckland.

ADMIRALTY.

January 13th, 1848.

MY DEAR BHOLANATH,—

I will not allow you to leave England without writing a few lines to you to say that I wish you well. I would add too that you have given very great satisfaction to me and to your other friends, by the earnestness with which you have pursued your studies, and by the distinctions which have attended your success in them.

I should like you to take away with you some token of

remembrance from me, and I will beg you to purchase one that may be agreeable to you with the enclosed draft.

Yours most truly, &c.,

(Sd.) AUCKLAND.

With the amount of this draft Dr. Bose bought a gold watch, which, according to the terms of the late Doctor's will, is to be preserved as an heirloom in the family.

A strong effort was made by the late Earl of Auckland, Sir Edward Ryan, Mr. C. H. Cameron, and other influential persons, to obtain for Dr. Bose admission into the Covenanted Medical Service of India. But the late Honorable Court of Directors were then of opinion, that the time had not yet arrived to admit the natives of India into that service. The Home Government, however, sent instructions to the Local Government that Dr. Bose should be treated in every way, as if he were a Covenanted Medical Officer. Soon after his return from England in 1848, he was first appointed Surgeon and Superintendent of the Sukea's Lane Dispensary and Hospital in Calcutta—an institution which in fact was established solely to employ him in town.

He died on the 22nd September, 1882, of a carbuncle on the neck.

CHAPTER II

THE HON'BLE SIR T. MUTHUSWAMI IYAR. K. C. I. E.

He was born of a poor but respectable family in the village of Vuchuvadi in the Tanjore District, in January 1832. His father, Venkata Narain Sastrial died while he was young. In 1846, he found a patron in Muthuswami Naiken, otherwise known as "Butler—Tehsildar," presumably because Mathuswami Naiken began life as a butler to Sir Henry Montgomery.

The following anecdote, we cull from the *Madras Standard* of May 21, 1894 ;

The Tehsildar was struck with young Mathuswami's intelligence and industry, and even foresaw a bright future for him. The way in which the Tehsildar happened to form a high opinion of Mathuswami's intelligence and habits is testified to by the following anecdotes. One day the Tehsildar received a report informing him of a breach in an adjoining river-belt, and being anxious to obtain some information about it, he sent for a clerk in the Cutcherry. But there being none in the office at the time, young Muthuswami made bold to approach the Tehsildar and await orders. The Tehsilder put the report into Muthuswami's hands and asked him if he knew anything about the breach. The boy said he would obtain the required information immediately, and taking the report with him, he went to the spot, ascertained the dimensions of the breach, inquired where the materials for its repair would be had, and in a short time submitted a written report furnishing all the necessary information. The Tehsildar, though at first not inclined to credit the report submitted by the boy, signed the paper owing to the urgency

of the occasion and sent it at once to the office for effect being given to
it. Meanwhile, the Head Clerk turned up and on reference being made
to him by the Tehsildar, he found that the boy's report was accurate. On
another occasion, a certain Mirasidar called on the Tehsildar to know how
much his arrears of tax amounted to. He owned lands in more than
twenty villages which lay scattered in the Taluq, and the Tehsildar was
not able to give the information without consulting his clerks. Finding
however, young Muthuswami standing close by, he asked him if he knew
anything about it ; and to his surprise he received an answer which, on
verification, was found to be correct. These two incidents raised young
Muthuswami in the estimation of his master.

THE HON'BLE JUSTICE MUTHUSWAMI IYAR AND NEWAB SIR SYED AHMED OF THE NORTH-WEST.

Some years ago, the Hon'ble Justice Muthuswami Iyar
came to Allyghur and went to Sir Syed Ahmed's house to
pay him a friendly visit. Without giving any previous intima-
tion of his visit, the Hon'ble Justice Iyar called at his house
just at daybreak, when he was told by the Newab's servants
that he would not rise from his bed till the usual customary
hour of 9 o'clock. Ordinarily dressed as he was in his usual
Maharatta garb, the Newab's servants took him to be an
ordinary visitor and paid no attention to him. Nor a seat
was offered till the appointed hour of the expected visit. The
high-minded Maharatta noble man did not care much about
the want of courtesy shewn to him unwittingly, and instead
of coming back to his lodging, he determined to wait till the
appointed hour, and took his seat upon one of the low walls
surrounding the spacious confound of the Newab's palace at
Allyghur, with the fierce sunshine falling on his face. In
this way he sat on the outer walls till 9. A. M.,
when, on coming to learn, that the Newab had risen from his
bed, he sent in his card. No sooner the bearer handed it
over to him, than the Newab himself came down from the up-
stairs and received the distinguished Maharatta visitor with
all the honor and courtesy which, an oriental scholar and a

perfect master of oriental etiquette like the distinguished Newab could shew on the occasion. The visit lasted for pretty a long hour, and. the Newab himself again came down to see the visitor off. Immediately after his departure, the Newab naturally enquired of his servants as to when the visitor came to see him. On coming to learn that the Maharatta Judge had to wait outside for many a long hour without being allowed a seat in the visitor's room, he ran up to the Judge again and begged to be excused for what the servants had unwittingly done. Justice Muthuswami, it is said, simply smiled and assured the Newab of the pleasure he derived from the visit. The simplicity of this Maharatta Brahmin Judge ought to teach a lesson to those who, under the veneer of English education, get offended with any the least want of show of courtesy.

Mr. ANANDA CHARLU OF MADRAS.

Mr. Ananda Charlu is a zealous supporter of the Indian National Congress. Mr. Ananda Charlu having been engaged as a pleader in a case, was, unavoidably detained in one of the border districts of Madras, travelled through the Ganjam Forests, for want of any other conveyance, and attended the Allahabad meeting of the National Congress held in 1892. Such an example of endurance of unusual hardships has become almost rare among the ease-loving English educated natives of India.

Mr. M. VENCATA ROYALOO OF MADRAS.

Mr. M. Vencataroyaloo, Telugu Translator in the Petition Department of the Government Office at Madras was dismissed from the public service on the 11th January, 1848, under the orders of the Governor of Madras, for having abstracted public records from the office. He brought an action for libel in the Supreme Court of Madras against Mr. H. C. Montgomery, officiating Chief Secretary to the Madras Government who

signed the notification for his dismissal. The case was dismissed by the Madras Supreme Court on the ground that the
Court had no jurisdiction in the matter over the local Government. (F. I. May 4, 1848.)

Mr. PATCHEEAPAH MOODELLY OF TANJORE, MADRAS, AND HIS INSTITUTION.

Patchcapah Moodelly Esq. of Tanjore, a devout Hindoo of
Madras died in 1794, bequeathing a fortune of about 14 lakhs
of rupees. The value of his estate was considerably reduced by
litigation and bad debts, but in August, 1841, a sum of seven
lakhs of Rupees remained at its credit, which the Madras Government, the Supreme Court, and the Home Authorities
concurred in appropriating to the establishment of an educational Institution at Madras. (F. I. June 21, 1849.)

SIR, T. MADHAVA RAO. K. C. S. I.

We read the following in the *Hindoo Patriot* of Oct, 4,
1875 :—

Sir Madhava Rao is shewing his metal. According to the *Times of
India* Sir Richard Meade had recommended that Gujanun Vittul, should
have a jaghir of a village of Rs. 750 a year, the Police Inspector, who
distinguished at the Baroda trial, out of the Baroda State, as a reward
for his services during the Baroda Commission. Sir Madhava Row refused
to sanction the gift on the ground that Gujanun rendered no services to
the Gaekwar, and that therefore the Gaekwar's Raj should not be en-
cumbered with any gift to him. Whatever services Gujanun rendered
beyond the discharge of his ordinary duties he rendered, the dewan considers, to the British Government, whose servant he is, and the reward
should be from them. We are informed that the Viceroy also takes
this view of the matter, and, considering that Gujanun already draws a
very handsome salary, has declined to accede to the recommendations
of Sir Richard Meade. It is also stated that the opinion of competent
lawyers is that as the British Government are simply trustees of the boy
Gaekwar during his minority, they cannot legitimately give away lands and
villages in perpetuity for any number of generations.

Mr. LUCHMUNARSOO CHETTY OF MADRAS.

As chairman of a meeting of the Hindoo community of Madras, held on the 24th October 1846, he sent a petition to the Court of Directors, bringing serious charges against the Madras Government in shewing more favour to the Christains than to the Hindoos, and referred to the case of Malcolm Lewin who was removed from the High Court Bench on the 17th Sept. 1846. The petition was signed by 72,700 Hindoos. (F. I. March 4, 1847.)

NAMES OF RESPECTABLE FAMILIES OF MADRAS IMPOVERISHED BY LAW-SUITS.

An anonymous correspondent, "Gratiano" wrote to the *Madras Spectator* in its issue of October 18, 1841, giving the following list of persons impoverished by paying large sums of money to the lawyers in litigation.

HOUSE NAMES.	NAMES.	AMOUNT.
		LACKS.
Soonkoo.	Krishnamah Chitty.	10
Trondy.	Mooneyapah Chitty.	10
Smith.	Vurdapah Pillay.	7
Brody.	Chengalaroy Moodelly.	4
	Iya Pillay.	7
	Charmayah Moodelly.	4
	Moodukrishna Moodelly.	40
Coomundan.	Teroomiala Naik	2
Bombay.	China Pillay	4
	Colingaroy Moodelly	40
Rajah.	Moodukrishna Naik	7
Munro.	Moodu Moodelly	3
	Apparow Moodelly	1
Seetron.	Nagapah Moodelly	2
	Debunath Moodelly	1
	Moorooga Moodelly	1—80 thousand.
&c. *	&c * &c * &c *	&c.
Pettoor.	Cauzy Chitty.	10

We have no such authentic list for Bengal. It is said that the Ranaghat Pal Chowdhuries lost 79 lakhs of rupees in litigation. The Moharanee Surnomoye of Kashimbazar paid in 1847 Rs, 10,000 to his Attorney, the late Babu Horro Chunder Lahiri of Serampore when she obtained the property of her husband in that year, not to speak of the enormous sums of money paid to her Attornies and Barristers.

THE CASE OF GOLAM MOHAMED KHAN.

Captain Whistler commanding a troop of the 6th Madras Light Cavalry, stationed at Arcot, in February 1846 lost a diamond ring. Soon after this he was informed by one of his own troopers named Golam Mohamed Khan, that he, the trooper had picked up a ring which fell from the person of Syed Cassim, a servant of Captain Whistler, and that he had sold it in the bazar for one pagoda. On this Captain Whistler, voluntarily accompanied by the trooper, waited on the acting Magistrate of North Arcot, Mr. R, R. Cotton, and informed him of his loss, and of what the sower had told him. He did not charge Golam Mohamed with the theft, and in fact it appears from his conduct throughout, that he believed the trooper perfectly innocent. But Mr. Cotton immediately subjected the man, as a prisoner, to examination by his office writers, and without accusation or evidence against him pronounced him guilty, and sentenced him to six months' imprisonment. Mr. Cotton remarked that "he was a mussulman, and all mussulmans were thieves, or else where could they get the fine clothes they wear at their feasts." The trooper was dismissed from the service and brought an action against Mr. Cotton in the Supreme court of Madras, but the Chief Justice ruled that the Court had no jurisdiction in the case. *Hurkura* Aug. 19. 1847

H. R. H. THE PRINCE OF WALES
AT THE MADRAS HARBOUR.

The *Madras Times* related the following anecdote in 1876.

"When the Prince of Wales was returning from laying the foundation stone of the Madras Harbour Works, he suddenly bethought himself that he would like to see the Grand Arsenal in Fort St. George. Soon the royal party arrived at the place, but found it all shut up, the day being a public holiday. An officer attached to the Arsenal was fortunately found in his quarters close by, however, and he soon got the outer doors of the Arsenal opened. At the top of the stairs, however, a glass office door barred the entrance to the great hall of the Arsenal, and no amount of coaxing or bullying would induce this faithful defenders of Her Majesty's material of war to give way, even to the Prince of Wales. The R. A. Officer in charge performed the acrobatic feat of getting in at a window, and tried to open the door from the inside. No go. It would not open. At length, His Royal Highness put his own stalwart shoulder to the outside, and with a "one, two, and all together," the door flew open and the Prince was thrown into the arms of R. A. inside. There was, of course, a glorious burst of laughter over the adventure, and if the Prince does not wear a medal for his victorious assault on the Grand Arsenal at Madras, it will be perhaps because he would not like to bring the garrison into trouble."

THE DUKE OF BUCKINGHAM.

In the *Hindoo Patriot* of Nov. 13, 1876, we read the following :—

A CARTMAN was convicted last month by the second-class Magistrate of Madurantakum in Madras of negligent driving, thereby endangering the lives of certain people at the sixty-second mile of the southern trunk road. The case attracted the notice of the Government of Madras, which has passed the following orders :

"His Grace the Governor in Council considers that the Cartman in this case was punished for an accident due to the 'neglect of the Railway Company to fence the pit which they had dug in dangerous proximity to the road and left without any kind of warning or watch. The Goverment consider that the Company should compensate the man for the punishment he has undergone by a money payment of say Rs. 30. The further steps in the matter will be taken in the Public Works Department."

He opposed the passing of the Vernacular Press Act. He was almost alone among the rulers of the land in holding that opinion.

THE EARL OF MORNINGTON.

The *Madras Mail* of 1861 thus wrote :—

"It is on record that the Earl of Mornington writing from Fort St. George privately to Sir Alured Clarke in Calcutta in 1799, said :—"I shall take an early opportunity of transmitting rules for the conduct of the whole tribe of editors ; in the meantime if you can not tranquilize this and other mischievous publications, be so good as to suppress their papers by force, and send their persons to Europe."

LORD HOBART.

We extract the following from the *Hindoo Patriot* of 1874 :—

THE FRIEND OF INDIA has a capital article showing up the administration of justice in India. The case under notice occurred in Madras One Sarawana Pillay, who is described as a "respectable man", "able and intelligent," was an Inspector of Police ; he had arrested a gang of dacoits, and it is stated that one of them died from torture practised by the Police. The Sessions Judge of Tranqueber convicted him of "constructive murder," but the High Court quashed that judgment, and sentenced him to two years' rigorous imprisonment for extorting evidence. The man still protested that he was innocent, and appealed to Lord Hobart for mercy. His Lordship rejected the petition, but Mr. Pillay threatened to go up to the Secretary of State. Our contemporary adds. "The Governor of Madras appears to have been considerably astonished. It would seem that he possesses a wholesome awe of the redoubtable Marquess, for rather than trouble Lord Salisbury, he called for further reports, the upshot being that Sarawana Pillay has been released from prison a pardoned man."

THE *MADRAS ATHENÆUM* AND ITS RUSTICATION.

We take the following from the proceedings of the Madras Government dated the 12th July, 1872.

"In its issue of Saturday, 29th June last, the *Madras Athenæum* newspaper, published at length the Proceedings of Government in the Judicial Department, No. 830, dated 19th June 1872, censuring the Acting Inspector-General of Police for the tone of his correspondence with the Jail Department, which Order of Government, as the Editor of the *Athenæum* must have been well-aware when the paper came to his hands had not been placed by Government at the disposal of the press. The Government have had repeated occasion to notice the publication by the *Madras Athenæum* of Government papers which had not been officially communicated, and this in breach of the understanding on which the Editors are furnished with copies of correspondence, the publication of which the Government deem unobjectionable or desirable. They resolve, therefore, in the present instance, to give effect to the G. O. of 30th November, 1865 on the subject, and direct the removal of the *Madras Athenæum and Daily News* from the list of newspapers to which papers placed at the disposal of the Press are supplied.

H. H. THE MAHARAJA OF VIZIANAGRAM
AND Mr. C. READE.

In 1859, Mr. C. Reade was Agent to the Governor of Madras in Vizagapatam. In September 1859, the public were startled by an accusation preferred by some of Mr. Reade's personal friends and official subordinates, charging him with pecuniary dealings with the Raja of Vizianagram and with falsehood, amounting to perjury, in endeavouring to conceal them. A Commission of enquiry was appointed, and Mr. Reade was proved guilty of little more than official imprudence in purchasing two horses and two elephants from the Raja when he was suddenly called out on public duties, and in borrowing two mirrors to adorn his drawing-room for the reception of Lord Harris. The result was that Sir Charles Trevelyan suspended Mr. Reade. Sir Charles Wood fixed the period of suspension at two years." (F. I. Aug. 22, 1861.)

Mr. GRANT DUFF AND THE MADRAS TIMES.

We take the following from the *Hindoo Patriot* of 1882.

He bungled in both the Chingleput and Salem Riots cases. Lately he has given a proof of bad temper and illiberal feeling, which we least expected from him. The *Madras Times* had published *in extenso* a minute of the Governor regarding his tour in July last. The editor was called upon to explain how he allowed himself to publish the minute, and he replied as follows :—

I beg to point out that your expression, 'how he allowed himself to publish,' implies some impropriety in the act. This I most respectfully but firmly beg to repudiate : for I am not aware of any law of morality, propriety or courtesy, which prevents an editor from presenting to the public a paper, (1) which was highly interesting, yet which contained no important State secret, (2) which publication was in no way calculated to embarrass the Government, (3) whose contents were already known among officials, (4) which, the public will agree with the press, ought certainly to have been communicated to the latter, (5) and of which a portion had already been published in the *Madras Mail* four days before, and copied by other papers.

This explanation did not satisfy the Governor, who has passed the following order on the subject :

"Order dated 1st December 1882, No. 1499. Public.

"In its issue of Tuesday, November 7th instant, the *Madras Times* Newspaper published at length the Minute recorded by His Excellency the Governor relating to his tour undertaken in July last, a confidential document which, as the editor must have been well aware when the paper came to his hands, had not been placed by the Government at the disposal of the Press.

"In reply to the enquiry made on the subject, the Editor expresses no regret for his conduct, but, on the contrary, takes credit to himself for having given publicity to a paper which he had irregularly obtained, refusing at the same time to explain how he became possessed of the same.

"3. In the circumstances the only course open to Government is to give effect to G. O., dated 30th November 1865, on the subject, and to direct the removal of the *Madras Times* from the list of newspapers to which papers placed at the disposal of the Press are supplied.

"4. Heads of Department will cease to utilize the paper in question for the publication of their advertisements.

RAM VURMAH, THE FIRST PRINCE OF TRAVANCORE.

In 1861, he wrote to a Madras Journal, suggesting that a nuzer in the shape of throne of solid gold should be presented by the Native Princes of India to Queen Victoria on her ascending the throne of India, He offered to subscribe Rs, 5000 to the fund required for this purpose. (F. I. Feb, of 1861,)

THE FIRST GOVERNORS OF MADRAS AND THEIR ANECDOTES.

We cull the following from the *Madras Standard* of Feb, 19, 1894,

"The first Governor of Fort St. George cannot have dreamed that his successors two centuries hence would develop into such magnates with Aid-de-camps and Secretaries, bands and body-guards in attendance. Mr. Aaron Baker, the first Governor, cannot have been a man of any consequence ; anyhow, it is worthy of note that Mr. Baker as the Governor of Fort St. George had under him not only all the factories on the Coromandel Coast but also those in Bengal. The man who then held the place of the present Viceroy at Fort William was, therefore, in those good old days subordinate to the Governor of Madras. The dignity of modern Governors is so great that it is impossible for any representatives of Her Majesty in India, to be imprisoned in this country. The severest punishment accorded to them is peremptory recall to their native land. But in days of yore, more than one Governor had to spend his days in prison, and one of the earliest of Governors who shared such a fate was Mr. George Foxcroft. Mr. George Foxcroft was a London Merchant, and he was deputed by the East India Company to succeed Sir Edward Winter as Governor of Fort St. George. Sir Edward Winter, however, did not quit India—Governors were not recalled in those days—but took his seat quietly as second in Council. But the second in Council soon proved to be too strong for the first. Sir Edward used as a pretext that the language of the new Governor was treasonable to the English Crown and on that ground, seized and imprisoned him with the assistance of the military, and it was only after Mr. Foxcroft was detained for over two years that Sir Edward yielded to a royal mandate sent out by the Commissioners. Several years subsequently, another Governor shared the same fate owing to some difference of opinion with his Councillors. Governors in those days were mere agents and were not in the receipt of more than three hundred pounds a year. The Governor or Agent was the first member of Council, the Book-keeper was second, the Warehouse-keeper was third, and the Customer was fourth. The Book-keeper drew a salary of one hundred pounds, the Warehoush-keeper seventy, and the Customer fifty. Under these, were factors, writers and apprentices. Factors were paid from twenty to forty pounds, writers received ten and apprentices five. Could the Governors, Warehouse-keepers and the rest of their kind have thought that their successors would ever receive such splendid salaries as they do now and render the administration of India the costliest in the world ?"

MR. JOHN DAWSON MAYNE.

We take the following from the *Hindoo Patriot* of 1872.

The MADRAS ATHENÆUM states that Mr. Mayne appeared on the 29th of last month before Mr. Justice Holloway, and made an application for a writ of mandamus against the Government of Madras to show cause why the Government did not summon him as a member of the Legislative Council to its meetings. He submitted that his resignation of the Advocate Generalship and Secretary to the Legislative Council did not touch his right as member, the statute of Parliament allowing a period of two years of service to each member after his nomination. *Rule Nisi* was granted, returnable in fifteen days.

It is said of him that he had a special servant whose business it was to waft the flies off his gown while he has engaged in addressing the Court.

MR. MALCOLM LEWIN, SECOND JUDGE OF THE SUDDER COURT, MADRAS.

He was suspended by the Madras Government together with two of his colleagues for having protested against the injustice done to the Hindoos of Madras in cases between Christians and Hindoos. He was presented with an address by the Hindoos of Madras signed by more than fifteen thousand people. (Vide *Madras Crescent* of 7th, Oct. 1846.)

The inhabitants of Madras presented him with a candelabrum at an expense of £170. The Court of Director's order on his dismissal appeared in the *Friend of India* of Novr. 30th, 1848.

The Hindu Community of Madras, in a meeting convened by the sheriff on the 7th Oct. 1846, voted an address to him. The full history of this case appeared in the *Friend of India,* March 23, 1848 in which the reply of Mr. Lewin to the address was reproduced from the *Madras Spectator* of March 9, 1848.

OPINION OF THE COURT OF DIRECTORS REGARDING THE REMOVAL OF THE THREE MADRAS JUDGES,

Extract from a private letter from the Hon'ble the Court of Directors, dated 20th January, 1847.

No. I.

Para 1. In your letter of the 22nd October, (No. 24 of 1846) you have furnished an explanation of the circumstances under which you have been induced to come to the resolution of removing from their office three judges of the Court of Sudder and Fouzdaree Adawlut, Mr. George J. Waters, Mr. Malcolm Lewin, and Mr. Thomas E. Boileau.

Para 9. The memorial itself did not relate to any personal grievance, but was in nature of an appeal from the authority of the government, to that of the Court of Directors, on a question of official duty; you therefore, very properly resolved, that it should be returned to the memorialists. Of the whole tone and tenor of the memorial, we highly disapprove, and we regard the comments made by Mr. Lewin, and Mr. Boileau on your orders of the 19th of May, unbecoming and unjustifiable.

Para 11. In the papers laid before the Government by Mr. Waters it was represented that official documents and information had improperly found their way into the newspapers, and this breach of duty was imputed by him to the authors of the memorial. We are surprized, that in drawing the attention of the judges and officers of the Sudder Court to the point, you did not refer expressly to the notification, copied in the margin, in which the principle, that public documents are only held in trust for the performance of public duties is so distinctly explained and the violation of that principle is so positively prohibited. We observe that Mr. Boileau, as well as the Registrar of the Court, and his Deputies disavowed having communicated any official information to the news-

papers ; a similar disavowal was not made by Mr. Lewin, who has even
denied the right of Government to question him on the subject, and Mr.
Waters acknowledged that on one occasion, he had himself published under a feigned signature a letter relating to discussions in the court.

Para 15. It is with deep concern that we express our entire concur-
rence in the propriety of removing 3 judges.

Para 17. Mr. Lewin was deserving of severe censure for the memorial,
and the minute relative thereto. Instead of atoning for that impropriety, he has greatly aggravated it, by the whole tenor of his subsequent
correspondence. He has reproached the government with being control-
led by party influence, and has disputed and insulted their authority.
He has assailed individuals whose conduct was not under his cognizance,
in the face of positive assurances furnished to him. He has persisted in
imputing wrong motives and views to the Government and giving way to
his excited feelings, he has thrown off all regard to subordination, and has
permitted himself to use language highly intemperate and offensive. He
has not only failed to take advantage of the opportunity afforded to him
to disavow, if he could do so, with a due regard to truth, having given
publicity in the newspaper to official information and documents relating to
subjects under discussion betwixt himself and his colleagues, and betwixt
the Government and the Sudder Court, but he seems to lay claim to a
right to commit this breach of the express orders quoted above, as well as
the most obvious principles of public duty." (*Englishman*, Nov. 27, 1848.)

The native Community of calcutta headed by the late
Babu Ashutosh Deb also presented an address to Mr.
Malcolm Lewin for his manly stand on behalf of the Hindus.

MEMORIAL OF THE MADRAS HINDU COMMUNITY
AGAINST THE MARQUIS OF TWEEDALE.

A grand meeting of the Hindoos of Madras was held on
the 7th Oct., 1846, at Patcheapah's School to present a memorial to the Court of Directors against the pro-Christian
tendency of the Madras Government. The sheriff, Mr. L.
Cooper opened the meeting, and Mr. Luchmee Narsoon chitty
was voted to the chair, About 10,000 people attended the
meeting. (Vide *Atlas*, Oct. 8. 1846.)

He was called upon by the Court of Directors not to use
the word "Heathen" in any public document. He was cen-

sured for it. The Madras Hindus took objection to it in their memorial in Malcolm Lewin's case. (Vide *Friend of India*, Aug. 12, 1847.)

SOME CURIOUS FACTS ABOUT THE SUPREME COURT OF MADRAS IN 1847.

Madras Atlas published a Calendar of the prisoners tried at the Sessions of Oyer and Terminer and General Goal Delivery held on the 15th April 1847. It contained only 13 cases in which the amount of property stolen exceeded Rs. 20; only four in which it exceeded Rs. 145, and only one of higher value than 5oo R's. It contained 14 cases in which the value of property was under one rupee, and two cases in which it was of the higher amount than two pice. (F. I. April, 29, 1847.)

REMINISCENCES OF THE MADRAS HIGH COURT.

We take the following from the *Hindoo Patriot* of May 8, 1876.

Scene No. 1.

An application came on, on Wednesday, before Mr. Justice Holloway with reference to the return of papers in a suit in which Mr. J. O. Wright had appeared in the first instance, Mr. Mayer next, Mr. P. B. Gordon after him, and Mr. P. Smith at the time of the application for the plaintiff. Mr. Gordon objected to giving up the papers asked for by Mr. Smith on the ground that Mr. Wright's costs had not been paid. Mr. Smith contended that as Mr. Wright had asked for no undertaking from the Attorney to whom he delivered the papers as to payment of his costs, it must be taken that he had waived them.

Mr. Justice Holloway :—In this case I do not think it can be said that Wright has lost his lien on the papers. The number of applications of this kind which come before the Court are perfectly disgraceful——

Mr. P. B. Gordon, interrupting—I have practised in this Court for a number of years, and my conduct has never up this time been impugned. If the term disgraceful is applied to me——

Mr. Justice Holloway.—I won't hear you, Sir. I won't be replied to. Sit down, Sir, sit down.

Mr. P. B. Gordon.—I must ask to be allowed to mention——

Mr. Justice Holloway angrily.—Sit down, Sir, I tell you. Hold your tongue, Sir.

Mr. Gordon seeing that it was useless his endeavouring further to be heard, collected his papers and left the Court.

Mr. Gordon is said to be a well-known attorney of the Madras High Court and highly respected.

Scene No. 2.

On Wednesday last during the hearing of a certain suit brought by Messrs. Lecot and Co. ; before Mr. Justice Kerman, the defendant had been examined and cross-examined, and was about to leave the witness box, when the learned Judge said he wished to put few questions to the defendant.

It appeared in this case that the defendant had signed a certain contract the terms of which were certainly very stringent, and defendant was desirous of making out that when he signed the contract it had not been properly explained to him, and that he did not properly understand its stringent terms. His Lordship began to examine the defendant, as to whether he had informed his solicitor of these circumstances, and on defendant answering the question evasively, His Lordship repeated the question and was pressing defendant for an answer when.

Mr. Advocate-General said.—I think, my Lord, the communications of defendant with his solicitor are privileged, and that the question is one which your Lordship ought not to put. Kerman, J.—I never heard such an objection.

Mr. Advocate-General.—I make it under the Evidence Act. (Reads Sections.)

Kerman. J.—Sit down, Mr. Advocate General. I am perfectly astonished that any professional gentleman should raise such an objection. I overrule it.

MR. FITZGERALD.

Formerly, a Hussar officer advertised a book to be called a "Twenty year's History of Mysore" and published a prospectus containing what were deemed libellous, and seditious accusations against the Commissioner. He was immediately arrested by the order of Captain Halsted, 1st Assistant to the Commissioner, and thrown into prison, till he could find

bail to the amount of Rs. 500, which he was unable to do."
(F. I. December 7, 1848.)

MR. A. MACLEAN.

Third Member of the Board of Revenue, Madras, was arrested with the view of his being brought to trial before the Supreme Court, on a charge of having violated an Act of Parliament by making himself responsible for a loan of £13,000 lent by Mr. Arathorn, an Armenian merchant to the Nobab of Carnatic through Golam Mortiza Khan. Sir Henry Pottinger was then Governor of Madras. (F. I. July 6, 1848.)

MADRAS GOVERNMENT AND THE HINDU FESTIVALS.

From the Garrison Orders of the Madras Presidency, the *Friend of India* of Oct. 14, 1847, quoted the following announcement :—

"Fort St. George, 10th January 1836. A Royal salute to be fired from the saluting battery at noon to-morrow on the occasion of the Pongal festival. In days gone-bye Madras Government published idolatrous almanacs at the public expense, in which the opening sentence offered "salutation to Sree Gunesh," and circulated them officially to the public establishments through the Chief Secretary. It authorized the Collector of the District, whenever the rains fell short, to order the Poojah of the rainy god Varuna to be performed. It directed "all the dufturs (bundles of public records,) to be placed in the cutchery in a row, and the Brahmins of the town, together with the cutchery servants, to assemble to worship them in honour of the goddess at four o'clock. It sanctioned allowance from the public exchequer for the performance of the Belly god Feast being Venaygake Chouty.

POOJAHS IN THE COLLECTOR'S OFFICE AT CANARA.

We learn from the *Times* of October 12, 1840, that "Ceremonies in honour of Gonesh were performed annually in the Cutchery of the principal Collector of Canara on the occasion of the Feast called "Venagaka Chathurthee." The same ceremonies were observed in all the offices of Tehsildars. A statement of expenses amounting to Rs. 11 was submitted to Government which sanctioned them. Similar observances were observed on the Dussarah Festival. The expenses amounted to five or six rupees in all ! ! !

THE ATTENDANCE OF CHRISTIAN EUROPEAN GOVERNMENT SERVANTS AT THE HINDU FESTIVALS.

The *Hurkura* of May 4, 1840, published a Minute of Lord Auckland on this subject dated 1st of April 1837, in which he said :

"The salutes at Surat are a compliment paid to the return of the season when the coast, by the change of the Monsoon, is again open to the merchant, and industry and profit are diffused among the commercial seafaring classes. I would be extremely loath to discontinue any one proper demonstration etc. The day of these observances at Surat seems to be a popular holiday, on which joy is natural and responsible ; and if some thing of superstition be added to it, this will disappear as intelligence and civilization advance, whilst the holiday, and its festivities, as must be desired, survive. Something of paganism may be traced in our English Feasts of May Day and Harvest Home ; something druidical in the rites of Halloween ; more than is Catholic in the village mummeries of Christmas ; and with such observances, which ought to be upheld, while they are gay, innocent and popular, will doubtless much that is now distasteful in India, be ranked as instruction is spread, and classes are mingle and differences are softened."

The Governor-General laid stress upon the inadvisability of its "abrupt" stoppage and alluded to the "Dissenters" upon this subject among the High officials in Madras, particularly alluding to the resignation by Sir P. Maitland of his command of the Madras Army in connection with this subject. (Vide F. I. May 14, 1840.)

LORD HARRIS, GOVERNOR OF MADRAS.

We read the following in the *Hindoo Patriot* of 1871.

The *Friend of India* has raised the question as to whether Missionaries are prohibited from being employed as teachers in Government schools. In 1867 we drew attention to the orders of the Court of Directors on this subject, and although we were glad for the sake of those whose bread was at stake, that the rule was not stringently enforced against them on the ground that a man becoming once a missionary does not always remain a missionary, still we think the question may now be discussed again dispassionately, as there is no personal question at issue. The question was first raised in 1856, when Lord Harris had appointed the Rev. Mr. Richards an Inspector of schools. The appointment was cancelled, and the· Court of Director wrote as follows : *"As a general rule, we wish you to bear in mind that we already have discouraged and deem it undesirable to appoint the ministers of any religious persuasion as inspectors of schools."* In 1858 Lord Ellenborough, who was the President of the Board of Control, took broader view, and wrote emphatically as follows in a despatch to the Government of India :

"The primary object of the Missionary is Proselytism. He gives Education because by giving Education he hopes to extend Christianity. He may be quite right in adopting this course, and left to himself unaided by the Government, and evidently unconnected with it, he may obtain some although probably no great extent of success, but the moment he is ostensibly assisted by the Government he not only loses a large portion of his chance of doing good in the furtherance of this primary object, but by creating the impression that Education means Proselytism he materially impedes the measures of Government directed to Education alone."

THE MADRAS PRESS IN 1817.

We read in the *Friend of India* of September 23, 1858, the following para, on the above subject :—

"The collection of papers recently published concerning the Press in India is very amusing, especially those portions that refer to the actual working of the censorship as originally established. Thus in 1817 we find the editor and proprietor of a paper called the *Commercial Circulator*, which had been prohibited from publishing any "literary, scientific, or miscellaneous articles," complaining to Government that a newly established journal, the *Madras Advertiser*, did publish such articles." The

government accordingly ordered that the *Madras Advertiser* should confine himself to the same articles of intelligence as the *Circulator*. What
were those articles that were neither literary, scientific, or miscellaneous?
Again, the *Madras Gazette* was "called to account," for having advertised
a French Government lottery at Pondicherry? And the Chief Secretary,
the Censor, expunged in a proof sheet of the *Madras Courier* a political
article on the affairs of Spain! In June 1820 when Governor Elliot resigned, we find him recording in a minute "the principal objects of those
who desire the freedom of the press are to disseminate the worst political
doctrines of the times, to bring the constituted authorities of Europe and
Asia into contempt, and to provide profits for lawyers from prosecutions
of libels in Courts of Justice."

HISTORY OF SOME OF THE NATIVE JOURNALS AND POLITICAL ASSOCIATIONS IN MADRAS.

We are indebted to the Editor of the *Peoples' Friend* for
the following. In answer to our query, published in the
Madras Standard of the 12th March, 1894, the editor
wrote the following para, in its issue of the 14th March of
that year.

"The Madras Native Association" was started by Gajula Lakshminursu
Chetty, son of G. Siddulu Chetty, of Siddulu Chetty and Co. This gentleman was a true patriot, and was a man of high feelings and enlightened
principles. He was the leader of the Young Madras party of the time, and
as an educated influential and wealthy merchant, some of the best educated men of the day gladly joined his banners. The Association did
splendid work in collecting and diffusing political information of a most
valuable kind, and presented to Parliament a series of able and exhaustive petitions which were adopted at large meetings. These
petitions strengthened the hands of the India Reform Party in England,
who were agitating in and out of Parliament for a reform of the Government of India, consequent on the renewal of the Charter of the East
India Company. Like other institutions of purely Native origin in Madras
if not in India, the Native Association collapsed in 1855 or 1860 with the
decline of the excitement caused by the fierce discussions which then
used to rage at the time of the periodical renewal of the Company's
Charter. Mr. Lakshminursu Chetty was aided in his work by many able
men, chief among whom was Mr. Harley, Editor of the *Madras Crescent*,
which belonged to him, and upon which he sank in the course of its exis-

tance something like a lakh of rupees. Mr. Michael Madhusudhun Dutt, the famous Bengalee poet, then an Assistant Master under Mr. E. B. Powell, at the so called High School of the Madras University, the progenitor of the Presidency College of a later day, was also one of Mr. Lakshminursu Chetty's coadjutors in his political and journalistic propaganda. Though Mr. Lakshminursu Chetty subsequently declined in worldly prosperity and sustained many reverses in trade, he yet was rewarded by Government for his public services with a seat in the Madras Legislative Council, succeeding in that position that famous old Madrassee, Mr. Vembakum Sadagopa Charlu of the Madras High Court.

"The Madras Rising Sun" was started and edited by Venkatroyulu Naidu *alias* Abboy Naidu, a Vakil of the Madras Sadar Court, the first Appellate Court of that day. Abboy Naidu was a fearless writer and able man all round. Mr. P. Lakshminursu Naidu, an Assistant Professor in the Trichinopoly College, is a relation of Abboy Naidu. We have spoken about the *Madras Crescent* already in connection with Mr. Lakshminursu Chetty, its founder and proprietor, and Mr. Harley, its far-famed Editor.

The *Native Advocate* was started as a weekly newspaper in August 1867, by Mr. D. Narasiah, now the Editor and Proprietor of the *Peoples Friend*. Mr. Narasiah was then barely 18. It was the only Native paper then in existence in the Madras Presidency, and as such commanded some attention and respect, notwithstanding the inexperience of its youthful Editor, who however was brimful of zeal and enthusiasm in the prosecution of his self-imposed-labors. The paper was issued as a tri-weekly from January 1868, but had to stop publication in December 1868, from insufficiency of public support and other causes.

The *Native Public Opinion* was started in 1871, by Mr. Raghunath Row aided by a number of friends, and flourished for some years, as it enjoyed the countenance and literary help of many able men including the late Mr. L. C. A. Vankatramana Pant, and Professor Rungauadham Modelliar &c. It gradually, however, sank lower and lower, until it was entrusted to the editorial care of the late Mr. John Venkatramiah, eldest son of the Rev. A. Venkatramiah, a convert of the famous John Anderson of the Free Church Mission. Mr. Venkatramiah was a singularly able writer, but he had to work single handed, and the circulation of the paper for a weekly was so small, partly on account of the high rate of subscription charged, namely one rupee a month, that he at last in 1884 or 1885 gave up the job in despair, and so died the "Native Public Opinion," notwithstanding that it had been started under very favourable auspices and enjoyed all along the countenance and patronage of all the leading Natives of the day.

CHAPTER III.

THE LATE HON'BLE VISHWA NATH MANDLIC OF BOMBAY.

We extract the following from the *Hindoo Patriot* of August 10, 1873.

"He was originally Personal Assistant to Sir Bartle Frere in Scindh, and subsequently in charge of the Income Tax Commission Office under the present Hon'ble Mr. Gibbs.

When Sir Bartle came to Bombay as Governor, he urged Mr. Viswanath to qualify himself for the Native Bar, holding forth to him the example of the late Babu Romaprasad Roy of Calcutta. Sir Bartle related that whenever Babu Romaprasad was retained in any case, the opposite party was invariably obliged to engage the most eminent talent available on the original side of the High Court. Mr. Viswanath kept this ideal before him and now divides the palm of the leadership of the Bombay Native Bar with Mr. Shantaram Narayen. Unlike Mr. Shantaram, however, Mr. Viswanath has always taken a prominent part in all public movements and is one of the few public men of mark amongst the Natives in the captial of Western India. Mr. Viswanath is a great authority on the land tenure question in the Bombay Presidency, and in company with another young man of mark Mr. Javerilal Umiasankur Jajnik, also well versed in the landed tenures of Guzerat, has done not a little by their united writings in the Press to withstand the wholesale introduction in the western Presidency of that insidious policy, which under the ingenious euphuism of the "State proprietorship in the soil" the *Indian Economist* is doing much to bring into vogue."

He along with other native members of the Bombay Legislative Council opposed the passing of the Bombay Game Preservation Bill which, Lord Ripon vetoed in 1881.

HIS SERVICES IN CONNECTION WITH THE BOMBAY BRANCH OF THE ROYAL ASIATIC SOCIETY.

In the *Hindoo Patriot* of April 2, 1877, we read the following.

The Bombay Branch of the Royal Asiatic Society was originally called the Literary Society of Bombay. It was founded by Sir James Mackintosh in 1804. Although many valuable papers had been read before the Society, no journal of its transactions was published until 1841. The Hon'ble Vishwanath Mandalic C. S. I , a leading member of the Bombay bar, and a member of the local Legislative Council, one of the best-educated and active native gentlemen of the Presidency, has now supplied this gap. He has edited and published three volumes of the early transactions of the Society at his own risk. In these volumes he has given some of the most valuable papers elucidating Indian history, philosophy, and antiquities, to which he has added a few references in order to show how the subject-matter stands at the present day. He has given brief notes of the lives of the members, who attended the first meeting of the society and also of the authors of the papers contained in these volumes. The work has been more than a labor of love with the editor, for h e has taken upon himself the money responsibility of the publication.

HIS LETTER ON THE ILBERT BILL.

He telegraphed at his own expense a letter to the *Pall Mall Gazette* describing the real character of Mr. Ilbert's Bill, and representing native views on the subject for the information of the British public.

Calcutta, Friday 19th February.

SIR,—Lord Ripon is being unjustly assailed by the *Times* and other papers—first, for a Bengal Rent Bill which is not yet in existence so far as the public knows, and therefore criticism is necessarily imaginary ; secondly, for a Criminal Law Amendment Bill approved by all Local Governments throughtout India with the exception, perhaps, of one back- ward district, and also approved by the independent European papers and all the Indian papers ; and, thirdly, for furthering local self-govern- ment which was introduced forty years ago, and extended by men like Lord Lawrence, Sir Charles Trevelyan, Sir W. Grey, Mr. Harrington, Sir Henry Maine, Lord Napier, Sir W. Muir, Sir Bartle Frere, and others, confirmed by Lord Mayo's measures, approved by successive State Secretaries, Liberal and Conservative and announced to Parliament annually. It is now a necessity of the days. Is the contentment and happiness of two hundred millions worth nothing ? Such conduct on the part of public English writers causes astonishment and regret. Great indignation is felt by the people at the circulation of wrong facts and worse arguments, and the attributing of low motives to such high statesmanship as is uniformly exhibited by the present head of Britain's greatest dependency.

Hon. V. N. MANDLIK, C. S. I.
Additional Member of the Legislative Council
of the Government of Bombay,

MR. CHISHOLM ANSTEY.

The *Hindoo Patriot* thus noticed the death of this great barrister in August 1873.

We are sincerely sorry to record the death of Mr. Chisholm Anstey at Bombay on the 13th instant. Notwithstanding imperfections of temper he was a remarkable man. About two years ago he came to Calcutta for a short time to defend Ameer Khan in the celebrated Wahabi case, and by a few days' practice here he brought back the glory of the old Calcutta bar. A man of vast legal erudition, wonderful eloquence, and thorough indendence, he was indeed an acquisition to the Calcutta bar, though unfortunately he was net possessed of quite an amiable temper. Indeed his temper was his greatest enemy. We take the following particulars of his life from the *Indian Daily News*. His father was a gentleman of the southern hemisphere, being connected with Tasmania. Mr. T. C. Anstey was, however, educated in England and was called to the Bar in 1839. He was of the Roman Catholic faith ; and took in early life an active part in the measures affecting that church. In 1847 he was elected to the House of Commons as member for Youghal in Ireland, which place he represented till 1852. He was there, as he has been in India, an awkward customer, and by way of getting him out of the way, he was appointed to the Attorney Generalship of Hongkong, which office he held for about four years, when, not being able to agree with the Governor and others in the island, he resigned his appointment, and returned to England. He practised chiefly at the bar of China and and Bombay ; for a short time he officiated as a Judge of the Bombay High Court. His labors in India will be chiefly remembered for the force and eloquence with which he used to elucidate the contitntio ʳˡ ˡ⁻w. He used to affirm that under the English law Her Majesty's Indian subjects enjoyed the same freedom which it was the good fortune of British-born subjects to enjoy. His last triumph was the Parsee Towers of Silence case. Mr, Anstey was 57 years of age.

DUSTOOR IDULJEE DORABJEE SUNJANA,
HIGH PRIEST OF THE SHAHINSAHEE PARSEES.

He died in September, 1847. The *Bombay Telegraph* of 30th August 1847, thus spoke of him :—"He was the most learned *Zend* and *Pehlvee* scholar among the Parsees of Western India. He was consulted at different times by eminent European, Scholars. He was the author of several works published in Bombay regarding the *Kubeesa* controversy, and Parsee religion. Among these the ablest one were *Khoreh Vaheejuk, Mojiza-i-Zurtoshtee,* and a Guzrati translation of the *Khourdah Avesta.* He knew the ancient languages of Persia which have fallen into disuse for more than twelve centuries. He knew Sanskrit also, The deceased had prepared a correct verse of the *Vendidad Sade,* one of the sacred works of the Parsees."

THE HON'BLE JUSTICE MAHADEO GOBINDA RANADE.

In the *Hindoo Patriot* of March 8, 1875, appeared the following para.

"Two Native Gentlemen of Bombay, Mr. Ranade and Mr. Permanand are on a visit to Calcutta. The first is a Barrister-at-law, who was not condemned to eat the customary dinners in an Inn of Court, but was enrolled under Sir Richard Couch's rules, and is now a Subordinate Judge of Poona, and the second holds a high appointment in the Bombay Secretariat. Mr. Ranade was for several years the English writer of the *Indu Prokash,* and Mr. Parmanand conducted *Native Opinion* for about three years."

SIR MUNGOLDASS NATHOOBHOY..

The *Pall Mall Gazette* wrote the following about Sir Mungoldas Nathoobhoy of Bombay in 1875.

"Sir Mungoldass Nathoobhoy is' a representative of one of the oldest Settia families of the Island of Bombay. They were settled there before the arrival of the Portuguese, and 'generation after generation of them were commissariat contractors, both to the Portuguese and the British Governments. Sir Mungoldass is a man of wealth and enlightenment and liberality. He took leading part in the foundation of the Victoria and Albert Museum and Gardens, in Bombay, as a memorial of the transfer of the Government of India to the direct rule of the Crown. In 1858 he has founded and endowed a handsome dispensary, and was one of the earliest benefactors of the Bombay University. But his greatest public services have been in connection with the Legislative Council of the Western Presidency, to which he had been three times appointed, and would have been re-appointed again this year but for his breaking health. Sir Philip Wodehouse has done at once a wise and graceful act in recommending him to the Queen for the highest honour that can be granted to a Native of India. Sir Mungoldass belongs to the Central Party among Native India Public Men —the Whigs of India—and expressed the difficulty of men in his position between the orthodox Settias and the educated party of "Young India," in the happy phrases, "we are like miserable drum, bitten at both ends." At another time, arguing with a zealous raw missionary, insisted that Hindoos being Christians by nature needed not to be converted, and added, "But I thank God that you English were converted to Christianity, or you would by this time have eaten of the world to the bone."

R. D. LUARD ESQ., C. S.

Collector of Continental Customs, a gentleman who had been degraded from his position as Judge of Surat, published a letter in the Bombay *Telegraph* and *Courier*, in its issue of the 12th March, 1853, reflecting on the character of Messrs Bell and Simson. Mr. Luard requested the Bombay Government to leave the injured parties to sue him criminally in the Supreme Court. But the Government did . otherwise and suspended him. (F. I. May 12, 1853.)

Mr. REEVES AND Mr. SETON-KARR.

We have it on the authority of the *Bombay Telegraph* and *Courier* that the appointment of Resident at Baroda was offered to Mr. Reeves in 1852, but he being a begotted Christian, declined the offer on the ground that he could not as a devout Christian, take part in the ceremonies and processions in honour of Hindu deities, as ordered by the Supreme. Government. The appointment was therefore given to Mr. Seton-Karr.   (F. I. June 23, 1853.)

SIR R. SHAKESPEARE, RESIDENT AT BARODA AND THE MUTINY.

In 1858, during the Mutiny, this officer reported that the Maharattas used "twigs" as the "chapaties" were by the Mutineers to warn the villagers of the approach of a revolt. The Police circulated these "twigs." Mr. Le Geyt, at a meeting of the Legislative Council referred the report to the Committee on the Criminal Code. Transmission of secret signals was considered a penal offence. (F. I. June 17, 1858.)

"Dried fish" were similarly circulated. The dried fish typified that the vitality of the English Nation was exhausted.

WORSHIP OF THE STATUES.

The *Bombay Telegraph* and *Courier* states that the Hindus of that Presidency worship the statue of Lord Cornwallis. The figure is washed with brandy, cocoanuts broken, and fruit and other offerings placed before it. In Madras the natives, it is said, hate the memory of Sir Thomas Munro, and believe that the birds cover his statue with filth in consequence of his crimes.   (F. I. February 11, 1858.)

MR. GREGOR GRANT AND MR. LE GEYT.

They were Judges of the Sudder Court of Bombay.   The former held the appointment from 1849 and the latter from

1846. Mr. Grant was, since his removal from the Bench on the charges brought by Mr. Knight in the *Bombay Times*, offered the place of Post Master-General, but he declined it. Mr. Le Geyt was transferred to the Court of Poonah. (F. I. June 9, 1853.)

The *Bombay Times* accused the first gentleman of shameless adultery, and of losing half a year's salary in a single night at a gaming table, and Mr. Le Geyt of being mixed up with the intrigues at Baroda, of being entangled in pecuniary transactions with a native subordinate, and of being generally in a condition of disreputed indebtedness. Lord Falkland the Governor of Bombay considered their explanations insufficient and they were transferred.

COLLISION BETWEEN THE SUPREME COURT OF BOMBAY AND THE LOCAL GOVERNMENT.

In December 1857, one Luxmon Dhejah was arrested on a charge of treason and confined in the Mazagon Jail. On the 2nd of January, he was by order of the Governor in Council removed from that jail to the Tanna jail without the jurisdiction of the Supreme Court. It was illegal on the part of the Government to arrest the man who was within the jurisdiction of the Supreme Court. Sir William Yardly ordered that a writ of *Habeas corpus* should be issued to the jailor of Tanna. The European bailiff who went to arrest the jailor of Tanna was kept in confinement by Captain Walker under the order of the Bombay Government. The Court therefore yielded, acknowledging its inability to resist Military force" F. I. February 23. 1858.

THE BOMBAY GOVERNMENT AND THE JUDGES.

We take the following from the *Hindoo Patriot* of 1883.

"There has been a social war in Bombay. The Government of Bombay and the Judges of the High Court have fallen out. The Chief Justice called the attention of the Governor to the indignity to which the Judges were subjected by being made to stand at his last levee where his Body-Guard used to stand. The Judges took this as an affront, and the Chief Justice, as their spokesman, wrote to the Governor on the subject, asking His Excellency "to return to his old ways." His Excellency replied that he had made the change as a matter of convenience. The Chief Justice did not see the validity of this excuse, and remarked that if a line was to be drawn, why not below the Judges? The Governor has refused to do so and has ostracized the Judges from Government House. His Excellency writes.

I cannot consent to revert to a system which I found to be so inconvenient as I have explained, even on a threat on the part of the Judges of not appearing at my *levee*. which of course would preclude me from receiving them at Government House."

DR. BUIST.

Was born at Tannadice, Forfarshere, on the 17th Nov. 1815. At twelve years of age he was sent to St. Salvador's College, St. Andrew's, and was licensed as a preacher in 1826 In 1840 he came to India as Editor of the *Bombay Times*, In July 1842, he was placed by Government in charge of the Astronomical, Magnetic, and Meteorological Observatory, Bombay. The appointment was unsalaried. In 1841, on the death of Dr. Heddle, Dr. Buist was appointed Honorary Secretary to the Bombay Branch of the Geographical Society. In 1859, he was appointed Superintendent of the Government Printing Press. In 1860 he died at Calcutta. He was called "Bloody Buist" for his support of the policy of shewing no mercy to the Indian people, during the Mutiny of 1857.

MR. MACLEAN OF THE BOMBAY CIVIL SERVICE.

The *Madras Spectator* of September 15th, 1848, states that Mr. Maclean endeavoured to obtain the benefit of the

Insolvent Act. The Chief Justice did not hear his case because of his friendship with him. Sir W. Burton heard his case and remanded the Insolvent to jail for six months for a fraudulent concealment of his debts (F. I. Sept. 8, 1848.)

A BOMBAY CASE IN WHICH A FEMALE JURY WAS EMPANNELLED IN 1861.

We read in the *Friend of India* of April 25, 1861, that:—

"In the Bombay Supreme Court, before the Chief Justice and the Puisne Judge, a Jury of Matrons was summoned in order to investigate the plea of pregnancy put forth by the woman Gunga, under sentence of death for the murder of a child. The Jury with their foreman, retired with the prisoner for half an hour and decided that she was not with child. The Jury consisted of 12 matrons" ! ! !

REFUSAL OF THE BOMBAY GOVERNMENT TO USE THE TOWN HALL.

In 1876, the Bombay Government refused to the public of Bombay the use of the Town Hall for a public meeting against the Bombay Revenue Jurisdiction Bill.

ALI MORAD OF KHYRPORE IN SINDHE.

A correspondent wrote to the *Bombay Times* thus ;—

"He offered Lady Dalhousie, as a present, a chair set with diamonds worth Rs.150,000. Her Ladyship refused the present for herself, but took it for the benefit of the Hon'ble Company. Ali Morad had to mortgage two villages to a Mahajun for the large sum required in preparing the chair. As soon as the Governor-General left the place, Ali Morad peremptorily required the unlucky sahoocar (capitalist) to restore his villages and requested him to realize the money from the Governor-General. (F. I. May 23, 1850.)

SIR ERSKINE PERRY.

We take from the *Bombay Gazette* of 1880, the following particulars regarding the efforts of the late Sir Erskine Perry for the advancement of the welfare of the natives of this country.

As president of the Board of Education from 1846-52, Sir Erskine laboured unceasingly to promote higher education among the natives. He encouraged female education, and materially helped the first pioneers of it, Mr. Dadabhoy Nowrojee, Mr. Nowrojee Furdoonjee,_ and others. The formation of zillah schools was during his time fostered and extended. The Poona College was reorganised under his influence, and he took a warm interest in the success of the new institutions. The Mechanic's Institution and the native General Library were founded under his auspices, derived considerable support from him in their infancy. On his recommendation, several alumni of the Elphinstone College were appointed Deputy Collectors and Magistrates, among whom may be mentioned Messrs. Dadoba Pandurang, Nana Morojee, Nowrowjee Byramjee, etc. With a view to encourage a taste for literature among educated natives, he awarded prizes out of his own purse for the writing of competitive essays on subjects of general utility. After an extended tour through Upper India, Sir Erskine wrote a very interesting paper on "The Geographical Distribution of the principal Languages of India, and the feasibility of introducing English as a Lingua-Franca." He travelled to Nepal and Ceylon; and his leisure hours were employed in literary works, as examples of which may be mentioned his "Letter to Lord Campbell on Law Reform," his translation of Savignee's "Rechtdes Besitzes," and his well-known "Oriental Cases." On his departure from Bombay in November, 1852, numerous addresses were presented to him by various public bodies such as the Mechanics' Institution, the Students' Literary and Scientific Society, the members of the Native General Library, and the native communities of Poona, Madras, and Bombay. Rs. 50,000 were subscribed for a testimonial, and the sum was devoted to the establishment of the Perry Professorship of Jurisprudence in Bombay.

SIR ERSKINE PERRY.

The *Bombay Times* reports a curious scene in the Supreme Court of Bombay in 1849. Sir Erskine Perry during the investigation into the great swindling case, summoned the committing Magistrate to appear as a witness, and declared that he ought to be in attendance in the Court during the trial of all cases committed by him.

The Magistrate replied that this was impossible, as the

Company's regulations directed that the Court in which he sat should be opened every day. The Judge replied that he did not care about the Company's regulations, that he was placed upon the Bench to administer English law, and that he would fine the Magistrate Rs. 1,000 the next time he was absent. (F. I. October 18, 1849.)

SIR ERSKINE PERRY AND SIR JAMSETSEE JEEJEEBHOY.

The *Rast Goftar* related the following in 1869.

"Sir Erskine Perry, in his evidence, before the select Committee of Parliament in 1854 related, that once he invited Sir Jamsetsee Jeejeebhoy to dine with him. He advanced no such shallow pretext as religious prohibition or the like; the only reply he gave was that at his advanced age he had not sufficient strength and courage to bear obliquy or the odium of such an act."

SIR JOHN PETER GRANT.

As a Judge of the Bombay High Court, he closed his court altogether, because Sir John Malcolm, the Governor, would not order into his jurisdiction, the Zillah Judge of Tanna, who had refused to give up a criminal in Jail, under sentence, who had hired a lawyer to subpœna him in the Supreme Court. He wished to commit the Zillah Judge for contempt of Court. Sir John Grant declared on the Bench that "he admitted no superior in India, but God Almighty". His colleagues on the bench were Sir Harcourt Chambers, Chief Justice, and Sir Edward West, puisne. West soon died, leaving two Judges, and anon the Chief Justice too died, leaving Grant master of the situation. In one case, that of Moro Rughunath, in which the Court issued a writ of *Habeas Corpus* on Rughunath's grand-uncle Pandurang Ram Chunder, the delivery was opposed by a military guard placed for his protection by Sir John Malcolm, the Governor of Bombay. Sir John Peter Grant upheld the dignity of the law, but Sir John Malcolm could ill resist so good an opportunity of crushing the powers of the hated Court. At last, however, Sir John closed his Court, on the 21st April, 1829. The case was then referred to Lord Ellenborough, the Indian Minister of that time who, instead of lending help to the King's Court at Bombay, condemned Sir Peter Grant, and sanctioned the nomination of Mr. Dewas, the Advocate-General to the office of Chief Justice by way of checkmating the cantankerous Judge. Sir John Malcolm, it is said, produced this confidential despatch at his breakfast table, and no wonder, that its content soon passed from mouth to mouth till it appeared in the local newspapers. Thus defeated, be it said in honour of the British Nation, the conscientious Scotch Judge resigned his apppintment.

He then came to Calcutta to practise in the Supreme Court where he commanded such success, and inspired such confidence in his character and abilities, that he was again promoted to the bench of the Supreme Court of Calcutta. He finally retired from India in 1848.

Sir John Peter Grant was fond of chess, and averse to out-door exercise. He slept the best part of the day and rose late in the afternoon, and reserved all night for work and enjoyment.

DR. BHAU DAJEE, SHERIFF OF BOMBAY.

Mr. Atmaram Sadumund brought an action against the Sheriff in 1869, to recover Rs. 5,000 damages for false imprisonment. The plaintiff was arrested for a debt of Rs. 75, alleged to be due for unpaid calls on shares in the Khatiwar Financial Association. At the time of his arrest, plaintiff denied ever having held any such shares, but the bailiff refused to believe him, and after the prisoner was taken to the Deputy Sheriff's office, the bailiff stated that plaintiff had been pointed out to him by the liquidator. On being taken before the Judge, he was ordered to pay the costs, which he did under protest, and was then liberated. It appeared from the evidence that plaintiff had been employed in an office with another man of the same name, and that the writing of the two was very similar. However, the shares were intended for the other clerk, and as plaintiff had been wrongfully arrested, he was awarded Rs. 200 damages." (*Englishman*, October 23, 1869.)

MESSRS. JEHANGEER NOWROJEE AND HIRJEEBHOY MERWANJIE, NAVAL ARCHITECTS OF BOMBAY.

They left Bombay for England on the 29th March 1838 with Mr. Dorabjie Muncherjie to acquire a correct knowledge of the construction of steam vessels and ships. Mr. Jehangeer Nowrojee was the son, and Mr. Hirjeebhoy Merwanjie nephew of Mr. Nowrojee Jamsetjee, the master builder in the Hon'ble East India Company's dockyard at Bombay. Their grand-father's name was Mr. Jamsetjee Bomanjie, who was also for several years master builder of that yard. This family was called "Lowjee Family," because the Bombay dockyard was built in 1735 by one of their ancestors, named Mr. Lowjee Nassarwanjee. Before the year 1735, all vessels were built at Surat. The Bombay Government contracted with a Parsee builder at Surat in that year to build a ship called the "Queen". Mr. Lowjee superintended this vessel in the capacity of a foreman, and Mr. Dudley who was sent to Surat by the Government of Bombay to see her properly built was so much pleased and struck with the attention and ingenuity of the foreman, that he persuaded him to accompany him to Bombay, in order to establish a building yard there. To this he consented, and having brought 12 or 14 shipwrights with him, selected the present spot for the dockyard, and thus laid the foundation of that establishment which is now considered the finest naval arsenal in India. Lowjee afterwards brought up his two sons, Manockjee and Bomanjee, to his profession, who each had a family of four sons, some of whom were also brought up as shipwrights, but Jamsetjee the son of the latter, built the largest, and first ship for the British navy the "Minden" of 74 guns, and afterwards six other ships of the line. Several members of the Lowjee family have distinguished themselves in other points. Hormasjee Bomanjee was well known in England and India for his commercial enterprise; and the extensive trade which he carried on in conjunction] with the celebrated house of Forbes & Co., (the oldest in Bombay) tended much to benefit Bombay by paving the way for others. Pestonjee Bomanjee was also a partner in the well known firm of Bruce, Fawcett and Co., now Remington & Co. Nassarwanjee Manockjee, also a member of the same family, encouraged French commerce, and his son Jehangeer Nassarwanjee carries on the same business. Almost all French ships that come to Bombay are consigned to him, as also French ships of war." (*Courier* 30th July, 1841.)

LIBERALITY OF A PARSEE-GENTLEMAN

(One Lakh of Rupees.)

We take the following from the *United Service Gazette* of November 20, 1840 :—

"Owing to the increase of Parsee population, the building of an additional "Dhukma," or Tower of Silence, has become exigent, and a large subscription, amounting to Rupees 85,009, were raised for the purpose among the people of this tribe, both rich and poor men, women and children. But at a religious congregation of the Parsees last Saturday; in their "*Austush Bheram*," Mr. Cowasjee Eduljee, *alias* Capias Kao offered a Lakh of Rupees for erecting the Tower.

SIR HENRY ROPER, CHIEF JUSTICE OF BOMBAY.

The Bombay merchants presented a petition to Parliament on the 26th April, 1841, against the Chief Justice, complaining of the unjust aspersions made by him on Mr. Charles Forbes in a written Judgment passed by the learned Judge

on the 12th February 1840, when he was a puisne Judge of
the Bombay Supreme Court. The *Calcutta Courier* in its
issue of November 29th, 1841, thus explained the cause of
the animus entertained towards Sir Henry Roper by the merchants of Bombay :—

"When a British subject dies in the Bombay Presidency, leaving
property within its Supreme Court's Jurisdiction, but having no executor
or next of kin within that Jurisdiction, the Law directs that the Ecclesiastical Registrar shall administer. The Law gives it to him as his right,
and to deprive him of it is to illegally withhold from him his due. Yet,
despite this clear direction, the merchants of Bombay have been in the
habit of evading it, and in the particular instance which called forth
Sir H. Roper's animadversions, an agency house, Messrs. Forbes & Co.,
actually kept a gentleman's will in their desk for a whole twelve months
after his decease until probate could be taken out wrongfully in England,
and they were appointed agents. Instead of so acting they should have
given up the will to the Ecclesiastical Registrar, and thus avoided the
wrong of keeping the testator's legatees out of their property during a year,
merely for the sake of obtaining 5 per cent. upon 40,000 rupees."

Sir. H. Roper also hauled up before him the proprietors
of the leading journals of Bombay on the charge of contempt of Court far having allowed the editors to ventilate the
grievances of the Bombay merchants.

Sir Roper summoned the following proprietors of the
Bombay Times, and the *Bombay Courier* to attend the court
on the 27th March, 1841, for contempt of Court.

PROPRIETORS OF THE *Times*.

Messrs. C. B. Skinner.	H. G. Gordon.
" F. Martin.	J. C. Stuart.
" E. M. Davidson.	J. A. Russel.
" T. Cardwell.	J. Wright.
" R. Richmond.	Framjee Cowasjee.
" W. Mackie.	

PROPRIETORS OF THE *Courier*.

Messrs. H. Fawcett.	W. Henderson.
" R. W. Crawford.	Reginald Frederick Remington
" James Remington Hadow.	
" Jamsetjee Jeejeebhoy.	

Mr. Herrich appeared before the Court on behalf of Mr. Framjee Cowasjee, and stated that he (Mr. Framjee Cowasjee) entertained the highest respect for the Chief Justice, and expressed regret for the "scandalous" paragraph that had appeared in the *Bombay Times*. A similar explanation was offered on behalf Mr. Jamsetjee Jeejibhoy, and the Chief Justice was pleased to excuse them. On behalf of the Europeans proprietors Mr. Cochrane appeared, who expressed his unwillingness "to offer any apology on behalf of his clients". The Chief Justice thereupon issued a rule against these Proprietors. The case was finally heard in April, and Mr. John Cochrane having "disavowed all feelings of hostility towards the Judge," the rule was discharged.

The people of Bombay presented a plate to Mr. John Cochrane, as a mark of their approbation of the able and independent manner in which he defended the Proprietors of the above papers.

A CONGRATULATORY ADDRESS TO HER MAJESTY THE QUEEN, ON THE BIRTH OF THE PRINCE OF WALES.

On the 26th January, 1841, a public meeting of the inhabitants of Bombay was held for the above purpose. The Chief Justice moved the first Resolution, seconded by Mr. Framje Cowasjee Esq.

"That a loyal and dutiful address of congratulation to Her Majesty and Prince Albert, on the auspicious birth of the Prince Royal be prepared for signature." The address was then read and moved to be adopted by the Lord Bishop of Bombay, seconded by Mr Juganath Sunkersett. Esq. (*Bombay Times*, Jan. 27, 1841.)

PUNDIT BISHNU PARUSHRAM SHASTREE.

This gentleman who was called the "Vidyasagur of Bombay" died in 1876. In 1864 he joined the establishment of the *Indu Prokash* as its Marathi Editor, and subsequently became its proprietor." (*Hindoo Patriot* May 15, 1876.)

THE FIRST COTTON MILL IN BOMBAY.

The first mill built in Bombay by an enterprising Parsee merchant named Cowasjee Nanabhoy Daver was erected in 1855. (H. P. April 16, 1877.)

NAMES OF SOME OF THE BOMBAY JOURNALS.

1838 to 1840.—*Gazette, Courier, Times, Oriental Christian Spectator*, and *Herald.*

1841.—*Gazette* died. *U. S. Gazette* came into existence.

1843.—*U. S. Gazette* died. *The World* and *Gentleman's Gazette* established.

1844.—The *World* died and the *Witness* was established.

1846.—*Courier*, and *Witness* died, and *Telegraph* established.

1847.—*Times, Gentleman's Gazette, Telegraph* and *Courier*, and *O. C. Spectator.* (*Bombay Times*, Jan 2, 1847)

THE BOMBAY PERIODICALS.

The earliest of these were those of the Bombay Literary Society, printed in London in three quarto vols., in 1817. It was discontinued for want of support. In its place, at an interval of twenty years came the *Transactions of the Bombay Branch of the Royal Asiatic Society*, by which the Literary Society had been absorbed, commenced in 1841 at the suggestion of Dr. Malcolmson, and under the editorship of Professor Orlebar. The latter gentleman went home in May, 1842, and the editorial management of the paper was taken up by Dr. Malcolmson who died in 1844. Dr. Bird then conducted the paper which was about to be discontinued in 1846. (*Bombay Times* August 22, 1846.)

The *Bombay Sporting Magazine* was edited by Captain Morris. Its publication was continued for two or three years. At a long interval, it was succeeded by a namesake edited by Captain Crockett, and published at the *Bombay Gazette* office. After the third number it was given up. The prefacial portion of the *Bombay Magazine* of Selections began in 1840, and was discontinued in 1841.

ROMA BAI'S MARRIAGE.

In 1880, the *Hindoo Patriot* wrote as follows.

The Marriage of Roma Bai with Babu Bepin Behary Das, M. A. B. L. of Sylhet is an event of no mean significance. This is the first time the Maharatha Lady has chosen a husband not only out of her caste but also of her nationality. Mr. Beveridge, the Judge of Patna, took great interest in the marriage. The marriage was effected under the Civil Marriage Act. The district registrar acted the padri.

A MEMORIAL OF THE NATIVE GENTLEMEN OF BOMBAY TO THE LEGISLATIVE COUNCIL OF INDIA TO RESTRAIN THE MISSIONARIES, AND SUBJECT THE CONVERTS TO CIVIL DISABILITIES.

In 1839, Sree Goburdhunjee Nathjee Maraji, Framjee Cowasjee Esq. and 2,113 inhabitants of Bombay presented a memorial to the Governor-General to enact laws against native converts. Their memorial was refused. (*Englishman,* May 11, 1840.)

MR. ROBERT KNIGHT'S DEPARTURE FROM BOMBAY IN 1873.

The friends of Mr. Knight at Bombay gave him an entertainment before his departure for Calcutta. In responding to an address from Mr. Venayekrow Juggonath Sunkersett he said among other things:

"You all know I'dare say that I am entering the service of the Government of Bengal. It is no doubt an experiment at my time of life, with habits of insubordination, I am afraid, I must say, pretty fully developed, to be entering into official harness ; but I am drawn to Bengal by two or three powerful attractions. In the first place the work that is offered me is exceedingly congenial to my tastes. It is many years since I wanted the Government of this Presidency to give me work of the same nature, and I am now to get it elsewhere. Then, again, I confess frankly, that I have a high admiration for the character of Sir George Campbell. He is a strong and wise ruler in spite of some local unpopularity, and the very man we want at the head of affairs there. And there is, lastly the condition of the people of Bengal, at once so full of interest and perplexity. I cannot reasonably expect I suppose to work many years longer in India, but the prospects of spending them—few or many—in association with a Government which is labouring earnestly and with so much enlightenment for the amelioration of the condition of the people is to me very attractive."

Mr. Robert Knight accepted the appointment of Assistant Secretary to the Bengal Government in the Statistical Department, in 1873, and continued to hold it till the middle of the year 1875.

MR. ROBERT KNIGHT.

In July 1868, Mr. Robert Knight sold his proprietary right of the *Times of India* to Mr. Mathias Mull, on condition that he shall not carry on, edit, or become, or be in any way directly or indirectly in property or otherwise connected with the carrying on, or editing of any other newspaper or periodical within the Presidency of Bombay, except the said *Times of India.* Agreeably with this contract, Mr. Mull objected to his publishing the *Indian Economist* from Bombay. (Vide *Englishman*, Aug. 23; 1869.)

MR. ROBERT KNIGHT AND MR. MATHIAS MULL, AS JOINT PROPRIETORS OF THE *TIMES OF INDIA.*

These Joint-partners quarrelled with each other in regard to its editoral management. We learn from the *Bombay Times* of 3rd February, 1869, that Mr. Robert Knight moved the local- High Court through his barristers Mr, White and Mr. Dunbar for a rule *nisi*, restraining, Mr. Mathias Mull from interfering with, or obstructing him from acting as sole Editor of the *Times of India*. By an agreement made on the 28th of November, 1868, it was mutually agreed that the said partnership should be dissolved from the 1st of July, 1868. It was agreed also that Mr. Robert Knight (plaintiff) should sell his share in the partnership property to Mr. Mathais Mull (defendant) on the terms mentioned in the agreement, and it was further provided that the unpaid portion of the purchase money of the plaintiff's share in the partnership property and outstandings should be secured by a mortgage of the said newspaper and printing office. It was provided that the plaintiff (Mr. Robert Knight) should be and remain sole editor for 12 months from the 1st of July 1868, on a salary of Rs. 1,300 per mensem, which should be paid regularly. On the 28th January, 1868, Mr. Robert Knight was informed that he would not be permitted to discharge the duties of editor. It was stipulated in the agreement that Mr. Knight should receive Rs.40,000 in cash at once, Rs.40,000 on the 3rd June 1869, and the balance Rs. 20,000 to be paid on the 3rd June 1870. The following letters were then read to the Court.

January 28, 1869.

To B. KNIGHT, Esq.

Sir

    I have heard with considerable consternation that while I was in England in 1862, you entered into a negociation affecting the reputation and interest of this office, which demands immediate explanation and refutation, if that be possible.

    I am informed by Mr. William Sim, of Bombay, that you tendered him the first inspection of telegrams coming to this office, the consideration for which privilege was sum of Rs. 4,000 (four thousand) paid to you. No such sum, of course, appears in our books, as it was a private transaction in which you induced Mr. Sim to enter.

    If no satisfactory refutation of the alleged transaction is furnished

me during business hours to-day, I shall take what course I deem necessary in the matter.

I am, &c.,
M. MULL.
January 23, 1869.

To M. MULL, ESQ.

Sir

I do not deign to answer the insolent and calumnious charge. You
must know it to be false as well as I do.

Yours obediently.
R. KNIGHT.

We have not space for other letters in which the parties
incriminated each other.

The Court then issued an order *nisi* for injunction *Adinterim*
giving Mr. Knight access to the editor's room till the Court
orders otherwise, if it on the further hearing does order
otherwise. (*Englishman*, February 8, 1869.)

SIR JAMSETJEE JEJEEBHOY, BART.

The *Times of India* quoted the following remarkable facts
of his life from the *Rast Goftar* of 1869.

"His praise worthy conduct during the celebrated "dog-hobble" of
of 1832 is cited by our contemporary in proof of his good sense and judgment, for when the generality of his race joined in opposing the orders
of the authorities to kill the wandering pariahs in the streets of Bombay,
the late Sir Jamsetjee stood aloof from all this trouble and disturbance,
much to the disappointment of the leaders of the community. Five years
after this riot the agitation against *post mortem* examinations by the
coroner was commenced among the Parsees. This blind opposition was
followed up by memorials and such other measures, but the worthy
Baronet refused to support them; he had to suffer so much in consequence
that he published a book in self-defence. He was the first founder of
hospitals and schools by private charity. He was the first in establishing schools in the mufusil. When the "students Society," by the
material aid of Professor Dadabhoy Nowrojee, first started their girls'
schools, they had to face a strong opposition. But when he went to the
Baronet for his assistance, he was there and then informed that he (Sir
Jamsetjee) had himself resolved to open girls' schools on his own account.
He gave English education to his daughter Purosbaee."

THE NAMES OF VERNACULAR JOUNALS OF BOMBAY IN 1853.

The *Bombay Somachar.* The *Bombay Chabook.* The *Bombay Jami-Jamshed.* The *Vepper Samachar,* The *Somachar Darpan.* The *Rast-Goftar.* The *Pariee Reformer.* The *Akbal Arai Sodagur.*

THE NAMES OF BOMBAY JOURNALS IN 1847.

PLACE & TITLE.	HOW OFTEN.	ANNUAL SUBSCRIPTION.	EDITOR.	NUMBER OF VOLUMES.
Gentleman's Gazette.	Daily.	48	P. J. Mckerine Esq.	7
Telegraph & Courier.	Do.	46	T. J. A. Scott Esq.	1
Bombay Times.	Bi-weekly.	40	G. Buist Esq L. L. D.	10
Spectator.	Weekly.	20	T. J, A. Scott.	1

(Vide *Bombay Telegraph* and *Courier,* June 16, 1847.)

THE BOMBAY ADDRESS TO HER MAJESTY THE QUEEN VICTORIA, AND HIS HIGHNESS ALBERT, FRANCIS, AUGUSTUS, CHARLES, EMMANUEL, PRINCE OF SAXE COBURG GOTHA, ON THEIR HAPPY MARRIAGE.

A public meeting was held in Bombay on the 20th April, 1840, under the presidency of the Sheriff (G.F. Hughes, Esq.,) to vote an address to the royal pair. Sir J. W. Awdry, the Chief Justice of Bombay read the address which was published in full in the *Bombay Courier* of 1st April, 1840.

SIR SALAR JUNG IN ENGLAND.

The London Correspondent of the *Pioneer* wrote the following in 1876 :

"There are strange stories afloat in London Club Land concerning the sojourn within our gates last summer of Sir Salar Jung. In several instances His Excellency gave mortal offence by refusing to see both native and European gentlemen who called upon him. It is now said that du-

ring the whole time, he was in England, Sir Salar Jung was put by the
India House under the surveillance of certain Mr. Eitzgerald (son of Sir
Seymour Fitzgerald, who was Governor of Bombay from 1867 to 1872),
who holds the somewhat anomalous appointment of Political A. D. C. to
the Secretary of State for India. It seems that Sir Salar could not, and
excepting certain cases when, gentlemen came to see him who could not
be turned back, he did not see any one unless the individual was
approved of by Mr. Fitzgerald. The two categories of men who were
specially interdicted from having interviews with His Excellency were
journalists and natives of India residing in London. At the time there
were several complaints made by persons who had known Sir Salar well
in India, that he refused to see them in England ; and the refusals were
set down to His Excellency being so much made of by "swells." that he
would not receive older and more humble friends. But it now turns out
that the unfortunate did not know of a tenth of the refusals on the plea of
his being busy, or his not being well, that were made to his former ac-
quaintances. The Political A.-D.-C., who by the way is not, and never
was, in the army, and does not speak a word of any native language, allowed no one he did not approve of to go near Sir Salar. And
this, so it is said, by special orders from the Secretary of State for India.
Truly we live in curious times. If this is the way a distinguished native
Indian gentleman like Sir Salar is "looked after," as if he were a
convict at large, the liberty of the subject must be somewhat cramped in
the E-st. But the most wonderful part of the whole business is that the
snug, almost sinecure, well-paid appointment of Political A.-D.-C.
should be held by a gentleman who never belonged to the army, or to any
of the Indian services and cannot speak a word of a native language,
and whose only qualification for the post appears to be that his father
was once Governor of Bombay.

EAST INDIAN ANNUAL REGISTER—A GAZETTEER.

A valuable work of this sort was for sometime published.
in Calcutta but abandoned because it was unprofitable as a
speculation. In 1841 an East Indian Gazetteer was projected
in Bombay, but the project failed for want of support.

MR. BOSANQUET OF THE BOMBAY CIVIL SERVICE.

The facts of his case were thus related in the *Indu-Prokash.*

Only very recently when the young Nawab of Junjira was to leave his State to go to Rajkot, a number of the Nawab's subjects assembled to bid farewell to His Highness, and as he was going to be separated from them for some time to represent to the Nawab as well as to the Ass. Political Agent, the grievances they were suffering from under newly introduced forest rules. So far as can be seen from the evidence forthcoming, there was no show of force but Mr. Fitzgerald unfortunately took into his head that the people had assembled there to prevent the Prince from leaving Junjira. Some of the men were prosecuted before Mr. Bosanquet, who, while the trial was pending cut off all communications with Mr. Fitzgerald and ultimately discharged the accused as there was no evidence against them. Mr. Bosanquet was however soon after reduced and a Resolution of Government was issued, ordering a retrial of the case. And, we are informed, the accused have been retried and convicted. The worst of the matter is that the case cannot come for appeal before the High Court, for if it could, the Government would not have discredited itself by so high-handed a proceeding. (H. P. May 3, 1880.)

THE SITTING OF THE BOMBAY LEGISLATIVE COUNCIL IN 1862 UNDER ACT 24 AND 25 VICTORIA, CAP. 67.

The Council met on the 22nd January, 1862 under the Presidency of His Excellency Sir George Russel Clerk, K: C. B. K. S. I.

The following native non-officials were appointed to the Council, (1) The Honourable the Nawab of Savanoor, (2)The Honourable Mr. Rustomjee Jamset Jejeebhoy, (3)The Honourable Mr. Madha Rao Vittal Vinchoorkur, (4) The Honourable Mr. Jagernath Sunkurset, (5) The Honourable Shet Preamable Hemabhaee.

· We learn from the *Friend of India* of February, 1862, that at the first sitting of the Legislative Council, the Honourable Nawab of Savanoor took off his shoes at the door of the Council room. Mr. Madha Rao however appeared in a pair of "stunts."

CHAPTER IV.

PROFESSOR RAM CHUNDRA OF DELHI.

We read the following in the *Friend of India* of Nov. 7, 1861 :—

"We have received from the well-known native mathematician, Ram Chunder of Delhi, specimen of a new method of the Differential Calculus, called "the method of constant ratios." His former work on Problems on Maxima and Minima by Algebra, though purely speculative, was highly thought of by so great an authority as De Morgan. The Baboo deserves great credit for the zeal with which he pursues his Mathematical studies for their own sake. In this respect he is an example to his countrymen both heathen and, like himself, Christian."

His treatise on problems of Maxima and Minima solved by Algebra was published in 1850.

HIS MISSION TO PERSIA.

We take the following interesting account of the Hindu member of the Japanese Mission to Persia from the Bushire letter of the *Times of India* published in 1880.

Mr. Ram Chunder, the Hindu, who accompanied the Mission, hails from Muthura in Oudh. He was educated in Switzerland and Germany, and has lived for a long time in Russia. There is, I believe, some understanding between the Russian and Japanese Governments respecting the mission. Mr. Ram Chunder is said to have suggested the mission. Having been a fellow-student in Berlin with the present Crown Prince of Japan, and the

Minister of Marine, he interested them with the affairs of Persia and Central Asia.

DR. RAJ KRISHNA DEY AND OTHER BENGALI DOCTORS IN THE N. W. P.

The *Eastern Star* of 1840 said —

"He was the first Hindu who used a dissecting knife, and though his example was speedily followed by others, he may be thus regarded as the leader of a reformation in Medical Science among his countrymen. Babu Rajkrishna Dey entered the Hindoo College on the 13th September, 1833, and left it on the 20th April, 1837. During the latter part of this period he was also pursuing his studies in the Medical College. He took his degree from the Medical College in 1838 and accepted service in the North-West. The Dispensary in Delhi having been newly opened in August 1839, it was placed under the charge of Dr. Rajkrishna. He died in 1840. Babu Shyama Churn Dutt was placed in charge of the Dispensary at Allahabad in 1839. Babu Uma Churn Sett was in charge of the Agra dispensary at this time. They made a great name in the North-West.

MAJOR CARNAGIE, MR. MARTIN OF THE CIVIL SERVICE, MR. WILLIAMS AND MR. FORSYTH.

In a Resolution recorded by Lord Canning and his Councillors in 1861, and published in the *Friend of India* of October 21, 1861, the first gentleman who was Deputy Commissioner, City Magistrate, and one of the Lucknow Prize Agents was dismissed for having purchased Notes aggregating Rs. 1,38,900 at rates much below the market value of good paper and for other offences. The second gentleman, who was a Deputy Commissioner then in England on leave was similarly charged. He was, on his return to India, was reproved. The third, an Extra Assistant Commissioner purchased Notes of the value of Rs. 61,000 at a lower rate, was suspended from office for one year without pay. As regards Mr. Forsyth, Secretary to the Chief Commissioner, he was reproved for his transactions. Mr. V. H. Scalch, then Commissioner of Chittagong was sent as a special Commissioner to enquire into these cases.

SUDDER COURT OF AGRA.

From a decision of the Sudder Court at Agra published in the issue of the *Englishman and Military Chronicle* of July 31, 1846, it appears that, in a civil case between Sreekishen and Ramkishen vs : Rai Hur Bux, the judgment in the above case by the Zillah Judge of Benares, having been given on *Nag Punchami*, a vacation day, was cancelled by the Sudder Court, and the file of the case was returned to the Zillah Judge for re-trial.

LAHAUN SING OF THE PUNJAB.

A Sheik Sirdar,. wrote a correspondent to the *Bombay Durpan* in 1840, was a man of learning and kept several astronomers with him. He held debates with Europeans, and also communicated to them such parts of the astronomical works as he was acquainted with, asking them for further illustrations and proofs. Lord Auckland while at Gwoalior presented him with a. curiously constructed celestial globe of brass, and an instrument for taking observations. (F. I. May 14, 1840.) -

---

LALLA JOTEE PROSAD.

In the *Mufussilite* of 1861 we read the following :—

"When informed; one morning by the late Mr. Coverly Jackson, that the Jumna's course would in a few years undermine the foundations of the. Taj, and that the edifice would fall into the river, he replied :—"No. It shall not, 1 will build a Ghat, which will turn the course of the river." The tolerant Hindoo did it, at a cost of £ 10,000 sterling.

H. H. THE MAHARAJAH OF PATIALA
AND HIS ARISTOCRATIC FEELINGS.

His Highness Norendra Sing Maharajah of Patiala, K. C. S. I., was by a notification dated 16th January 1862, appointed an Additional Member of the Supreme Legislative Council by Lord Canning. The Maharajah felt "indignation and annoyance to sit with Rajah Dinkur Rao.Rughunath Bahadoor, and Raja Deonarain Sing Bahadoor, on the ground that the former was a servant of a brother Feudatory Chief, and the latter, a mere Raja. He was however *sumjaod* and yielded afterwards.

A SHIEK AND A MAHOMEDAN MILLIONAIRE IN ST. PETERSBURGH IN 1831.

The *Friend* of *India* in a leading article under the above heading, dated June 15, 1861, thus described them.

"Some thirty years ago, a faqueer of the Khutree caste, but known as Roy Brahmin, left his native village in the District of Jhung in the Punjab. His professed object was to visit the Shiek shrine at Astracan. He made his way from Astracan to St. Petersburgh where he settled as a merchant and accumulated a fortune of three millions of roubles, equal to nearly half a million sterling. Either desirious that his friends should share his good fortune, or anxious for the companionship of his own people, some six years ago, (1855) he wrote a letter to one Ram Das in Jhung, inviting him to join him. At the same time a Mussulman of the name of "Moolah Oooh", as rendered by the Russians, also resident in St. Peters- burgh and having made a fortune of some twenty thousand pounds, invited an old friend, called in the Russian official papers, "Galarman Chowk", of Sharpore in Oudh, to join him. The two seem to have set out together for the distant Russian Capital. On reaching Moscow they were robbed, but on appealing to the authorities their property was recovered, and they were told they would find it at Nijni Novgorod. They pressed on to St. Petersburgh however, and found that their rich friends, Roy Brahmin and Moolla Ooch, had both died a month or two before their arrival. Ram Das presented his letter of invitation to the Russian agent of Roy Brahmin, but was unceremoniously turned out of doors with the gratuity of one rouble. Disconsolate yet determined to have Justice, he appealed to the Emperor with whom he got an accidental interview. Galarman

Chowk also told his story to the authorities in 1856. Both cases were therefore reported to the Foreign Secretary in London through the Russian Minister. The Russian Government admitted the wealth of Roy Brahmin and Moola Ooch, which consisted chiefly of claims against the State. The papers were then sent to India for enquiry. Meanwhile, to complicate the matter Ramdas died, but Golarman remained in St. Petersburgh awaiting the issue in his own case.

The Calcutta Foreign Office instituted an enquiry into the matter. The Punjab authorities reported that Roy Brahmin left India as a faqueer in 1830, and that Ram das followed him in 1855. Ram Das had two brothers one in Jhung and another in Amritsahar."

We do not know how their case was disposed of.

CAPTAIN CUNNINGHAM.

The celebrated author of a work on the annexation of the Punjab was dismissed from his appointment as Political Agent of Bhopal for having made use of public documents in his work." (F. I. August 2, 1849.)

MAJOR SMYTH.

He was, like Captain Cunningham, publicly reprimanded at Muthura for the publication of his work called a "Secret History of the Lahore Durbur," as calculated to bring into disrepute the services of the army." (F.I.September 27, 1848.)

DOST MOHOMMED KHAN AND THE HON'BLE
MISS EDEN.

The following anecdote occurs in Dr. Mouat's lecture on the Mussulmans of India. It refers to a game of chess between Dost Mahomed, the Ameer of Cabul, and the Hon'ble Miss Eden, sister of Lord Auckland, the then Governor-General of India.

Miss Eden challenged the Ameer to play; he accepted the challenge. They sat down in the centre of one of the marble saloons of what is now the palace of the Viceroy of India; and all who could approach,stood round, a gay and brilliant throng, to watch this tournament between the captive ruler of the Afghans and an English lady of high birth and rare accomplishments. The little conversation that ensued, was interpreted to the players, respectively, by the Hon. Henry Elliot, and Mr. Henry Torrens, both master of Persian, and men of remarkable ability. Miss Eden won the first game, apparently with out much difficulty, and clapped her hands in high glee, at having vanquished so renowned an antagonist. The Dost took his defeat with grave courtesy and much good humour, and prayed the lady to grant him a renewal of the contest, to retrieve, if possible, his fallen fortunes; adding in elegant Persian that it was "the only defeat he had ever sustained in which pain was a pleasure." The old warrior king looking round upon the uniforms of the gallant soldiers by whom they were surroun ded, now put forth his whole strength, and soon showed th at he was a m aster of the craft, checkmating the lady in a rapid serie s of moves that were pronounced by those present to exhibit the hi ghest skill. He then apologised for his apparent rudeness in defeat ing a lady who had done him so much honour—telling Major Nicolson afterwards that it would not do to be beaten by both sexes of the great nation whose guest he still was."

DOST MOHOMMED AT GOVERNMENT HOUSE IN 1841.

(From a correspondent in High Life. *Hurkura* 26, May.)

"The Government House party, on Monday night, in honor of Her Majesty's entrance upon the 23rd year, went off with great eclat. The Ex-Ameer, Dost Mohommed sat for some time with Lord Auckland, in the full enjoyment of the rich conversational exhuberance, for which that nobleman is so celebrated, and afterwards seated himself to a quiet game of chess with Honourable Miss Eden. His gallantry would not permit him to win the first game, but he checkmated the lady in the second, after a few moves. He said, that he would have checkmated old Sale too, out in the Kohistan, if Sekunder Burnes had not been so active with his money-bags. When he took Miss Eden's second Knight, he observed with a smile, that the Horsemen of the British were always soon cleared off the board. "Yes" said Miss Eden, smiling and suiting the action to the word, "but we know how to take your castles." "Ah !" rejoined the Dost good humouredly, "but if the Father had been there instead of the Son, you would have heard less about your Guznec Victory."

The conversation that passed between the Ex-Ameer and the Governor-General was as to the social customs of the British. The Dost was very eager to know what the gentlemen said to their partners, between the figures of the dance, and Captain Nicolson was accordingly ordered to interpret, *sotto voce*, what was passing between Mr.——and Miss ———; but the Ex-Ameer soon stopped him, observing, "you blame as Moslems for saying that our women have no souls, and yet you British talk to your women as though you were fully convinced of the fact."

H. H. THE MAHARAJAH OF KAPPURTHALA
AND HIS MARRIAGE WITH A EUROPEAN LADY.

The late lamented Dr. Sumbhu Chunder Mukerjee, the Editor of *Reis* and *Rayyet* thus wrote on the subject in its issue of 13th October, 1893.

"The late Maharajah Sir Randhir Singh Bahadoor, G. C. S. I. married a White Girl. He died on his way to Europe at Aden in 1870. The Maharajah was succeeded by his son Raja Kharak Singh, who died in 1877, leaving a minor five or six years old, the present Ruler. The news of the sheik Chief having wedded a Christian created a great sensation in Society, both European and native. Although ratified by an accommodating *Padre*—an American Missionary,—the connection was scarcely one for Anglo-Indian Society to boast of. The Lady Randhir Singh was not only accepted at the Viceregal Court but actually petted. The Chief had employed Europeans and had gone in for public works in his territory. He had endowed missons and built churches. The *Friend of India* devoted a leading article to him, in its issue of 20th February, 1862, the drift of which may be imagined from its heading "Almost a Christian." He never advanced beyond "almost," on the contrary, it seemed as if he gradually receded. All India was startled by the news that the whole Christian colony had broken up and dispersed. The Lady had gone for a drive and never returned. Engineer and builder also had taken French leave. The reverend Gooroo too had gone on a discreet visitation to British territory. The *padre* and the Rajah's European relations had not accounted for large sums."

THE DISSOLUTION OF THE MARRIAGE.

We read the following in the *Indian Public Opinion* of 1869.

"The Kuppurthala authorities have solemnly pronounced a dissolution of the marriage between the Rajah and the Miss Hodges, which was celebrated in 1859, in Jullundhur. At a conference between Mr. Cunningham on the part of the Rajah, and Mr. Jardine on the part of the lady, it was agreed that a moderate provision should be made for her and her two daughters."

MR. COPE AND THE *DELHI GAZETTE*.

He edited the paper for the last 8 years and severed his connection with it in 1849, and proposed to start paper at Lahore. The *Delhi Gazette* realized a profit of from Rs.200 to Rs. 50 p. c. (F. I. November 1849.)

THE ORGAN OF THE BRITISH INDIAN ASSOCIATION OF THE TALOOKDARS IN OUDH.

Babu Dhukhinarunjun Mukherjea invited in 1862 the late Dr. Shumbhu Chunder Mukherjea, to be the Secretary to the above Association.

The *Shamachar Hindoosthani* edited by Dr. Sumbhu Chunder Mukherjea appeared in January, 1862. It was a revival of the *Akbar Hindoosthani* which existed only for a short time. (F. I. January 16, 1862.)

MR. MELVILLE, A CIVILIAN WHO EMBRACED ISLAMISM.

The *Pioneer* received the following telegram about the Civilian, who embraced Mahomedanism in 1873.

Murree 16th October. Mr. Melville, of Sirsa, is the Civilian who has turned Mahomedan. He is transferred as Assistant to Delhi, and suspended pending orders of Government. His new name is Shaikh Abdul Rahaman. The object in changing his religion was to marry a khansama's daughter from Lahore.

NEWAB ASADULLAH KHAN *ALIAS* GHALIB, THE FAMOUS URDU POET OF DELHI.

Indian Public Opinion of 1869 noticed his death thus :—

"He expired on the 15th February, 1869, at Delhi at the advanced age of 73 years. Since the days of *Sonda* and *Meerdown* to the times of *Zoak* and *Momen*, who both died shortly before the mutiny, and in whose days *Urdu* is said to have reached its perfection, no poet can vie with Ghalib of Delhi. The productions of his genius will be regarded by orientalists as models of the best *Urdu* ever spoken or written in either verse or prose. His verses in the Persian language vie with the *Urfi* of Shiraz, *Baidill*, *Sayeb* and Ghani of Cashmere. His beautiful verses in Persian when produced at Ispahan and Teheran were highly appreciated by the literary men there. His pupils in the Science of poetry will be found in the remotest parts of Hindoostan wherever *Urdu* is the language of the country."

MAHARANEE JUND KOONWAROR CHUNDA OF LAHORE.

The *Friend of India,* of December 21, 1848, contains a full report of the case instituted by Mr. Newmarch, as Agent of the Ranee before the Supreme Court of Calcutta for her release from Benares as a state prisoner. Mr. Peterson appeared for the Ranee. Sir Lawrence Peal, Chief Justice rejected the application.

Reminiscences and Anecdotes of the Judges of the Supreme and High Courts.

CHAPTER V

A CASE OF COLLISION BETWEEN THE SUPREME COURT IN 1879 AND THE GOVERNMENT.

We extract the following from the Hindoo Patriot of 1883. Babu Ashutosh Mukerjea, M. A. B. L., Premchand Roychand student, and a Vakil of the Bengal High Court, published another pamphlet entitled " the Annals of the British Land Revenue system in Bengal from 1698 to 1793." They give a brief but connected history of the British land-revenue system in Bengal. He wrote thus,

At length a case arose in which the disputes between the executive and judicial powers arrived at a crisis. In 1779, a suit was commenced in the Supreme Court against the Raja of Cassijorah, in Midnapore, by one Kassinath Babu, his agent at Calcutta. By the rules of the Court, no process was issued against any native of Bengal, unless the plaintiff swore that such native was subject to the jurisdiction of the Court, and added in his affidavit circumstances which rendered him so subject. Upon the affidavit of Kassinath Babu, which affirmed that the Raja was the zemindar of Cassijorah, employed by the East India Company in the collection of the revenues of his zemindary, a *capias* was ordered to issue, in which bail to the amount of three lakhs and a half was allowed to be taken. The Government referred the matter to their Advocate-General, Sir John Day, who gave it as his opinion that " zemindars were land-holders, and held their lands and right by inheritance." A literal translation of this opinion was sent to the Raja, who was also instructed not to pay obedience to the process of the Court. The writ of *capias* having been returned as unexecuted, on account of the conceal-ment of the zemindar, another writ was issued to sequester his land

17

and effects. In the execution of this writ, the Sheriff dispatched to Cassijorah an armed force, consisting of sixty men, headed by a serjeant of the Court. The Governor-General sent orders to the officer commanding to apprehend all persons answering to the description which had been given of this detachment. The orders arrived too late to prevent the violation of the Rajah's zenana, and of his religion, "the former having been forcibly entered, the women and children having indeed been conveyed away upon the first alarm; the door of his temple broken open and his idol taken and packed like a common utensil in a basket, and sealed up with the other lumber," as Mr. Hastings, described the affair in a private letter. "But the whole of the party sent by the Sheriff were afterwards seized. Affairs having come to this extremity, the Governor-General and Council issued a notification to all zemindars, chowdhries, and Talookdars, in Bengal, Behar and Orissa, that except in the two cases of being servants or British subjects or bound by their own agreements, they were not to consider themselves as subject to the jurisdiction of the Supreme Court, or to obey its process.

The Supreme Court thereupon issued a rule to show cause why an attachment should not issue against the company's attorney and the officers who were instrumental in seizing the Sheriff's officers and their attendants at Cassijorah, and the Governor-General and Council themselves were served with a summons to answer to Kashinath Babu in a plea of trespass. But a reconciliation was soon after effected between the governing Council and the Supreme Court, by the bestowal of an office of great power and emolument dependent upon the pleasure of the Council, upon the Chief Justice, Sir Elijah Impey.

MR. COURTNAY SMITH.

A Bengal Judge of the "Highest Court in the country was removed from it in 1828 for refusing to receive 'a deposit of Government paper as security in some suit under his cognizance." (F. I. November 3, 1848.)

HENRY THOMAS COLEBROOKE.

The Saturday Review wrote thus in 1873.

"He was never sent to any school at all, but he was evidently a lad of quick perceptions and studious habits, and, after a home education, he landed in India at the early age of seventeen, well grounded in classics and mathematics, with a considerable command of French, and with some knowledge of German."

"He appears to have spent about three years in Calcutta, hunting, shooting, and studying the languages In 1786 he was appointed Assistant to the Collector of Tirhoot, a rich and populous district of Behar, and in 1789 he was transferred to the next district of Purneah. The inquiries which terminated in the Perpetual Settlement of Lord Cornwallis were then in full progress ; and doubtless, in these districts Colebrooke laid the foundation of that intimate familiarity with Hindu usages and modes of thought which secured him an early elevation to the Bench, and eventually a seat in Council. 1793 the year of the said Perpetual Settlement, Colebrooke was placed in charge of the huge district of Rajshahye."

"Nattore, the head station of Rajshahye, was some thirty miles from the left bank of the Ganges, and for five months of the year it was a mere island in a vast sea of rice. That station was abandoned subsequent to Colebrooke's time, and a second fatality characterised the new choice of a centre. Civilians who had been struck down by malarious fever at Nattore were transplanted to Rampore Boalia on the crumbling banks of the Ganges ; and in the space of the last thirty years, court-houses have vanished and alleys lined with splendid trees have been eaten up by the simple process of diluvion and erosion. From this swampy feverish district of Bengal Colebrooke was transferred to the drier climate and more congenial society of Mirzapore and Benares. By this time his character and attainments received their due reward and recognition, and he was sent by Wellesley on a diplomatic mission to the Raja of Berar, which enlarged his experience and occupied him for more than two years. On his return he was appointed Judge of the highest Court of appeal, known for seventy years as the Sudder Adawlut, and some time afterwards he was made Chief Judge of the same tribunal—a position which he had practically filled in the estimation of suitors and of colleagues from the time of his appointment. In 1807 he became member of the Supreme Council. In 1810 he married ; and his wife dying after four years of what appears to have been unalloyed domestic happiness, he finally quitted the service in 1814. Previously to his departure he had been President of the Asiatic Society of Bengal. In his retirement he continued the same course of laborious research and scientific inquiry which had illustrated his Indian career. Though in 1823 he declined the offer of the first Presidentship of the Royal Asiatic Society, he accepted a similar post in the Astronomical Society in the next year. His later life was tried by failing health, by loss of sight, by domestic sorrows, and by some family annoyances ; and he gradually sank, and died on March 10, 1837, in his seventy-second year. (H. P. June 9, 1873.)

SIR BARNES PEACOCK, KNIGHT.

We take the following facts of his early life from the *Friend of India* of September 12, 1861 :—

"Sir Barnes Peacock began life as a pupil of Mr. Coleman, an eminent special pleader. After some years of uninterrupted success as a special pleader Mr. Peacock was called to the common law Bar on the 30th of January 1836. He at first went to the Western Circuit, then considered only less profitable than the Northern. He then deserted the Western for the Home Circuit including London and its vicinity. Here he secured a large junior's practice of the most solid and valuable character, both in Westminster Hall and in the city. In 1837 he came prominently forward in consequence of the novel and startling application reported as Bourne vs : The king in 2 Nevile and Perry's reports, page 248. In this case, the prisoners, who had been sentenced by the Monmouth Quarter Sessions to various terms of transportation for burglary, were released, through his bold advocacy of their cause. In 1844 he put the seal to his reputation by his argument before the House of Lords in the case of Daniel O'connell reported in 11 Clarke and Finneley page 155. In 1850, he was made Queen's Counsel. Shortly after, he was selected by the Court of Directors legal member of the Indian Council. In 1859, on the retirement of Sir James Colville, the Presidency of the Calcutta Supreme Court was offered to Mr. Peacock, and he took his seat, as Chief Justice, on the 22nd of June of that year.

SIR BARNES PEACOCK AND THE HON'BLE JUSTICE DWARKA NATH MITTER.

Mr. William Tayler who was formerly a member of the Bengal Civil Service and dismissed from it by Sir Frederic Halliday for his dereliction of duty during the Mutiny of 1857, when he was Commissioner of the Patna Division, became a vakeel of the late Sudder Court, and upon the amalgamation of the Supreme and Sudder Courts was enrolled as a vakeel of the High Court. He subsequently carried on business as a Muktear in the district of Patna where he was formerly a Commissioner. Among other clients he was retained by Ranee Usmedh Kower, the elder Ranee of Ticaree. He brought a civil suit in 1865 against the Ranee for the recovery of a certain sum of money due to him as fees by the Ranee. The case was reported in the 2nd Vol. Weekly Reporter, page 86. The civil suit brought by Mr. Tayler against the Ranee, was dismissed, but in a counter case instituted against Mr. Tayler, which ultimately came before the High Court on appeal, Mr. Justice Dwarka Nath Mitter remarked that a "fraud has been perpetrated against her (Ranee Usmedh Kower) by Mr. Tayler in concealing from her the fact that the estate sold by a decree of Court."

Aggrieved at this remark, Mr. Tayler wrote a letter in the *Englishman* charging the learned Judge with "wanton insult and unfounded assertion" This famous letter appeared in the *Englishman* of the 2nd of April, 1869. Thereupon the Chief Justice, to vindicate the honour of the court, arrested Mr. Tayler while he was on the point of leaving Calcutta in a mail steamer for England. It is said that Sir Barnes Peacock went personally to Dwarkanath's house while he was sleeping, roused him from his bed, showed the letter of Mr. Tayler and told him of his intention to arrest Mr. Tayler immediately. He prepared a seal of his own for the immediate arrest of Mr. Tayler as the office seal was not to be had at the time.

The first letter of the 2nd April 1869, by Mr. Tayler against the Hon'ble Justice Dwarkanath Mitter runs thus :—

———

"My reputation, Iago, my reputation" Othello.

"TO THE EDITOR OF THE ENGLISHMAN.

'Sir,—I was in hopes long ere this, I might have sent you for publication the proceedings of the High Court in the matter of my application for the review of my judgment in the case in which Mr. Justice Dwarka Nath Mitter did me the honor to record that I had 'perpetuated a fraud' ; but as I have not yet been able to obtain an authenticated copies, I do not wish to delay any longer the remarks which I consider myself called upon to make in justice to myself in regard to this *insulting*, and as I shall show, *utterly unjustifiable charge.*

Condemnation or censure passed by a Court of Justice on a suitor (if without sufficient ground or reason) is the most mischievous, the most intolerable of slanders. The Judge on the Bench, like the parson on the pulpit, has it all his own way for a time, but the preacher attacks man in general, the Judge deals with the individual. General condemnation hurts no one. Individual censure may be ruin to the object of it.

"I now propose to show, and that by *clear and unanswerable evidence,* that this dishonouring and unmeasured imputation judicially cast upon me by Mr. Justice Dwarkanath Mitter, *has been recorded by him without one tittle of evidence to support it, that it is wholly untrue and manifestly absurd ; and I beg you to observe that the learned Judge who placed it on record has not condescended to give one single reason, ground, or argument in support of his denunciation.*

"If a *District Judge had so acted, he would in all probability have been suspended,* or at all events subjected to some such ordeal as Mr. Beaufort underwent not long ago ! Whether elevation to the Bench of the High Court carries total exemption from responsibility with it remains to be seen."

Besides this, he wrote two more letters to the *Englishman,* one on the 12th April, and another on the 13th, criticizing the judgment of Mr. Justice Mitter in Regular Appeal No. 67 of 1868, dated the 19th November, 1868;

Mussumut Zuhurrun appellant, vs : William Tayler respon-dent.   On the 19th April, he was arraigned before the Court and on the 24th, convicted of contempt of Court and sentenced to suffer imprisonment for one month and to pay a fine of Rs. 500 which was paid. Mr. Tayler then published a letter of apology in the *Englishman* of the 22nd April, as suggested by the Chief Justice and was subsequently released from the jail, and left for England on the 28th. The full Judgment of this case appeared in a supplement to the *Englishman* of 3rd April, 1869.

THE PROSECUTION OF THE EDITOR AND PRINTER OF THE *ENGLISHMAN* FOR THE SAME OFFENCE.

Mr. Alexander Banks, the Printer of the *Englishman*, and Mr. George Roe Fenwick, * the Editor appeared before a Divisional Bench consisting of the Chief Justice and Justice Macpherson, on May 3rd 1869, to answer to the charge of contempt of Court for having published in its issue of the 16th an article condemning the Chief Justice in the follow-ing terms :—

"We suspect that Sir Barnes, if he attempts to carry out his dictum too far, will raise a storm not easy to quell. The Editor wrote another article on the 19th and also invited public subscriptions from Europeans to pay off the fine imposed upon Mr. Tayler. These were the counts of the indictment against the Editor. Mr. Alexander Banks, the Printer was let off, and Captain Fenwick escaped punishment by having withdrawn through Mr. Paul who with Mr. Kennedy, defend-ed the Editor, all imputations of improper motives on the part of the Chief Justice, and explained that the word "cruelty" was not intended in a bad sense but merely as meaning

* In 1840, he was the Editor of the *Commercial Advertizer*. He then quitted the editorial chair and proceeded to the mufussil to practise as an attorney.

severity (see full reports of this case in the *Englishman* of
the 7th and 8th May, 1869.)

SIR BARNES PEACOCK.

In 1861, he opposed the passing of the *License* Bill and
moved an amendment :—

"That except so far as relates to arrears of duties in taxes
due, or to offences committed, or to acts previously done, the
provisions of this Act and of Act 32 of 1860 and of Act 39 of
1860, shall cease to have any force or effect, if at any time
the revenue of India shall become chargeable with any new
or extraordinary pensions, or gratuity, or with any increase
of any extraordinary pensions, or annuities granted in any
one year, or any one period of twelve calendar months,
amounting in the whole to more than Rs. 200,000, or £20,
000 sterling, or with the payment of principal or interest of
any other promissory note, or other Government security
issued after the passing of this Act, and made payable to any
person or persons by way of pension or gratuity, or without
adequate consideration given."

Sir Barnes Peacock then exposed in detail the mistakes
made by Sir Charles Wood in his defence of the Mysore
gratuity. He made the following speech anent his separa-
tion from the Council :—

"In all probability this Council will shortly cease to exist,
and I rejoice to see that non-officials are proposed to be introduced as members into the body which is to succeed us.
&c. &c. &c.

For my own part I shall cheerfully resign the trust which
has hitherto been committed to me, and shall look with
confidence to those whom Parliament in its wisdom shall appoint to succeed us. But as long as I have the honor to hold
a seat in this Council and are called upon to assist as a member of the Legislature of the country, I shall, through good

report and through evil report pursue that which I conscientiously believe to be right, and then when the time arrives for relinquishing the trust, I shall have the consolation of knowing that I can lay my hand upon my heart, and truly declare that I never gave a vote in this Council which I did not at the time believe to be just and correct."

Noble words are these and should be written in characters of gold.

The License Bill was passed in 1861 with two dissentient votes of Sir Charles Robert Mitchell Jackson and the Chief Justice of Bengal.

SIR BARNES PEACOCK, KT.

The *Hindoo Patriot* wrote thus :—

"None perhaps more bravely defended the position of the Court than Sir Barnes Peacock. Sir Barnes would not yield an inch, and he generally carried the day. A brother Judge had applied to Government for leave without going through the Chief Justice, and the Government had granted his application, but Sir Barnes protested, and the Government cancelled its order and told the Judge to come through the Chief Justice, and this was done. The Government had asked for the opinion of the Court extrajudicially in a Sylhet case, just as it did in the Fuller case, but Sir Barnes refused to express the opinion solicited in such an irregular manner, and Government had to give in."

SIR EDWARD RYAN.

The *Mofussilite* has the following about the late Sir Edward Ryan.

Sir Edward Ryan's name takes us back to a dark period of Indian history, when men's minds were wrought to fever heat of excitement by the appalling disaster which befel our army in that dreary passage through the Cabul gate, whence only one remained to reach the goal at Jellalabad. Among these who administered the sweets of consolation to the troubled

18

mind of the Governor-General as he paced up and down the terrace of Government House, it was Sir Edward's genial face and gentle nature which spoke comfort to Lord' Auckland far more than any others who approached that nobleman in the hour of his country's humiliation, which was charged to his account."

Sir Edward Ryan was the best friend of the educated natives in his day. In England he used to take great interest in Indian youths who went there for education or professional advancement. (H. P. September 27, 1875.)

SIR EDWARD RYAN.

He retired in 1841. The students of the Hindoo College presented him with a handsome silver vase and salver, as a slight testimonial of their gratitude for his generous exertions in the cause of Native education in Bengal. The members of the Agri-Horticultural Society voted a bust in his honor for his having been its President from 1829 to 1841. The bust was placed in the Metcalfe Hall. The address presented to him by the students of the Hindoo College was read by Babu Gobin Chundra Dutt.

A PUBLIC MEETING IN HONOUR OF SIR EDWARD RYAN.

A public meeting was held in the Town Hall on the 30th December, 1841. About one hundred European and two hundred Natives assembled on the occasion. Mr. W. H. Smoult, the sheriff was in the chair. Mr. Turton moved the first resolution that a committee consisting of Sir. W. Casement, the Hon'ble J. H. Cameron, Mr. Turton and Mr. Halliday be appointed to present an address. It was resolved to raise a portrait in his honor. (*Courier* 31st, Dec, 1841.)

SIR JAMES COLVILLE KT.

The *Hindoo Patriot* noticed his death thus in 1880.

In 1845 he was appointed Advocate-General, Calcutta, in 1848 a Puisne Judge of the Supreme Court when he was knighted, in 1855 Chief Justice and in 1859 retired. On return to England he was appointed assessor to the Judicial Committee of the Privy Council on Indian Appeals, being at the same time sworn in as a Privy Councillor. In November 1865, he was appointed a member of the Judicial Committee ; and in November 1871, he was appointed to act as one of the paid members on that body, but he soon after retired. Sir James Colville was a zealous friend of the cause of native education. He was President of the Council of Education and used to take a lively interest in his work. He also served for several years as President of the Asiatic Society, and contributed much to its prosperity by his wise counsel and personal influence. As Vice-President of Lord Dalhousie's Legislative Council he took an active part in passing the Widow Marriage Act. Sir James Colville was a clever writer, and his literary skill was not unfrequently availed of by both Europeans and Natives. A remarkable instance occured at the memorial meeting in honor of Lord Hardinge. There was a division at the meeting, one party headed by Mr. Longueville Clarke, Mr. Theodore Dickens, and Mr. James Hume proposed a public building, while the other party headed by Babu Ramgopal Ghose proposed a statue. Babu Ramgopal carried the day, but the wording of his resolution was not accepted by the meeting. Several gentlemen present tried their hands, but they did not prove successful. At last Sir James Colville came to the rescue, and the resolution draft by him was unanimously agreed to. Sir James counted some of his best friends among native gentlemen of Bengal.

Sir James Colville was the first Vice-Chancellor of the Calcutta University on its creation in 1857.

THE HON'BLE JUSTICE FRANCIS BARING KEMP.

The *Hindoo Patriot* wrote the following in 1878.

He came to India in November 1831, and has thus seen 47 summers in the service of this country. After an Indian career for nearly half a century Mr. Kemp leaves for his native land next month.

He was an Etonian, and largely inherited the fine spirit of his *alma mater*. After passing through the usual noviciate he became Commissioner of the Sunderbuns and the settlements made by him, as a contemporary justly remarks, "were among the most equitable settlements of this time." He afterwards served in several districts, but he distinguished himself most as District Judge of Backergunge. Mr. Kemp may be said to be gifted with a judicial temperament. Passion does not disturb his temper ; bias does not warp his judgment.

He established his judicial reputation in Backergunge. His connection with that district was made memorable by the Baropakhya case. There are not many left in these days who recollect the facts of that case. It was a case of riot, on one side of which were ranged two zemindars, and on the other the Baptist Missionaries of Backergunge. It is not necessary at this distance of time to recall the facts of this case. Mr. Kemp, bold and uncompromising as he has always been, gave his judgment against the Missionaries. As usual the Missionaries raised a long howl, and Sir Frederic Halliday, who was then the Lieutenant Governor of Bengal, and a personal friend of Father John of the *Friend of India* was very much dissatisfied with Mr. Kemp's judgment. There was no appeal from it, but Sir Frederic, if we remember aright, brought it under the notice of the Sudder Court as a Court of General Revision and, Superintendence. The Sudder Court upheld Mr. Kemp's judgment, but at the same time expressed an opinion that the zemindars' people might have been punished. This gave Sir Frederic a good handle, which he did not fail to use. He came down with sledge-hammer upon Mr. Kemp. The Missionaries were also not the men to keep quiet, and kept on a running fire upon the poor Judge in the shape of letters to newspapers, leaders in the *Friend*, pamphlets and reports. But Mr. Kemp was made of a stern stuff; he clung to his own judgment, and appealed to the Government of India against the censure passed upon him by Sir Federic Halliday. Sir John Peter Grant was then Member of the Supreme Council, and he went through all the papers in the case with his usual judicial calmness. He supported Mr. Kemp, and the Government of India accordingly cancelled the censure recorded by Sir Frederic Halliday. But Mr. Kemp was long left in the cold in consequence of this escapade. On the establishment of the High Court in 1862, he was appointed a judge of that Court, and if there was a judge of the High Court respected by his colleagues, by suitors, and advocates alike, it was Mr. Kemp. Gentle, generous and just, all had equal confidence in him. He would not hesitate to condemn the Government strongly, if he saw good reasons to do so, when it stood as a suitor before him, but on no other occasion would he take any notice of the acts or conduct of the Government, though as a warm-hearted friend of the people, and an uncompromising lover of justice he could not always approve of them in his own conscience. Mr. Kemp's retirement is a loss to the High Court as well as to the country.

THE HON'BLE JUSTICE MARKBY.

Mr. Justice Markby retired from the High Court Bench in 1878. He opened a law class in his own house where he used to deliver law lectures to students. He contributed a remarkable article to the *West Minister Review* in which he expressed his opinion that Native Judges were much superior to the European Judges. He helped the native community with his advice and influence when the great controversy about high education was raging in the time of Sir George Campbell. Mr. Markby's equable temper was shewn to the greatest advantage in the late controversy about Dr. Mohendra Lal Sirkar's election to the Medical Faculty.

THE HON'BLE JUSTICE GLOVER.

Justice Glover died at Galle in 1876. He was, as was believed by the late Hon'ble K. D. Pal, part proprietor of the *Englishman* newspaper. (H. P. August 14, 1876.)

THE HON'BLE JOHN PAXTON NORMAN,
OFFICIATING CHIEF JUSTICE OF
THE CALCUTTA HIGH COURT.

He was assasinated on the 21st September 1871. It is said that he once declined to hear a case against the E. Indian Railway on the ground that he held shares in it.

Mr. Norman, was born in October 21, 1819. His father was the late Mr. John Norman of I wood House, Congresbury, and of Claverham, a Magistrate and Deputy-Lieutenant for the county of Somerset. His mother, who is the representative of the old Border family of Paxton, survives to mourn his loss, and resides with her son, the Rev. A. M. Norman, Rector of Burnmoor, in Northumberland, Mr. Norman was educated at the Exeter Grammar School, and subsequently at Exeter College, Oxford, where he graduated in 1851. After studying at the Temple he practised for many years as a special pleader, but was called to the Bar in 1862. He was the author of many legal treatises and papers, the most important of his writings being "A Treatise on the Law and Practice Relating to Letters Patent for Inventions," and the *Exchequer Reports*, of which jointly with Mr. Hurlstone, he was editor for several years previously to his leaving England. In May, 1861, Mr. Norman was appointed, under Lord John Russell's Administration, one of the Judges of the High Court of Bengal.

THE HON'BLE JUSTICE LOUIS STUART JACKSON.

We take the following from the *Hindoo Patriot* of 1880.

He first came to public notice, though not to his credit, as Joint-Magistrate in charge of the Serampore Sub-division. Father John then flourished at Serampore, and Mr. Jackson committed an illegality towards the Gossains of that town, for which he was hauled up before the Supreme Court of Calcutta, and we believe was made to pay damages. This was of course the indiscretion of youth. Whilst on the bench we are sorry to say he was not quite fair to the junior members of the native bar—he used to find fault with their dress, with their manners, with their mode of delivery, and with their law and argument. He had not the toleration and magnanimity of Sir Barnes Peacock. He used also to make sometimes an invidious distinction between the European Barrister and the native pleader, and from his external manifestation, not latterly, he did not seem friendly to the advancement of the native to the bench of the High Court. We had it from the late Justice Dwarkanath Mitter himself that on his elevation to the bench he was looked upon by Mr. Justice Jackson with a gruffness which he could account for only by the many passages-atarms he had with him whilst at the bar, but it was said that when he saw that Sir Barnes was Dwarkanath's friend, and that the latter was not a man to be put down by gruff looks, he quieted down, ayé, became one of the warmest friends of Mr. Mitter.

Mr. Louis Jackson contradicted the above statements,

but Babu Kristo Das Pal, published the following judgment to substantiate his assertion.

No. 68418.

Pleas at Fort William in Bengal before Sir Lawrence Peel, Kt. Chief Justice and his Companion Justices of our Sovereign Lady the Queen of the Supreme Court of Judicature at Fort William and Bengal of the second Term in the year of our Lord Christ, One thousand eight hundred and forty-seven and in the Tenth year of the Reign of our Sovereign Lady Victoria by the Grace of God of the United Kingdom of Great Britain and Ireland Queen Defender of the Faith and so forth.

Gungaprosad Gossain, and Gopeekristo Gossain the Plaintiffs in this action by William Thomas Denman and William Henry Abbott the younger their Attornies complain of Louis Stuart Jackson, the Defendant, in this action who is a British subject residing in the Province of Bengal and an Inhabitant of the Town of Calcutta and therefore a person subject to the Jurisdiction of this Hon'ble Court of a Plea of Trespass. For that the Defendant heretofore to wit on the 15th day of March in the year of Christ One thousand eight hundred and forty-seven with force and arms &c. broke and entered a certain stable of the Plaintiff's situate and being at Serampore in the Province of Bengal, and stayed and continued therein for a long space of time to wit for five days and then seized, took and drove away one horse one mare and one pony of the Plaintiff's then and there found and being of great value to wit of the value of Company's Rupees Two hundred, and then converted and disposed thereof to his own use and other wrongs to the Plaintiffs the Defendant then did against the Peace of our Lady the Queen and is the damage of the Plaintiffs of Company's Rupees five hundred and hereupon they bring suit &c.

Fort William in Bengal to wit.

Plaint filed on the 8th June 1880.

Plea of General Issue . . . And now in this third Term in the same year that is to say the fifteenth day of June in the year a foresaid, the Defendant by Thomas Bruce Swinhoe his Attorney; comes and defends the wrong and injury when &c. and says that he is not guilty of the said Trespasses in the said Plaint above laid to his charge or of any part thereof and of this he puts himself upon the Court &c.

Replication of Similiter. . . . . and the Plaintiff as to the Plea of the Defendant by him above pleaded and whereof he hath put himself upon the Court doth the like.

And now in the said third Term in the same year that is to say the Twenty-ninth day of July in the year aforesaid at which day here come the parties aforesaid by their Attorneys aforesaid, and the Justices of the Court of the Lady the Queen here having heard the respective allegations of the said parties as justice doth require and having examined the truth thereof and duly considered the evidence produced on both sides say that the said Louis Stuart Jackson is guilty of the said Trespass in the said Plaint above laid to his charge in manner and form as the said Gungaprosad Gossain and Gopeekristo Gossain have above complained against him and the said Justices adjudge the Damages of the said Gungapersad Gossain and Gopeekristo Gossain by the reason of the premises aforesaid over above their costs and charges by them about their suit in this behalf expended to Company's Rupees Fifty. Therefore it is considered that the said Gungaprosad Gossain and Gopeekristo Gossain do recover against the said Louis Stuart Jackson the said Company's Rupees Fifty for their damages adjudged as aforesaid and the said Louis Stuart Jackson in mercy &c.,

Judgment signed, the 2nd day of August 1847. W. Theobald, Prothonotary.

Let the Seal be affixed.
(Sd.) M. O. Wells.

(A true copy.)
(Sd.) W. Theobald Officiating Keeper of Records and Muniments.

MR. LOUIS JACKSON ON TOUR.

We cull the following from the *Hindoo Patriot* of 1876.

Mr. Justice Louis Jackson's report of his tour, visiting the Mofussil Courts, is replete with interest, and ought to have been published. We give the following extract from it containing a bitter personal complaint.

"The only point which I have now to notice is one of a somewhat personal kind, but which appears to call for attention.

During my recent journey I of course received every proper attention from all District Judges with whom I had actual business, but, with some exceptions my official visit was past unnoticed by the administrative district officers.

I name the exceptions: 1st from Mr. Peacock, the Officiating Commissioner at Dacca, from the District officers at Darjeeling, Mr. Edgar and Mr. Paul, and from the Magistrate of Purniah, Mr. Kemble, I met with the utmost courtesy; Mr. Barton, the Magistrate of Backergunje, was also attentive and obliging.

But the Magistrates of Dacca, Tipperah and Rajshaye and the Deputy Commissioner of Sylhet, omitted even the compliment of visit. I am far from wishing to imply that the inattention on the part of these officers was purposely discourteous, and a point of private courtesy is one upon which each person judges for himself. But I conceive that a Judge of the High Court of Judicature visiting a civil station on public duty is entitled to expect that the chief authorities of the station should wait upon him and offer their services.

I am persuaded also that the Lieutenant-Governor would consider this a part of their duty.

It may therefore, if my colleagues agree, be fitly brought in a demi-official manner to the notice of His Honor in order that gentlemen who are ignorant of this duty in this respect may be therein instructed.

Apropos of Mr. Justice Louis Jackson's complaint of want of attention to him on the part of District officers whilst he was on tour during the last Dusserah vacation, the *Bengal Times* gives the following anecdote. A trading firm in Calcutta once sent Mr. Jackson a bill directed "Lt. L. S. Jackson." It was the merest oversight. Foaming with rage says the *Times*, came Mr. Jackson, bill in hand, and summoning the head of the establishment, *repudiated* in set terms of bitter sarcasm the *honour* of serving Her Majesty as a Lieutenant! "I would have you know, Sir," he exclaimed, "that my title is the Honourable Louis Stuart Jackson, one of the Judges of the High Court of Judicature at Fort William in Bengal, and *not* a Lieutenant, Sir, *not* a Lieutenant, and he who is ignorant of the fact can know very little."

SIR CHARLES ROBERT MITCHELL JACKSON IN THE LEGISLATIVE COUNCIL IN 1861.

Sir Charles Jackson moved "that a message be forwarded to the Right Honourable the Governor-General in Council requesting his Lordship in Council to inform this Council what progress had been made in erecting a prison at the Neelgheries, and what accomodation such prison will afford for European and American convicts sentenced to penal servitude."

Mr. Laing opposed this resolution on the ground that the Council had no power to ask such questions.

Sir Barnes Peacock supported the motion. The Council then divided on the motion as follows :—

Ayes.	Noes.
Sir Charles Jackson	Mr. Laing
Mr. Erskine	Mr. Beadon
Mr. Sconce	Sir Bartle Frere
Mr. Harington	
Sir B. Peacock	(Vide F. I. March 14, 1861.)

It was in 1862, Sir Charles Jackson convicted, for the first time in the history of Criminal Administration of this country, a European soldier by the name of John Rudd of the murder of a native at Sealcote, and sentenced him to be hanged. The non-official European Community headed by Mr. Longueville Clarke raised a howl against this just sentence and appealed to Lord Elgin, but to no purpose. (Vide our book called "*Record of Criminal cases as between Europeans and natives.*

THE HON'BLE JUSTICE BUDD PHEAR AND THE CALCUTTA UNIVERSITY.

The *Englishman*, in its issue of March 10, 1869 thus wrote as to why the Hon'ble Justice Phear resigned his seat in the Senate :—

"Well: the Vice-Chancellors since the establishment of the University in 1857 have been, Sir James Colville, Mr. Ritchie, Mr. Erskine,——*protem*,. Mr. Maine, Mr. Maine again, and Mr. Seton-Karr. Soon after the appointment of Mr. Seton-Karr, Mr. Phear resigned his seat in the Senate. If all that we have heard be true, the provocation that he received was quite enough to explain his subsequent conduct. It is no secret that Mr. Maine recommended Mr. Justice Phear as his successor, and the Viceroy, in neglecting that recommendation in favour of a civilian put a slight upon that gentleman." .

The Hon'ble Justice Phear was a great friend of the natives. At a social party he requested the Hon'ble Justice Dwarkanath Mitter to receive the lady of a European Civilian. This was taken as an insult by the Civilians and non-official Europeans, and it is said that in consequence Mr. Justice Phear was almost out-casted.

CALCUTTA SUPREME COURT JUDGES AND SOME BARRISTERS AND WHEN THEY WERE CALLED TO THE BAR.

Sir E. Ryan	...	June 23, 1817
Sir J. P. Grant	...	Feb. 1, 1802
Sir H. W. Seton	...	June 20, 1809
Mr. Prinsep	...	June 1, 1817
M. Turton	...	Feb. 6, 1818
Mr. Clarke	...	June 25, 1819
Mr. Lawrence Peel	...	May 7, 1824

CHAPTER VI.

An anonymous correspondent wrote the following in the *Statesman* of May 16, 1877, on the subject of Government officers contributing to the press.

I shall begin by going back to a date when the oldest daily, the *Englishman*, had no existence. The Reverend Dr. Bryce, a Scotch divine, though not a Government chaplain, still held an appointment under Government, conferred upon him, as it was supposed, on account of his systematically supporting the Government, and was the acknowledged editor of the *John Bull.* (i) The *India Gazette* (ii) had at one time or another, contributors upon its staff, who were also in the service of the state. The journal was merged in the *Bengal Hurkura*, (iii) and it would be vain to attempt to enumerate all the public servants that wrote for that once influential journal, belonging to every branch and department of the Government Service. A few names may be given, some of which may perhaps call up interesting associations. Henry Meredith Parker of the Civil Service, one of the most gifted

---

(i) The *John Bull* assumed the name of the *Englishman* and the *Military Chronicle* in 1835.

(ii) It was edited by Mr. Adam.

(iii) The *Bengal Hurkura* was first established in 1795. The first proprietors were Babu Dwarka Nath Tagore, Colonel Young, and Mr. Samuel Smith.

·men that ever came out to this country, was a constant writer in the columns of the *Hurkura*. Some of his fugitive literary productions are still read with pleasure, in the volumes bearing the quaint title of *Bol Ponjia*. His dashing and valuable letters, under the *nom de plume* of the *Ghost of a Salt Officer*, attracted the attention of Lord William Bentinck, who used to say that there was nothing like the *Ghost of a Salt Officer*. It is needless to add that Parker was not removed from his appointment, until he was promoted. One of his contemporaries, Dr. John Grant, who belonged to the regular Medical Service, and held the appointment of Apothecary-General in Calcutta, was a prolific writer for the local press, specially for the *Hurkura*, and avowedly so : and he scribbled on to the end without let or hinderance from the authorities. Charles Becket Greenlaw (i), the well-known Secretary to the Marine Board, and Coroner of Calcutta, but historically famed as the great Apostle of Steam Navigation, whose bust adorns the Town Hall, was a contributor to the *Hurkura*, and it was chiefly by his unflagging and vigorous agitation in the Press, that a speedy consummation of the Steam question was obtained for the public. James Sutherland, the immediate successor of Buckingham, afterwards the editor-in-chief of the *Hurkura*, was in the later years of this life forced to assume the livery of Government (ii); although in his journalistic capacity he had twice been threatened with deportation. He held first the position of a Collegiate Professor, and then the office of Secretary to

(i) A public meeting was held on the 27th January 1843, to present an address and a piece of plate to Mr. Charles Becket Greenlaw for his successful labours in the cause of Steam Communication between England and India. D. Elliot Esq, Mr. G. A. Bushby, Mr. H. Torens, Mr. F. J. Halliday, Messrs. Irving and McFier, Dr. Gordon, Mr. J. Allen, Mr. Adam Smith, Mr. George Thompson, Babus Dwarka Nath Tagore and Prosunna Kumar Tagore attended the meeting. The venerable Archdeacon T. Dealtry was in the chair. Babu Dwarka Nath Tagore moved the presentation of a piece of plate. Mr. George Thompson made a masterly speech on the occasion. (B. H. Jan. 28, 1843.)

(ii) He was made a school-master at Hooghly, by Lord William Bentinck in 18‥

the Marine. But througout his official career, he never ceased to write leaders for the *Hurkura*.

And then I may mention Lieutenant J. W. Kaye of the Artillery, afterwards Sir John Kaye, the so-called "Historian of India." He first tried his "prentice hand" on the *Literary Gazette*, which was issued weekly from the *Hurkura* Press, and was acknowledged to possess greater merit than its London namesake. The young artillery officer fired off his first round of squibs and crackers in the columns of the *Calcutta Literary Weekly*, but he had a Herculean humourist to compete against in the columns of the *Englishman*, under the sobriquet of Number Nip, also a military officer. The contest, week after week, was found to be unequal, and the artilleryman had in the end to surrender at discretion to the bayonet charge of the infantry officer. All the times Kaye was writing of the *Literary Gazette*, he was also contributing leaders for the *Hurkura*. And it must not be forgotten that throughout this part of his career, he was borne on the effective roll of the Bengal Army, and not the shadow of an objection was ever suggested to the connection of a military officer with the press. The *Literary Gazette* referred to, calls to mind Captain David Lester Richardson, (i) better known at the time as D. L. R., and remembered with affection by Degumber Mittra and natives of his class, education, and age. D. L. R. (ii) was on the Government educational staff and while thus a public servant, never abated his habitual lucubrations, but continued to wield the pen literary as well as the pen political, and was never called upon by authority to desist from his occupation. Before leaving the *Hurkura*, it will not be *mal a propos* to revert to the letters of *Ghost of Goinda* published in that journal, which stirred up Lord Dalhousie to appoint a police commission, that brought to light an organised system of iniquity that would have been denied credence but for undeniable and absolute proof of the fact. The author of this great *expose*, which caused so much local excitement at the time, was also a servant of Government, as in the case of another *Ghost* mentioned above, and was the instrument of saving the Goverament from further disgrace and the public from further depredation. *Number Nip* of the *Englishman* also throws back memory to pleasant literary reminiscences of long, long ago. Who was he ?

(i) From the middle of the year 1829, to the end of 1836, he was employed in editing *the Calcutta Magazine, the Calcutta Literary Gazette, and the Bengal Annual*.

(ii) In 1836 he was appointed Professor of Literature in the Hindoo College.

Why, another military hero like Kaye, more valiant and irresistible with his pen than his sword : to wit, Captain Robin Adair McNaughten, also of the Bengal Army. His facile, fascinating, and powerful pen was wielded from Agra to Calcutta while he was still in the army, and holding an appointment in the Judge Advocate-General's Department ; and he was never charged with conduct unbecoming an officer for writing in the papers. At the period I am alluding to, the *Friend of India* of Serampore, with John Clarke Marshman at the helm, who also was proprietor of a flourishing paper mill, drew a good deal of public attention on account of its exclusive Government information as it was thought, and its proprietor having the monopoly of supplying paper of a certain quality to all the Government establishments all over the country. In all such cases, some little invidious innuendo and exaggeration is always to be expected, and the expectation was not belied in this instance. The general feeling ran high in this direction, and the Calcutta dailies kept up the fire day after day in such a manner, that the equanimity and gravity of the Serampore hebdomadal were shaken for once and in an article, meant to be sarcastic and satirical, it met the taunt of being a hireling organ, with the well-known distich—

I am His Highness's dog of Kew,

Pray tell me, Sir, whose dog are you ?

This brought forth a stinging article in the columns of the *Indian Times*, which was under the joint editorial management of Captain Frank Palmer—a retired cavalry officer and the eldest son of the famed John Palmer, the prince of Calcutta merchants and good fellows—and Mr. Chick. As might have been expected, the *Friend* of those days, who was very pious, took to a "serious" mood forthwith. But as a key to the clear understanding of what has been stated respecting the *Friend of India*, it is only necessary to mention that several in the service of Government, such as Henry Lawrence, Havelock, R. Temple, contributed to that much-favored, and no doubt very able journal, and amongst others no less a personage than Frederic Halliday Esquire, the first Lieutenant-Governor of Bengal. Harking back to a somewhat anterior date, it is possible to produce a lengthy list of names of public servants, who, though writing for the Calcutta Press, were not brought to grief. Just one or two names may be given here. Mr. Michael Crow, (i) who at the time of his death was holding the post of Collector of Calcutta, regularly wrote for the Press, and avowedly so, and yet it did not prejudice his official prospects. Mr. Blackburn was a clerk in a Government office, because to one of his class it was not open to him to be anything else except perhaps a butler, or cook. Moderately educated, while driving the quill at his desk, he put himself through a laborious course of literary culture. His maiden efforts gave encouragement ; he went further and prospered, till he was induced in a short time to throw *keraneedom* to the dogs, along with the grinding and ungrateful service in a Government office. He took up a position more suitable to his independence of spirit and taste, that namely, of sub-editor of the *Englishman*. The enterprising, spirited, and gifted gentleman I am referring to, went to England, and for many years was the proprietor and editor of the London *Spectator*. All the time, however, that Blackburn remained in a Government office he wrote for the Press, as was generally known at that time, without detriment to himself from official quarters. One other name I shall only here note, that of Mr. William Kirkpatrick. He was one of the most extraordinary men of the time, of rare ability and varied and sterling talent, but of a peculiar moral temperament and want of tact, which combined, very much counteracted the force of his fine intellect. He did not always put himself in official harness, but he was an inveterate "scribbler" always. He was for a time Registrar of the Sudder Court, a most important and difficult office, and even then he "scribbled" for the Press, for the *cacoethes*

(i) He was the Editor of the *Reformer* and was for many years employed as head draftsman in Quartermaster General's office, and afterwards as Interpreter of the vernacular languages in the Calcutta Police Court, and was the Uncovenanted Head of the Settlement Department under Mr. Lowis. He was then appointed a special Deputy Collector for the purpose of measuring Calcutta and Punchannagram. Mr. James Prinsep, the Assay-master of Calcutta also edited the *Calcutta Courier* for some time.

is a disease which the Faculty are unable to deal with up to this day. Yet Kirkpatrick was never brought to task for his *cacoethes scribendi.* But I must hasten on to a close, although I might have prolonged my garrulous gossip almost indefinitely. I have made allusion to the *Friend,* the *Hurkura,* and the *Englishman,* I have had quite enough, as you will probably say, of "calling o' names" regarding the *Hurkura.* To the nomenclature connected with the *Friend,* I could, if time permitted, make extensive addition. I shall, however, add only one more—a man for the times, ambitious and of good address. I refer to a stage of existence of the Serampore journal when Dr. George Smith was editor, &c. It was then that George Kellner wrote for that paper, and that paper wrote for him ; and yet, although a Government servant, the Government promoted him. I fear I am encroaching on your patience and space. I shall refer just to one or two Calcutta journals and some particulars connected with them and I have done.

The first is the *Eastern Star,* a weekly, that became strong enough to be a daily, entitled the *Calcutta Star.* The projector, proprietor, and editor was James (i) Hume, barrister. A troop of literary friends assisted him in his enterprise, the history of which is apart from the present purpose. Amongst his friends, James Hume was ably supported by the contributions of Henry Torrens, Civil Servant, and Col. Broome. Neither the one or other of Hume's coadjutors came to grief, or was ever called to question on account of their press connection. It should not for a moment be forgotten that the main object of this paper, is to shew that the connection of Government servants with the press has not, in local history been regarded with the same inimical eye as of late. Perhaps no stronger example can be quoted than that of the *Phœnix* in 1857. That journal was started the year before, Mr. Chick being editor and part proprietor, while he was at the same time in Government service in the Marine De

---

(i) He was the Police Magistrate of Calcutta and Justice of the Peace. He was Secretary to the races. He was proprietor and editor of the *India Sporting Review,* and Secretary to, and General correspondent of the Agricultural and Horticultural Association. He was the acknowledged proprietor and editor of the *Calcutta Star.* He was a Director of the Inland Steam Navigation Company.

partment. It is not necessary to revert to the excitement caused in Calcutta by the terrible events of '57. The *Phœnix* was the best informed journal of the day, alike in respect to priority, correctness, and completeness of its intelligence. And how did this happen to be so ? At a time of public commotion, excitement, and panic, the Editor applied in the proper quarter to be furnished, from time to time, with authentic intelligence, on the condition that he would studiously refrain from giving publicity to bazaar rumours and sensational gossip. The application was immediately granted, and in accordance with the arrangement a short-hand writer was sent daily to the Military Secretary, General Sir Richard Birch, for the substance of all intelligence of the day received by Government. The Private Secretary likewise, at all hours, sent items of news of importance to the editor, and if of urgency, even at midnight. Very different this from the principle and practice of the present *regime*, and so much for the idle and narrow-minded objection raised against the connection of Government servants with the press. Just one more, and the most recent and most condemnatory example, which I shall state in two words and conclude. The *Observer*, (i) a weekly, started only a very few years ago, was uncompromising, scholarly, and clever; and that very able journal, in the literary getting up, represented, in *personnel*, the Civil Service, the Army, its Education Department, and the Uncovenanted Service. What more shall I say ?   C. E.

THE ORIGIN OF THE ENGLISHMAN.

Mr. Joakim Hayward Stocqueler, thus described the establishment of the *Englishman* newspaper in 1835.

"I had not a shilling, but I had faith in the chapter of accidents. Time was allowed for the payment of the capital, and I looked about for a friend to supply me with the means of commencing operations. I found in Dwarkanath Tagore—a Hindoo who loved Englishmen and generously encouraged every enterprize from Ram Mohun Roy's dream of Hindoo conversion to the extinction of Toryism, which he knew meant obstruction. Adieu to the *Bengal Herald* and wel-

(i) The *Indian Observer* was first established in February, 1871. The paper ceased to exist in 1875, when its good-will was purchased by Mr. Robert Knight, editor of the *Statesman*

come the *Englishman,* for so I now named the paper which had so long offended liberal nostrils as the *John Bull.*"

Mr. Stocqueler thus described the moral atmosphere of Calcutta in 1835 when he started the *Englishman* newspaper :

"Sam. Smith of the *Hurkura* dared not tell Alexander and Co. they were scoundrels ; he owed the house seven lakhs of rupees. Wm. Adam could not allow Macintosh &c Co. to be abused in the *India Gazette,* for it had been their paper ; and George Prinsep, who edited the *Courier,* was an ex partner of the great house of Palmer & Co. "Rogues all !" Happily I had no such scruples. True I had bought the *effete John Bull* [then edited by a Mr. Bignel, who always fell asleep at dinner before the cloth was removed] from the assignees of Cruttendon & Co ; but though they would have *burked* the expression of opinions adverse to the Agency Houses, if they could, I knew that I was in a condition to bear their hostility and so opened the pages of the *Englishman* to the complaints of the sufferers —the destitute widow—the indigent orphan—all, in fact, who had lost their property."

He said that when he founded the *Englishman,* he had Sir John Peter Grant, a puisne judge of the Supreme Court of Calcutta, and Mr. Leith, Q. C. as contributors. He had also another Barrister on his 'staff'. He thus wrote about him.

"I found a suitable henchman in Charles Thackeray barrister by profession, nothing in particular by practice. Bachus claimed him, and he had long yielded to the seductive influences of the rosy deity. In a word he was drunk every day of his life, and consequently never was employed by attorneys. He despised *briefs* and adored brandy. Sending for him I proposed that he should join the staff, and do the grievance bussness. He consented. The terms were 10 rupees and a bottle of claret for each heading article, long or short. Every day at eleven he came to the office only *half* gone from matutinal, 'pick-me ups.' I put him into a room with a sheet of foolscap, pens, ink and the bottle of claret. By 1 P. M., the article was written, the bottle emptied, and the 10 rupees sacked. Thackeray staggered home. The editorials were vigorous homethrusts, *in vino veritas.* Nor did Thackeray confine himself to the Agency rascalities. He became a thorn in the side of the Magistrates and the judges of the Small Cause Court. Detecting the Judges' flaws in their decrees he held them up to popular scorn in withering articles which would have led the O'Hanlons, Blaquieres, Macfarlanes and Hares to resign the po ts they so inadequate-

filled, but that the *dives pecunia* supplied a balm to their wounded pride."

In July 184:, the *Englishman* passed into the hands of Captain MacNaghten.

Joachim Hayward Stocqueler, Proprietor and Editor of the *Englishman* got the benefit of an Insolvent in 1841.

(*Hurk.* January 11, 1841.)

THE *ENGLISHMAN* AND THE *MILITARY CHRONICLE*

IN 1837.

It was published by Mr. Rushton for the Proprietor. Mr. J. H. Stocqueler, in his issue of the 3rd January, 1837 stated that he got permission from the Sudder Dewany Adalut "to publish, occasionally, the letters of the Sessions Judges, reporting criminal cases, together with the orders, circulars &c. of the court. The Sudder Board of Revenue also permitted the Editor to publish its proceedings. (*Eng.* Jany 3, 1837.)

Mr. A. HILLS VERSUS HURISH CHUNDER MUKHER-JEA, THE EDITOR OF THE *HINDU PATRIOT*.

We take the following from the *Friend of India* of February 13, 1862.

"During the height of the indigo controversy the *Hindoo Patriot* charged Mr. Archibald Hills with having carried off and violated a native woman named Huromony. The Missionaries, Messrs. Long and Bomwetsch, had brought similar charges of a vague character. He brought a suit against the printer and editor for defamation of character before Babu Taruk Nath Sen, Principal Sudder Ameen of the 24-Pergunpahs and laid the damages at Rs. 10,000. Mr. Bell, the barrister, appeared for the plaintiff, and Mr. Montriou for the defendants. Finally an apology was offered and accepted. A verdict to be entered for the plaintiff for nominal damages, but costs to be paid to the plaintiff upon the amount of suit as brought."

The Patriot Hurish Chunder died penniless in the cause of the down-trodden ryots of Bengal—an unique example of journalistic self-sacrifice, in the meantime, and his house at Bhowanipore was attached in execution of this decree for costs which were paid afterwards by some of the members of the British Indian Association. It appears from the *Hindoo Patriot* of 3rd March 1860, that the plaintiff in this case was not Mr. Archibald Hills, but one Mr. George Meares. Mr. Hills brought a criminal suit against Babu Hurish Chunder Mukherjea and his printer in the Supreme Court which refused his petition.

Mr. ROBERT KNIGHT ON THE PERMANENT SETTLEMENT QUESTION.

The late lamented Mr. Robert Knight, Editor of the *Statesman and Friend of India* was very kind to us. Since he started the above paper in 1876, we began to contribute to its columns, first as a mufusil correspondent from our native town of Krishnaghur, then as its paid reporter, and lastly as one of its paid mufusil correspondents. In this way, we had the good fortune of coming in contact with this great journalist.

The following letter, Mr. Knight wrote to us, in answer to our query as to whether he had had any recollection of any particular controversy with the late Babu Kristo Das Pal for whose biography we were in 1886 collecting materials.

The Statesman;

Chowringhee.

Calcutta, September 13, 1886.

My Dear Mr. Ram Gopal,

I think I was editing the *Times of India* from about June 1868 down to the end of November 1868, but I do not remember any special discussion of the Permanent Settlement Question at the time. It was a very old conviction of mine that the Permanent Settlement was a fatal economic mistake, but my great battle in opposing its introduction into other Provinces of India was fought from 1859 to 1863. Sir Charles Wood's famous despatch sanctioning a permanent settlement for all India was dated I think July 1861 or July 1862. It was to get this despatch cancelled that I strove earnestly in England, and in 1866, I had the satisfaction of seeing it given up.

Yours Sincerely

Babu Ram Gopal Sanyal.   (Sd.) R. KNIGHT.

MR. BUCKINGHAM, THE EDITOR OF HICKEY'S *CALCUTTA JOURNAL*, ESTABLISHED IN 1781.

"On one occasion, Bishop Middleton was "put in a huff" by a letter on the duties of chaplains—though it was not half so pungent or offensive as the *Englishman's* imaginary dialogue between the statue of Bishop Heber and that of Lord William Bentinck. His Lordship "peremptorily called on Government to enforce the restrictions on the Press," and the then Chief Secretary, Mr. Butterworth Bayley, was reluctantly constrained to inform Mr. Buckingham, that "if he continued this course of conduct, his license to reside in India would be at once annulled, and he would be required to furnish security for quitting the country at the first convenient opportunity." But Mr. Buckingham set the rules at defiance, and was deported from the country not by Lord Hastings but by his successor. (F. I. September 23, 1847.)

THE CALCUTTA EDITORS REWARDED BY THE GOVERNMENT PRIOR TO 1840.

The. *Englishman* of January 30th, 1840, thus wrote on the subject.

"We are happy to announce that the steady and zealous advocacy of Government, on the part of our Sreerampur contemporary, has at last received its appropriate reward. Mr. John Marshman has been appointed Translator of Drafts, Acts, and other public documents with a salary of Rs. 800 per mensem. It is a fashion now-a-days to reward Indian Editors for their services and dis-services.

Mr. James Sutherland of the *Hurkura* was made School-Master at Hoogly, in consideration of his good opinion of Lord Wilam Bentinck towards the close of his Lordship's administration.

A military Editor of the *Literary Gazette* was created an aid-de-camp, in consideration of his dedicating *Annuals* to Lady William Bentinck. He further more obtained a snug place in the Hindu College." (i)

Mr. William Adam, Editor of the *India Gazette*, was appointed head (and tail) of a commission to enquire into the state of Native Education on Rs. 1,000 a month, because he abused the government.

The Editor of the *India Gazetto* was, while in India, offered the appointment of Secretary to the Committe of Public Instruction, on a salary of Rs. 1,200 per mensem, but he demanded Rs. 1800, which being refused, he declined the appointment. He published a work from England called *the Indian Year Book* in 1841. (*Calcutta Literary Gazette*, January 3, 1841.)

THE EDITOR OF THE *BHASHKUR* NEWSPAPER, AND THE RAJA OF ANDUL.

Babu Sreenath Roy, Editor of the *Bhaskur* was kidnapped by twenty or twenty five armed Hindoosthanee door-keepers of Raja Raj Narain Roy of Andul, in the district of Howrah. At 8 A. M., of the 13th January, 1840, while the editor was getting into a hackery near the Patuldanga road, he was seized, gagged, assaulted, stripped almost naked, was taken to Pathuriaghatta, because nearly three weeks ago, he had published a letter in his weekly Bengali paper called the *Rushoraj*, alleging that the Raja had brought about a marriage of two Brahmins with low caste women,

---

(i) Captain D. L R. was appointed by Lord William Bentinck to succeed Mr. Troyer as aide-de-camp. In 1839, he was appointed an aide-de-camp to the Deputy-Governor, Col. Morrison.

and giving currency to a rumour that the Rajah's mother once threw him into the river, so that there might not be any interruptions of her pleasures.

A writ of *Habeas Corpus*, in the above case, was served on Raja Raj Narain Roy on the 13th January, 1840, at Mr. Higgin's office. The Editor was removed from Andool to a place three miles distant therefrom.

BEFORE SIR E. RYAN, SIR J. P. GRANT, AND SIR H. W. SETON.

Mr. Turton, the Advocate-General moved the Supreme Court for a writ of *Habeas Corpus* on behalf of the Editor. The affidavits stated that the deponents saw the Raja present in his own compound at Andool, and that his people were applying leaves (অৰ বিছুটী) which produced great pain and irritation to the flesh of Sree Nath Roy, who was apparently shrieking from agony and crying for justice.

On the following day, i. e. the 15th January, the return to the *Habeas Corpus* was made, and merely denied that Raja Raj Narain was liable to the jurisdiction of the Supreme Court.

Mr. Turton, with whom Mr. Clarke appeared, said he took an objection *in limine* to this. The affidavits stated that the seizure was made in Calcutta ; and that the Rajah had a residence within the town. The seizure, and the imprisonment were here, and it was too much to say one who had also a residence on the other side of the Maharatta Ditch might walk across, and commit such an outrage, and return back to the side from whence he came, and defy the power of this Court.

Sir E. Ryan then told Mr. Turton that the Court would hear him on that point.

Mr. Prinsep after quoting some authorities, and remarking upon the statements of the affidavits being vague, said, that he would maintain that the Court was bound to take

21

the facts as stated in the return to the *Habeas Corpus* to be true, though unsupported by affidavits ; and if so, the opinion of the highest authorities was that no one was subject to a writ of *Habeas Corpus*, unless he was *generally* liable to the jurisdiction of the Court, whereas the Raja at most was only liable for the particular offence, and for that an indictment might be made.

Mr. Leith argued on the same side.

Sir E. Ryan said that the Court would not trouble the Counsel on the other side to reply, the opinion of the whole Court was so strong that the *return was bad.* It was quite sufficient that the facts as stated in the affidavits raised a strong presumption sufficient to warrant the using of the writ of *Habeas Corpus.* In the present case the offence had been committed within the jurisdiction, and removing out of the jurisdiction subsequently cannot take from the Court the power to protect and to release in such a case the person oppressed.

Mr. Prinsep then moved for a leave to amend the return.

Sir E. Ryan. No. It is not a case for amendment.

Mr. Turton. My Lord, they had better mend their ways.

Return bad and an attachment 'was issued against Raja Raj Narain. (Vide *Englishman,* 17th March, 1840.)

On the 28th January, Raja Raj Narain surrendered to the Supreme Court to clear his attachment. Mr. Prinsep and Mr. Leith appeared for the defence to argue that upon the affidavits filed, the defendant was entitled to be admitted to bail to answer the necessary interrogatories.

Mr. Turton and Mr. Clarke stated for the prosecution that, not only on those affidavits, but on others contradicting them, the Raja ought to be committed for contempt of Court until he had answered the interrogatories.

Sir E. Ryan C. J. passed the following order.

"Raja Raj Narain Roy appears on an attachment issued from this Court. The affidavits filed on the opposite sides are totally contradictory, one stating that Sreenath Roy was liberated on the 17th, and the others that he is yet in custody. The Rule upon which he (the Advocate-General) relied is clearly laid down in *Blackstone's Commentaries* and various text books, and states that if it clearly appears that the party attached has been guilty of contempt, he must answer the interrogatories whilst kept in custody. Raja Raj Narain Roy's own affidavit confesses that he has been guilty of gross outrages; it further shews that the attachment was served upon him on the 14th, and yet he dared to retain Sreenath Roy in confinement. For this contempt of Court there is no justification. Let the Sheriff therefore take him into custody and detain him until he has answered the interrogatories.

On the 4th February, the Raja appeared again before the Clerk of the Crown to answer the interrogatories filed on behalf of Babu Sreenath Roy. Out of 39 interrogatories, only 8 were exhibited that day, but the Raja declined, as advised by his Counsel, to answer seven of them.

Mr. Prinsep moved for the expunging of the seven interrogatories and for bail. But the Chief Justice ordered the Raja to a further imprisonment until the 1st of March.

The Raja kept the editor in confinement not only in his house, but in the gardens of Babus Ashu Tosh Deb, and Kashi Prosad Ghose and shifted him from place to place.

The case was next heard on the 2nd March. Mr. Prinsep asked for bail which was refused.

On the 12th March, the case was again heard. Mr. Prinsep then moved to expunge certain of the interrogatories. After hearing the counsels on both sides, the Chief Justice ruled that the interrogatories which relate to the mode of treatment pursued towards Sreenath Roy, viz., the 8th, the greater part of the 9th, and the whole of the 10th, must be suppressed and referred back to the Clerk of the Crown office.

The case was finally heard on the 20th March, 1840 when Raja Raj Narain Roy was brought before the Court by *Habeas Corpus.*

Sir Edward Ryan, the Chief Justice delivered the following order

"Raj Narain Roy :—It now remains for this Court to ex-

press the opinion which it has formed of the contempt of
which you are confessedly guilty. You did not obey our,
writ, it has been said by one of your Counsel (Mr. Prinsep)
by his advice—that he advised you to return to the process
of this Court, that you were not liable to its jurisdiction; and
in the warmth of his advocacy he unadvisedly added that,
under the similar circumstances, he should again so advise.
With regard to the contempt committed, we shall certainly
lean to the side of mercy, because that contempt proceeds
no higher than to a contempt of the process of this Court.
You have already been a long time imprisoned. We have,
however, taken this length of imprisonment into consideration, and shall not add to it; but think the process of this
Court shall be sufficiently vindicated by imposing upon you a
fine of Rs. 1,000 to the Crown, until which is paid you must
continue in prison. (*Englishman*, March 21, 1840.)

THE HISTORY OF THE *SAMAOHAR DARPUN*.

It was first published on the 23rd May, 1818 and
stopped in 1841. Dr. Carey at first thought that the publication of such a Bengali journal imparting political knowledge to the people would not be liked by the Goverment.
But, on Dr. Marshman sending a copy of the first issue of
the paper to Lord Hastings, the Governor-General approved
of the paper. Soon after its appearance, Raja Ram Mohun
Roy established another Bengali paper, and the orthodox
Hindu community started the *Chundrika* under the editorial
management of Babu Bhobani Churun Bannerji.

In 1829, the *Darpun* became a diglot paper. During
Lord Amherst's administration several copies of the paper
were taken by the Government. The Editor published a
Persian edition of the paper, at that time.

In 1826, the Editor represented to the judges of the
Supreme Court that advertisements for the Sheriff's sales
should be published in Bengali in his paper, and the request

was granted. They subsequently appeared in the *Chundrika* and *Bhashkur.*

Lord Hastings, with the view of encouraging the under-taking, passed an order in Council for its being transmitted at one-fourth the usual charge for postage, and Lord Amherst subsequently subscribed on the part of Govern-ment for more than a hundred copies of it for the public offices. On the demise of this paper in 1841, another paper named *Sutya Prodip* appeared in 1850 from the Srecrampur Press. (F. I. Sept 19, 1850.)

THE ORIGIN OF THE "BOMBAY GAZETTE."

We take the following from the *Bombay Gazette* of 1894.

We cannot be much surprised—we certainly do not complain—that the *Calcutta Review* for July has been privileged to hear many particulars about the early ages of the *Bombay Gazette*, which, we confess, had escaped our memory. An anonymous writer, whose fine Roman hand, however, betrayeth him, in the course of some bright pages devoted to "Bombay Domestic Annals" gives a brief, but interesting, reference to the Press. The *Bombay Gazette* (i) and the *Courier* were established about 1790 ; and for forty years both papers continued to be weeklies. The *Courier* was founded by Mr. William Ashburner, of the Civil Service. It is satisfactory to know that in 1820 both papers were flourishing. On the last day of the next year, 1821, the then editor of the *Bombay Gazette*, Mr. Adolphus Pope, ex-Sheriff of Bombay, died at Poona. The Indian Press was greatly hampered at that period by the exorbitant postal charges for inland delivery. The Post Office, under a notification, published in England, refused to deliver a newspaper at any distance under half-a-rupee, which, at that time, meant one shilling and three pence, the rupee being from six pence to seven pence above the par of exchange. Is it not a case for some Dr. Faustus to implore the Demon—in default of a more beneficent Power—to roll back the cycle of seventy years ! In 1827, a certain Colonel M. Stanhope declared at the East Indian House, that although

---

(i) In the *Friend of India* of 1861, we read that the "first Bombay paper was the *Gazette*—not the same Journal of that name—which appeared in 1789. This discrepancy in these two statements, we were not in a position to correct. The *Bombay Gazette* became a daily paper in 1841, or as stated in the *Friend of India* in 1850.

Mr. Fair was the nominal owner of the *Bombay Gazette*, the real proprietor was Mr. Francis Warden (of Warden Road ?). This little circumstance seems to have given point to a remark that fell from the chief of the newly-constituted High Court   The first Chief Justice of Bombay deemed it his duty to declare that he would punish the editor and proprietor of the *Bombay Gazette* with both fine and imprisonment, and he deported Mr. Fair. His Lordship—Sir Edward West—also suspended five barristers including tde Advocate-General—a very terrible Chief Justice ! The year 1840 was disastrous to the personnel of the Bombay press. Within three months Mr. Rousseau, sub-editor of the *Courier*, died of cholera ; Mr. Callum, proprietor add editor of the *Bombay Gazette*, died of cholera at 29 ; Mr. Brennan, editor of the *Bombay Times*, and Secretary of the Chamber of Commerce, died of apoplexy, at the age of 36. We must not pass over an incident illustrative of the martial manners of the times. The editor of the *Bombay Gazette* in 1833 challenged Colonel Vans Kennedy ; the latter declined to fight, and was denounced in the columns of the paper as a slanderer and a coward. This led to an action for libel and a verdict in favour of the prudent Colonel for Rs. 500.

MR. GEORGE SMITH AND THE ANNALS OF
INDIAN ADMINISTRATION.

We take the following the *Hindoo Patriot* of August 10, 1874.

"As the Annals of Indian Administration has now reached its eighteenth annual volume, the present Editor, who has been responsible for its appearance since 1859, may thus put on record a few facts as to the origin and history of the publication. In 1856 Mr. Meredith Townsend submitted to Sir Cecil (then Mr.) Beadon, the Home Secretary, a plan for publishing an indexed epitome of the principal Reports annually issued by the Supreme and Provincial Governments, and of some of the Indian Blue-books laid before Parliament.

The first part appeared in that year. In 132 pages the Editor analysed just 2500. Soon afterwards he published a Thesaurus, or general index to all the published records of Government previous to 1856. Lord Canning then the Governor-General, expressed approval of the work, which continued to appear in quarterly parts. In 1863 Mr. George Smith L. L. D., obtained from Lord Elgin the appointment of the Calcutta Statistical Committee to draw up a uniform statistical system for the administration Reports annually submitted to Parliament. In that Committee Mr.

Bullen, President of the Bengal Chamber of Commerce, took charge of the commercial statistics, and Mr. R. H. Hallingberry of the financial statistics, both of which for all India are now promptly issued in monthly and annual volumes by the Financial Department. Dr. Smith drew up the plan and detailed tables of the present Administration Reports, and Sir George (then Mr. Justice) Campbell filled in the details of the Judicial portion of that plan. After a few years spent in referring the scheme to the Secretary of State and the Provincial Governments, it was finally adopted with a few modifications to suit local peculiarities. On the 23rd May 1873 the Government of India ordered the further development of the plan, by a division into five years' and one year's subjects."

RAJA KRISHNA NATH ROY BAHADUR,
VERSUS
THE EDITOR OF THE *RUSHORAJ*.

In the *Bengal Herald* of January 14, 1843, appeared the following.

(BEFORE SIR J. P. GRANT.)
January 13, 1839.

Raja Kishen Nath Roy Bahadur brought a libel suit "against the Editor for having accused him in his paper of unnatural crime," and his wife of—.Mr. Leith and Mr. Morton appeared for the prosecutor, and Mr. Hume, Mr. Theobald and Mr. Lang for the defence. He was convicted and sentenced to be imprisoned for six months, and to pay a fine of Rs. 500, and to enter into a recognizance in the sum of Rs. 1,000, and to find two sureties in the sum of Rs. 500 each, making it a condition not to publish any libel against the Raja for one year after the date of his imprisonment.

It was during this time, Raja Nursing Chunder Roy also brought a libel suit against Babu Gouri Shunker Bhuttacharjie, editor of the *Rushoraj*, and Sir John Peter Grant took a recognizance from him of Rs. 5000 requiring him to appear before the Court when summoned after the expiration of his term of imprisonment.

Mr. JAMES HUTTON, EDITOR OF THE *ENGLISHMAN*.

The *Madras Mail* wrote the following in 1877.

"The *Leader* was started some months ago by Mr. James Hutton, and it has been conducted by that gentleman with conspicuous ability ; but the metropolis seems a poor field for a weekly review, and Mr. Hutton leaves Calcutta for England in a day or two. He is one of the veterans of the Indian Press. He came out to this country as an Ensign in a Queen's regiment about thirty-five years ago, tumbled into a fine fortune, tumbled out of it, then applied himself to newspapering, and has edited the *Delhi Gazette*, the *Bengal Hurkura*, the *Englishman*, the *Madras Times*, and the *Leader*. His connection with this presidency was brief, and his retreat was not quite glorious ; but he gave us a taste of mature editorial qualities, and if he had not fallen foul of the Duke and Mr. Coleman, he would probably have been still among us ; but he lost his temper with those personages, and the *Madras Times* and Presidency lost him in consequence."

THE *PIONEER'S* ORIGIN.

Under Lord Mayo's administration the *Pioneer* was established as an independent organ, but we know that Mr. Girdlestone, a North-West civilian was permitted to edit the paper in its early days. The *Indian Observer* was suppressed by Lord Mayo, the Stracheys and Sir George Campbell who prohibited civilians not to write to that paper.

(H. P. May 24, 1875.)

MR. W. E. H. FORSYTH.

Mr. W. E. H. Forsyth, Clerk of the Crown, High Court, and Assistant Secretary to the Government of Bengal was for some time the editor of the *Indian Observer*. He was popularly beleived to be the author of the article called "*Tiberius*" published in the *Observer*. He died in 1881.

(H. P. February 28, 1881.)

THE *FRIEND OF INDIA*, MR. ADAM AND LORD HASTINGS.

In the Quarterly series of the *Friend of India* (i) published in 1819, a "temperate" article appeared against the practice of burning Shuttees. Mr. Adam, then one of the members of Council, and subsequently the Governor-General of India, went into Council with a proposal to suppress the *Friend* for that article. But Lord Hastings refused to interfere, as he saw nothing objectionable therein. (F. I. January 6th, 1848.)

SUBSIDY TO THE PRESS BY GOVERNMENT.

Lord Dalhousie at the time of his retirement allowed an annual grant of Rs. 8000 for its *Annals of Indian Administration*, commenced by Mr. Townsend as an independent publication in 1857. This subsidy was granted for his "unscrupulous advocacy" of the Annexation policy of that Governor-General. Lord Northbrook stopped this subsidy in 1875. It was Sir Cecil Beadon who first took away the paper contract from the Serampore press. The *Indian Economist* edited by Mr. Robert Knight while he was appointed Assistant Secretary to the Bengal Government during Sir George Campbell's regime was subsidized by Government to the extent of 800 copies or rupees per month.

THE *MUFUSSILITE*, AND MR. J. W. O'SULLIVAN.

We read the following in the *Hindu Patriot* of 1869.

"We are glad to see it announced that Mr. J. W. O'Sullivan has assumed charge of the *Mufussilite*. He is a veteran member of the Press. His life is a remarkable instance of self-culture. He was originally in the

---

(i) It became a weekly paper in 1835 with 45 subscribers, but at the close of 1858, the number rose to 3415. Such was the marvellous success of this semi-official and anti-native paper under the editorial management of Mr. Marshman, Mr. Meredith Townsend, Dr. George Smith, and Mr. James Routledge. It ceased to exist in 1875, after a prosperous and brilliant career of full forty years.

22

artillery, and for a few years served as an engineer in the Punjab on its occupation by the British. Being of an adventurous spirit he could not brook the fetters of an official life and joined the *Englishman* in 1865 as its reporter. He then became a teacher in the Hindu Metropolitan College. He again joined the staff of the *Englishman* as a contributor under Mr. Cobb Hurty. Subsequently, he became Editor of the *Phœnix* which he conducted with great spirit and independence. On the death of that paper he became a contributor to the leading papers of Calcutta and Bombay. For several years he was the Calcutta and Simla correspondent to the *Times of India*, and as such he had access to the highest society in Calcutta and Simla. He was the guest of Sir John Lawrence while at Simla. He was one of the few Anglo-Indian newspaper writers, who is at home on questions of local finance and land-tenures."

MR. WILLIAM RIACH, EDITOR OF THE *STATESMAN*.

Mr. William Riach edited the Calcutta *Statesman* from 1878 to 1883 during the absence of Mr. Robert Knight in England, with great ability and independence. He was a great friend of the natives whose cause he advocated with the warmth and ability of immortal Hurish Chundra Mukherjee. Mr. Riach's able articles on the Lokenathpur Murder Case, the materials for which were furnished by our humble selves and Mr. Mano Mohun Ghose of the Calcutta Bar produced a considerable sensation at the time. The history of this remarkable case will be found in the "Life of Mr. M. M. Ghose" in our work called "The Bengal Celebrities." Mr. Riach did a yeoman's service to the case of the free press of India, when he in a series of brilliant articles, opposed the passing of Lord Lytton's Gagging Act and ridiculed Mr. C. E. Buckland, the Press Commissioner, in an article written on the 5th July, 1879, for the miserable stuff he supplied to the public press. For this famous vituperative article, Mr. C. E. Buckland, with the sanction of Lord Lytton and his Council, stopped the press messages by way of revenge. But Mr. Riach in an elaborate letter published in the *Statesman* of July 21, 1879, cleared himself from the imputations cast upon him, and Lord Lytton was pleased to restore the press messages to the *Statesman.* We regret that, for want of space we can not reproduce here the official correspondence as well as the letters of Mr. Riach on this subject.

Mr. Riach was our great friend and patron. It was he who recommended us to Mr. Knight in 1879 for an appointment on the staff of the *Statesman.* As for the other anecdotes of this great journalist, we beg to refer our readers to "*The Bengal Celebrities*," p. 30—33.

An Evening Party was held at the Albert Hall in August 1883, in honour of Mr. Riach on his departure from this country. The Rev. Dr. K. M. Banerjee, Babu Kristo Das Pal, Dr. Mohendralal Sirkar, Babus Norendra Nath Sen and Surendra Nath Banerjee took a prominent part in this affair. About 150 native gentlemen, representing different sections of the educated community, were present

THE REMINISCENCES OF THE *AMRITA BAZAR PATRIKA.*

The origin of this Bengali newspaper, its gradual devolopment from a vernacular journal into a diglot one, its further rise from a diglot paper into a purely English weekly paper under the Gagging Act of Lord Lytton, and finally its transformation into a daily broad sheet journal immediately after the agitation of the famous Consent Act are subjects too long and exhaustive for this little volume. The history of this journal is unique of its kind, and requires a separate book. We therefore jot down below in this chapter some of the few stray reminiscences of this great journal which marks an epoch in Indian journalism conducted by the natives of this country.

THE *AMRITA BAZAR PATRIKA* AND ITS SATIRICAL WRITINGS.

One of the peculiar features of this native journal which insured its success to a no small degree was its satirical writings. In 1872 its famous editor Babu Shishir Kumar Ghosh perhaps wrote this political satire in that paper, which caused a considerable sensation at the time.

POLITICAL GEOMETRY CHAP 1st. DEF.

1. A Political point is that which is visible to the Government but invisible to the people.

2. A line of policy is length without breadth of views.

3. A Political figure is that which is enclosed in one side by ambition and another by hypocrisy.

4. A Political circle is a plane figure contained by one line of policy and is such that a certain point within this figure keeps the circumference firm and united.

5. And this point is called interest.

6. A Political triangle is a wedge which is usually gently introduced at the beginning of any new impost.

7. Parallel lines are lines of policy which though they never meet always tend to the same direction.

Chap, 2nd—Postulates.

1. Let it be granted that any tax may be imposed upon any sects or class of the people without their permission.

2. Let it be granted that any measure may be introduced or withdrawn at the pleasure of the Government.

3. Let it be granted that any promise may be made or broken provided there be a nominal pretext at hand.

4. Let it be granted that a deficit may be shown when there is a surplus.

Chap, 3rd. Axioms.

1. Might is always right.

2. England governs India for the good of the latter.

3. Things which have a black cover have also a black interior.

4. Things which have a white cover have also a white interior.

5. Black can never be white, neither white black.

6. The promise or opinion of one individual is equal to the promise or opinion of the whole nation.

PROP. 1st. PROBLEM,

Given a permanently settled Revenue on land to draw a road cess from it.
From the southernmost point of Bengal to the northernmost point

describe the condition of the Zemindars. Promise 19 guns to the Moharajah of Burdwan (Post 3) and impose (Post 1) an income tax. Take this point, which draw the cess and produce it to the ryots :

For one Zemindar the Rajah of Burdwan promised to pay the income tax and it is therefore binding on all Zemindars. (axiom 6.) Then because as the Road cess is drawn from the point where the income tax intersects the permanent settlement they are therefore parallel and the road cess is therefore drawn &o. &o.

Q. E. F.

Obs. Latterly Stifle attempted to prove this proposition by axiom 1st only.

Exercises on Prop. 1st.

1. Given the Road cess find the Educational cess, the Medical cess and other cesses.

THE *AMRITA BAZAR PATRIKA* AND SIR GEORGE CAMPBELL.

In 1872, a capital cartoon appeared in the pages of this paper by way of ridiculing Sir George Campbell's scheme of the appointment of Sub-Deputy Magistrates on their passing the test for horse-riding &c. The famous Bengali stanzas were these :

সেলামে মজবুত অশ্বারোহণেতে ।
শাঙুল স্থানে চেন কম্পাস কানেতে ॥
তিন হাত সাত ইঞ্চি দুই আঙুল পাছটী ।
আমাদের হুজুরের মনমত ডেপুটী ॥

(H. P. May 6, 1872.)

The cartoon was subsequently reproduced in the columns of the *Hindoo Patriot* then conducted by the late lamented Babu Kristo Das Pal to whom it was lent by Babu Shisir Kumar Ghosh, although there was great rivalry between these two journalists.

LORD LYTTON'S GAGGING ACT AND THE *AMRITA BAZAR PATRIKA.*

The late lamented Honourable Kristo Das Pal once told us that Sir George Campbell one day sent for him and requested him to exercise his influence over the Editors of the vernacular newspapers, with a view to moderate their tones, and also to speak to Babu Sishir Kumar to do the same.. He communicated the errand to him, but the *Amrita Bazar* fearlessly went on discharging its public duty, without giving the least consideration to this warning note. The paper became a thorn on the side of the Government, which at last thought of curbing its independence by enacting this execrable Act. But alas! even in this secret design, it was ignominiously. defeated. Babu Shishir Kumar Ghose and his brothers saw clearly with a prophetic political insight that the net was meant to be spread for them, and they rose equal to the occasion. They, on the other hand, secretly managed to get an English printer for their paper, and let it be said to their eternal credit and to the credit of Indian Journalism that on the very day, Lord Lytton and his Councillors passed the Gagging Act, the *Amrita Bazar Patrika* appeared in full English dress, to the great discomfiture of the rampant Anglo-Indian Government of that day, and to the bewilderment of friends and foes alike,

TABLE I. THE LIST OF *DEFUNCT* PAPERS BEFORE 1840.

The *Calcutta Christian Observer* for February, 1840.
furnished the following list of newspapers.

No.	NAMES.		EDITORS
	Weekly.		
1	Sumbad Kaumadi	...	Rajah Rammohan Roy.
2	do Timiranashak	...	Babu Kristo Mohan Dal
3	do Sudhakar	...	do Premchand Ray.
4	do Ratnakar	...	do Brojomohan Roy.
5	do Ratnavali	...	do Jagannath Mallik.
6	do Sarasangraha	...	do Benimadhab De.
7	Anubadhika	...	do Prasunna Kumar Takur.
8	Samachar Sabha Rajendra		do Moulavi Alimullah.
9	Sumbad Sudhasindhu	...	Babu Kali Sunkar Dutta.
10	„ Gunakar	...	Babu Grish Chandra Bose.
11	„ Mritunjayi	...	Babu Parbati Charan Das. (i)
12	Dibakar (monthly)	...	Babu Ganganarayan Bose.
13	Bigyan Swubodhi	...	Messrs N. W. Woollaston and Babu Gangacharan Sen.
14	Gyanodoy	...	Babu Ram Chandra Mitter.
15	Gyanashindhu Taranga	...	Babu Russik Kishen Mullik.
16	Animal Biography	...	Babu Ram Chandra Mitter.

(i) Nearly all verse, but not of good composition.

| No. | Names. | Editors. | Date of Commencement, Years. | Circulation Town/Dak. | | Monthly Price. | | | How Supported. |
				T.	M.	Rs.	As.	P.	
1.	Samachar Darpan.	1. J. C. Marshman.	1819.	350	160	1	0	0	By Subscribers and Sheriff's Advertisements.
2.	" Chundrika.	2. Babu Bhabani Charan Banerjee.	1822.	86	6	1	0	0	By the Dharma Sabha.
3.	Gyananahun.	3. Ramchandra Mitter.	1831.	45	4	1	0	0	By the Hindu Collegians.
4.	Shumbad Purnachundra.	4. Uday Chand Adya.	1835.	778	55	0	4	0	By Subscribers and Commisariat advts.
5.	" Probhakar.	5. Ishwarchandra Gupta.	1836.	124	7	1	0	0	By the Thakur Family and Sheriff's advts.
6.	" Sandamini.	6. Kaliachand Dutta and friends.	1838.	78	2	0	8	0	By Hindu Benevolent Institution.
7.	" Bhaskar.	7. Sreenath Roy.	1839.	70	15	1	0	0	By Subscribers and the Deb Family.
8.	Banga Dut or Bengal Herald	8. Raj Narain Sen.	1839.	50	0	0	8	0	By Subscribers and Baba Bholanath Sen.
9.	Sambad Roshoraj or Sentimental.	9. Kali Kanta Gunguli.	1839.	150	0	0	4	0	By certain native youth unknown.
10.	" Arunodoy or the Dawn.	10. Jagannarayan Mukherjee and friends.	1839.	500	70	1	0	0	

J. O. B. SAUNDERS, Esq.

We take the following from the *Englishman* of the 18th July, 1879.

The connection of J. O'B. Saunders with the Press in India dates back for at least ten years before the Indian mutiny, when he held a share in the *Delhi Gazette*. In 1849 he went to Delhi from his indigo factory at Hattrass, as manager of the paper, when Mr. Place returned to England. The editor of the *Delhi* in those days was the brilliant Henry Mead who used to say of himself that god made him an editor and the devil made him a speculator ; and it must be confessed that the diabolical influence was the stronger. He was ever going to make his fortune, in some clever speculation ; fortune, however, did not come except at last in the cruel form of a sudden and terrible death by drowning in the Hooghly. The story (i) of the accident by which he and others lost their lives may almost be forgotten now in Calcutta, although the doughty John Blessington Roberts, the sole survivor of the party, lives to tell the tale. Mead's latest effort of speculative genius was a method of solidifying castor oil for export so as, by diminishing the bulk of the ordinary cask stowage, to secure reduced freight. So far he was successful, but it was discovered, when the solidified castor oil got to England, that the cost of liquefying again came to double what the ordinary freight would have cost. Mead, who had been seduced from the *Madras Atheneum* to take the command of the *Delhi Gazette*, did not remain long as

---

(i) He was drowned in the River Hooghley on Saturday the 6th September, 1862. The Agent of the Oriental Inland Steam Company had invited a party to a private trial trip of the new Steamer *Ganges*. Mr. Mead who was then editor of the *Hurkura*, with several others took to an unsafe boat and was engulphed in the river. In the early part of his Indian career, he was Editor of the *Madras Atheneum*, which he left to engage in unfortunate mercantile speculations in Burmah. He then edited the *Delhi Gazette* in 1850. His connexion of a few months with the *Friend of India* in 1857 was remarkable for the article he wrote on the "Centenary of Plassey."

After a chequered career in England and Ceylon, Mr. Mead was made Editor of the *Hurkura* in 1862 when he died. (F. I. Sept. 11, 1862.)

23

editor of the latter journal. His fame is better known in
connection with the *Friend of India*, when, as temporary
editor of that journal in 1857, he wrote the brilliant article
which has now a place in the history of the mutiny,—"The
Centenary of Plassey," and brought down upon the paper the
angry wrath of the Governor-General in Council, which forced
Mead to resign the editorial chair in order to save the *Friend
of India* from suspension. At Delhi Mead was not a success
as an editor, so J. O'B. Saunders took up the reins himself.
He got from Mussoorie James Hutton, another name familiar
to Indian ears, recalling recollections of one who lives to
wield in London the brilliant, if somewhat biting, pen which
made foes fear him in the East. George Wagentrieber, editor
of the *Delhi Sketch Book*, which has had no worthy successor
yet, came as Sub-Editor ; and the *Delhi* flourished grandly
in those days. It was the most profitable and the most
powerful paper in India, and J. O'B. Saunders used often to
boast that no change of Time or circumstance could kill it.
So far the prophecy remains true, and the "Old *Delhi*" has
still many friends ; but time has not been merciful to it, nor
spared it for the bright old age which its editor, the subject
of this memoir, enjoyed. This, however, is a world of change
even for newspapers,—and *resurgam* may yet be echoed
from Agra.

In the autumn of 1851 was started *Saunders' Monthly Magazine for
all India*, with J. O'B. as conductor and a "galaxy of talent" as contributors. Amongst these, were John Sherer, H. G. Keene, Robert
Spankie, Captain Trotter, Cargill of the Delhi College, Harvey the
"Civilian," Fanshawe, Lumsden, Hutton and others more or less known
to Indian fame. There were giants of the pen in those days—days before
"the d—d daily post and doubly d—d hourly telegraph," as I once heard
an old Indian merchant characterise these triumphs of civilisation—
came to disturb the ease, and mar the serenity of temper, of contented
Anglo-Indians. They were the days when men wrote for pleasure more
than for profit ; when mofussil life was a happy, hard riding, hard drinking, devil-may-care kind of existence ; when hospitality flourished, and
friends could be trusted. They were "good old times," and some

autumn fruit still lingered unplucked upon the now barren pagoda tree.

In the beginning of the hot weather of 1852, J. O'B. Saunders took sick leave and sailed for England round the Cape. He met his "fate" on board the ship in the person of the good and gentle lady who survives him as his widow, and who was the second daughter of Captain Reid, well known in the Bengal Cavalry.

In this year, 1852, Place returned from England and resumed charge of the *Delhi Gazette*, with Wilby from the *Mofusilite* as editor. James Hutton went to the *Agra Messenger*, which had been for some time edited by Patterson Saunders, but in 1853 Hutton returned to England sick. The *Messenger* shortly afterwards died, and in 1854 *Saunders' Magazine for all India* ceased to enlighten and amuse India any more. Business cares occupied now the time and attention of the Saunderses until the storm of the mutiny broke out and the tide of ruin swept away the lives and wealth of many Englishmen. J. O'B. Saunders was in England then, but his brother, Patterson, was in India, and did gallant deeds at Agra and Allyghur, which brought honor to his name on the page of the historian, and more profitable recognition from the Government and the Queen, in the shape of a present of a *jaghir* of land of the value of one lac of Rupees. Pat. Saunders' achievements as an Agra volunteer, and the story of the charge in which his cousin Tandy fell mortally wounded, are not the least noteworthy of the stirring incidents of those dark hours, when English men, women and children, literally carried their lives in their hands.

The ruin of indigo properties in the North-West of course involved the Saunderses in the wreck. Commercial disaster also overtook the firm of Saunders and Larpent, and after upwards of 30 years of Indian toil and trouble, J. O'B. had almost to begin the world again. But he was a Scotchman, and held with Scotland's present poet that

"None should say that Fortune grieves him
While the star of hope she leaves him ;"

and this star never died in J. O'B.'s heart. In his contemplation of "the situation," he saw no chance of business matters righting themselves and princely fortunes coming back to merchants. All was panic and confusion throughout India ; one great house after another gone or going to smash. Credit had collapsed, and there was bankruptcy all around. But there was balm in Gilead. The *Englishman*

newspaper was then in the market; the celebrated Cobb
Hurry, as determined a champion againt shams and political jobbery as William Cobbett himself, had been editing the.
paper, but wished to go home.   Saunders joined him in purchasing the property, giving Walter Brett a share and the
editorship.   It is no part of this paper of mine to touch upon
the strange and romantic career and tragical end of the last
named; it is perhaps still sufficiently remembered in Calcutta.
Cobb Hurry went home to die. (i)   Walter Brett (ii) reigned
for some time over the *Englishman* and Calcutta opinion, until an unexpected Nemesis overtook him, and he disappeared
from the scene to find a lonely grave amongst strangers in
Australia. J. O'B. Saunders had then to fight the name of
the paper to popularity, for unpopular it had undoubtedly become.   The Anglo-Indian Press at that time was more
feared than respected.   It had become the enemy of all in
authority and was ever ready to attack the Government and
Government officials, with or without reason.   It admitted
all manner of letters into its columns, so long as the letters
were pungent and personal.   The personality was horrible
and the motives were of the basest kind, and the darkest in-
sinuations   were   unhesitatingly   published   against   men
in office, who had no means of replying, or vindicating themselves.   The civil and military authorities visited with condi-
gn punishment any subordinate found guilty, or suspected,
of writing for the newspapers, and so these papers became
chiefly Caves of Adullam for any discontented soldier or

(i)   In 1862.   He was for a long time Joint Secretary with Babu
Dwarkanath Tagore to the Landholders' Society established in 1838, the
precursor of the British Indian Association.

(ii)   Mr. Walter Brett moved the famous amending Resolution at the
Canning Memorial Meeting held by the natives, protesting against the
use of the name of Europeans in the address. presented to the Viceroy.
Mr. David Cowic, the Sheriff presided on the occasion. Brett's resolution
was not seconded by any one present at the meeting. He, as a representative of the non-official Europeans ·lodged a complaint before Sir Barnes
Peacock against the Sheriff for having refused to call a public meeting
in the Town Hall on the requisition of Europeans. We shall publish
these maudules hereafter in no our sum of of in book.

cashiered officer, or disgraced civilian, to howl in against his superiors in power. The abuse of Government and official dignitaries, which was the chief topic of the day, was frequently varied by the editors abusing each other, which they did with all the will, and considerably more than the vituperation, which distinguished the editors in Pickwick. In fact, nothing could have been lower than the state of the press of India immediately after the mutiny. There were exceptions, of course, to this rather sweeping condemnation—the *Friend of India* may be named as one—, but the normal attitudé of the majority of the Anglo-Indian press was one of studied hostility to the Government and all in authority. There was perhaps reason for this, on account of the insane policy of the Government towards the press during the mutiny, and the attempt to gag it, or strangle it by the celebrated "Black Act." I neither defend the Government of the day nor excuse it. There were faults on both sides ; and if the press abused the Government, Government officials were equally hearty in abusing the press.   *   *   *

J. O'B. Saunders never aspired to have a brilliant pen, but his humour, vast experience of men and manners in the East, his wide and deep knowledge of Indian subjects, inspired many brilliant articles from the pens of those who learned from him. He was sometimes hasty—perhaps rash—in his judgments, but his kindness of heart always won in the end against temper. His life was a pure and temperate one, and he was the idol of his own home. A man of genial humour, of strong feelings, shrewd and sensible, an old Scottish gentleman—such he lived and such he died. Light be the turf upon his grave. Old friends gathered round, and some who had been enemies with each other shook hands beside it. I need add no more. This imperfect sketch would merely seek to symbolise Ophelia's gift—

"Rosemary for remembrance and pansies that's for thoughts."

G. R. F.

THE NAMES OF NEWSPAPERS IN MADRAS IN 1847.

PLACE & TITLE.	HOW OFTEN.	ANNUAL SUBS- CRIPTION	EDITOR.	No. OF VOLS.
Madras Atlas.	Daily	30	Unknown.	2
Spectator.	Tri-Weekly	40	W.Glover Esq	2.
Athenæum.	do.	30	Unknown	7
Circulator.	do.	10	Rev. Mr. Traveller.	59
U. S. Gazette.	Bi-weekly	35	Unknown	11
Crescent	do.	24	do.	Unknown.

JOURNALS OF KURACHEE.

Advertiser.	Bi-Weekly.	30	M'Kenzie Esq	Unknown.
Moulmein, Chronicle; Free Press.		30	Abrus, Esq.	

JOURNALS IN THE NORTH-WESTERN PROVINCES.

Gazette.	Bi-Weekly.	35	H. Cope, Esq.	6
Meerut Mufasilite	do.	35	L. Long, Esq.	2
Bonares Recorder	do.	30	Unknown.	7

(Vide Bombay Telegraph. and Courier, June 16, 1847

NAMES OF ENGLISH NEWSPAPERS IN CALCUTTA.
IN 1847.

PLACE & TITLE.	HOW OFTEN.	ANNUAL SUBS-CRIPTION	EDITOR.	No. OF VOLS.
Serampur Friend of India ...	Weekly	Rs. 20	J. Marshmen Esq.	13
Calcutta Bengal Hurkura ...	Daily	64	Several writers.	91
Englishman ...	do.	do.	J. Cobb Hurry Esq.	9
Calcutta Star...	do.	do.	G. T. Heutty Esq.	8
Eastern Star...	Weekly	20	Unknown	9
Christian Advocate ...	do.	10	do.	
Hindu Intelligencer ...	do.	10	do.	2
Bengal Catholic Herald ...	do	10	...	Unknown
Calcutta Literary Observer ...	Fortnightly	5	...	...
Christian Observer ...	do	10	...	...
Christian Intelligencer ...	do	9	...	...
Freechurchman	1 in a month	...	8 The organ of the Freechurch of Scotland.	
Oriental Baptist	do.		3 do. of Baptist Missionaries.	
Oriental Observer	do.	...	3 Organ of the Hindu Community & conducted by native youths recently from school.	
Calcutta Review	1 in 3 months		4 Rupees per number.	

BENGALI IN 1847.

1. Provakur ...	6 in a week	10	
2. Purno Chundrodoy	do. ...	8	Babu Adit Churn Addy was its proprietor and editor who died in 1873.
3. Sungbad Chundrika	2 do.	10—5	
4. Sungbad Bhaskur	1 do.	8	
5. Sumachar Gyandurpan	do.	4—4	
6. Sungbad Rossoraj...	2 do.	4—4	
7. Pashunda Perun ...	1 do.	2	
8. Kabya Rutnakur ...	do.	1	
9. Durjan Manabadolun	2 in a month	2	
10. Nitya Dhurmaranjika	2 do.	3	
11. Twotyabodhinipatrika	1 do.	2	By Debendra Nath Tagore.
12. Sutya Suncharini Patrika ...	1 do. ...	3	Syama Churan Bose established it in 1846 as the organ of the Satya Sancharini Sava.
13. Jugutbundhu Patrika	1 do.	3	was conducted by the junior students of the Hindu College.
14. Hindu Dhurma Chandrodoy ...	1 do.	3	The organ of the Bishnu Sava. established to counteract the influence of the Brahma Somaj.
15. Upadesak (the Bengali organ of Baptist Missionaries ...	... 1 do.	1—8	
16. Bidya Kulpadruma	1 in 3 months	1—4 per number.	

———

⟶⟶○○⟶

CHAPTER VII.

For want of space, we beg to close this our humble publication with these miscellaneous matters, and hope to resume our work in a separate volume hereafter.

Mr. JOHN Mc. ARTHUR

versus.

SIR JOHN PETER GRANT, LIEUTENANT-GOVERNOR OF BENGAL.

We take the facts of this *cause celebre* from the *Friend
of India* of May 22 1862.

The *Friend* in a leading article under the heading the
"Last Libel Case," thus wrote on the subject :—

"Sir J. P. Grant is before us in a new character—a defendant in an action of libel. A Mr. John Mc. Arthur, assistant to the Manager of the Luckipaira Indigo Factory, is
the plaintiff. The alleged libel was contained in a book
called "Selections from the records of the government of
Bengal, number XXXIII, part III. Papers relating to Indigo cultivation in Bengal." It was in the form of a letter
from Mr. Lushington, Commissioner of Nuddia to the Lieutenant Governor, and contained an expression of belief that
the plaintiff had been accessory before the fact to certain
lawless acts during the recent disturbances, though there was
no hope of securing a conviction for a criminal offence. So
far as Mr. Lushington was concerned, this was a privileged

communication. But very soon afterwards the alleged offenders in those disturbances were aquitted by the Sudder Court, because the evidence adduced against them was worthless. It was endeavoured to bring home the knowledge of this acquittal to the late Lieutenant-Governor. Of course he had not remained ignorant of the result of a trial which was of interest to a man who more than any one is responsible for the unhappy disturbances out of which it rose. This knowledge however was immaterial, for he was officially and personally responsible for having published this libel without reasonable excuse. The Advocate-General submitted that though it was difficult to bring it within the class of cases as to privileged communications, yet the principle involved in these cases ought to be extended to a libel of this nature. But he did not proceed to show either the necessity or the advantage of doing so. The Chief Justice quoted the rule which had been laid down as to privileged communications. They must be made *bonâfide* in performance of a duty, or with a fair or reasonable purpose of "prohibiting the interest of the party" using the words. Nominal damages of one rupee were assigned to the plaintiff."

MUNIFICENCE OF KUMAR KRISNA NATH ROY
TO KULIN DEGAMBER MITTER &c.

The following letters which will explain themselves, appeared in the *Friend of India* of 1840. We could not lay our hands on these important letters, when we, in 1889, published a sketch of Babu Digumber Mitter. Nor Babu Bhola Nath Chunder, in his biography of this great man could publish them. After a diligent search for months together, we found them in the above paper, and publish them in this volume for the information of the present generation. This magnanimous liberal grant of a lakh of rupees to Babu Digumber formed a kind of nucleus to his future fortune.

My dearest friend,

It is with feelings of the greatest pleasure that I herewith enclose two Promissory Notes of number and dates as per margin, amounts in value to a lakh of Company's rupees, which you will

No. 6112, of 1835 —36 dated 31st. March, 1836, for Co's Rs 96,000, No. 2,534, of 1835 —36, dated 31st. March, 1836 for Co's Rs. 4,000.

do me a great favour by accepting as a small tribute of that gratitude and friendship which your services as well as your amiable character have inspired in me.

Far it be from me ever to flatter myself with an idea that this is a remuneration of that zeal and assiduity, which from the commencement of our friendship, you have always displayed in my cause, The acts that you have sprung from these sources are engraved in my mind, and nothing I could do would repay them ; but paltry as this gift may be, when compared with the valuable services you have rendered to me, and the sentiments of friendship which you cherish for me, yet allow me to assure you that the same friendly feelings which have induced you to devote your-self so zealously to the promotion of my welfare have prompted me also thus to furnish you with a small provision for your family.

Believe me, my dearest friend,
Most truly yours,
(Sd.) KUMAR KRISTNATH ROY.

- - -

.BABU (afterwards RAJA) DIGUMBER'S REPLY.

My dearest friend,

' The many proof I have had of your sincere friendship, not indeed only since I have been in a situation in your service of comparative comfort, but, also when prosecuted, I may say persecuted, upon fictitious charges, when deprived of my livelihood, and worse than that, when my character was tried to be taken from me, call forth from me an expres sion of gratitude that should last to the end of my existence.

But when you have crowned your disinterested friendship to this day by a present so princely, so magnificent, I do, my dear friend, sincerely declare that any attempt at express · sing my deep-felt thankfulness must be a lamentable failure. Pardon then my attempting it ; pardon my prayer that you will excuse my attempting it. But Oh ! give me credit for sincerity in declaring that my life shall continue to be devoted to your service ; that my humble efforts will be trebled in promoting the interests of one endeared with a heart far more princely than my princely domain.

I remain, my dear friend, with deep-felt gratitude, your devoted servant, and faithful affectionate friend,

(SD). Degumber Mitter.

To Kumar Krista nath Ray Bahadoor.
Banjutty villa,
Oct, 2. 1840.

RANEE HURASOONDURY DASEE
VS :
KOOMAR KRISHNA NATH RAY.

We learn from the *Bengal Herald* of September, 1839, that the Ranee Hurosoondury Dasee, wife of the late Raja Hurry nath Roy brought a criminal case before the Chief Magistrate of Calcutta against her son, Koomar Krishna nath Roy for his having on the 24th September, 1839, instructed Mr. Stretell to move 21 boxes from her premises to the house of the Joint Executor, Mr. J. C. C. Sutherland.

A police Pike deposed that Mr. Stretell entered the premises with 50 persons when the Ranee called out "we are -disgraced,—Christians have come in, and we have lost our caste."

Mr. Stretell stated that, at the request of the Rajah, he, in company with Mr. Lambrick, Babu Digumber Mitter, and two Portuguese females went there for the purpose of sealing the property belonging to the Raja. He asked Mr. Mac-

Cann to go like wise, to prevent breach of peace. On his arrival at the house he told the Raja to desire the ladies to go out of sight. Shortly after the Raja returned and told them you may now enter the room where the property is. Mr. Stretell and Babu Digumber Mitter then went in with the Rajah, Mr. MacCann stood at the threshold of the door to see that no property was taken away surreptitiously. The Rajah's servants took out the boxes, and Mr. Stretell caused them to be corded, and requested Mr. MacCann to seal them. This being done, these boxes were removed in hackeries to Mr. Sutherland's house. Mr. MacCann refused to protect the property on the road. Mr. Hedger, the Ranee's Attorney, with several Chowkidars, came up to Sutherland's house and endeavoured to take away some boxes from one of the carts, but they did not succeed. Mr. Leith appeared for the Ranee and Mr. Turton for the Rajah.

The further hearing of this case was reported in the *Bengal Herald* of Oct., 1839. In the depositions given by the Ranee Hurosoondury and Shoosamoyee (?) they stated that they were prevented from entering the Toshakhana by the two Portuguese Ayhas, who shoved them about the room ; and that when Ranee Hurosoondury closed the door, the Kumar forcibly opened it and severely struck her on the head. Twenty lakhs, and twenty-thousand rupees in Company's papers, which were carried away with the other property, belonged personally to Ranee Shoosamoye, (सुस्मयी ?) and were left by her late husband.

The case was again heard on the 30th September. 1839. Mr. Leith prayed that those who aided and abetted in the affair should be bound down. Mr. Turton objected. He refused to include Degumber Mitter, as no charge had been proved against him. The Kumar was bound down in his own recognizance in the sum of Rs. 5000, Mr. C. G. Stretell in his own recognizance in the sum of Rs. 3,000, Mr. I. I. Mac-

own recognizance and in the sum of Rs. 600 and that of
two sureties of Rs. 300 each.   Babu Degumber Mitter in his
own recognizanance, in the sum of Rs 500, and that of wto
sureties of 250 Rs each, and Bunoo Ayah, in her own recognizance in the sum of Rs 500, and two sureties of Rs. 250
each. Mr Leith wished Mr. J. C. C. Southerland. to be bound
down likewise, but there was no charge proved against him.

RAJA KRISHNA NATH AND BABU DEGUM-
BER MITTER AS HIS DEWAN.

We read the following in the *Friend of India* of April
23, 1840.

"We are happy to learn from the papers, that the young
Raj Kumar Kishennath Roy, has determined on giving
five prizes, valued at Rs. 5000, to the m st successful students
of the Calcutta Medical College, nd the Rajah's Dewan
Degumber Mitter, is now in correspondence with Dr. Goodeve upon the subject."

RAJA SHOOKMOY ROY.

He made a gift of one and a half lakh of Rupees for the
construction of the Juggernath Road from Pooree to Bissen-
pur via Cuttack and Midnapur. It was 261 miles long, with
816 bridges and drains. It was commenced in 1823 and
completed in 1830, at an expense of 5,415 rupees per mile.

(*Courier.* Aug. 27. 1841.)

MUNIFICENT GRANT OF A LACK OF RUPEES BY THE MAHARAJA MATAP CHAND BAHADOOR IN 1841.

The *Calcutta Courier* of that year wrote thus :—

"We are extremely glad to hear that the young Raja of Burdwan had placed at the disposal of the Government the princely sum of one lakh of Rupees, to be appropriated to support of the Lying-in-Hospital, the Medical College, and other educational institutions.

MAHARAJAH RUNJEET SING AND PROPHET MOHOMET'S DRESS.

The *Lahore Chronicle* of 1862 says that the British Government are the jealous custodians of the pyjamas, hair, shoes, walking-stick and other relics of Mohommet, which are kept under lock and key in the Fort of Lahore. Timour brought them to India. They descended through the various masters of the Punjab to Runjeet Shing who, though a Sheik, professed such veneration for them that he refused one lakh of rupees offered by the Nawab of Bhowalpur for one of the shoes of the Prophet. He used to keep them in the fort of Mokerian in the Hoshiarpur district. On one occasion the fort caught fire, but the flames could not touch the "Ziarut Shureef." Moharajah Sher Shing brought them to Lahore. (F. I. Dec. 25. 1862.)

THE GREAT EASTERN HOTEL COMPANY LD.

Messrs. D. Wilson & Co.'s firm assumed the above title in 1862, with a capital of 15 lakhs in 6,000 shares of Rs. 250 each. It was established in 1835. Mr. D. Wilson who was otherwise called "Dainty Davy" held 1500 shares in this Company. (F. I. June 16, 1862.)

BABU GOBINDA PROSAD PUNDIT OF SEARSOLE.

He died in 1862. He was a Cashmerian Brahmin and settled at Beerbhoom. He began life as a common sarkar in the employ of Messrs. Alexander&Co., the original proprietors of the coal mines now owned by the Coal Company. He then went to the Court at Hoogly, and became a Deputy Collector. He acquired a putnee of a piece of land at Searsole where his son-in-law built a house. The son-in-law sent some specimen of coal to Gobinda who saw at once its value and made arrangements for the working of the mine. At the age of 39 he was a Talookdar and the proprietor of an extensive coliery. He died in the Bankoora Jail, imprisoned for having taken part in an affray.

(*Indian Field*, 1862.)

THE SEAL'S COLLEGE.

On the 1st, March 1843, this College was first opened. Among the party assembled, were the Chief Justice, Sir J. G. Grant, Babu Dwarka Nath Tagore, Mr. George Thompson, the Rev. K. M. Banerjee, the professors of St. Zavier's College and the Barristers. Mr. Johnson of the St. Zavier's College was its first superintendent. (The B. H, March 4 1843.)

FINIS.

www.ingramcontent.com/pod-product-compliance
Lightning Source LLC
Chambersburg PA
CBHW020622030726
47497CB00007B/2376